# The Spine Chillers

By

Ben Clark

# The Spine Chillers

Written and drawn by Ben Clark
Lettering by Sean Tonelli
Edited by Alexander Finbow

## Guest comic strips

### Staple-head - page 107
Written by Alexander Finbow, art by PJ Holden, letters by Jim Campbell

### Dum Dumm - page 108
Written by Richmond Clements, art by Vicky Stonebridge, letters by Jim Campbell

### Lovecraft's Nightmare - page 109
Written by Alexander Finbow, art by William Simpson, letters by Jim Campbell

### Pull my Finger - page 110
Written by Dominic Finbow, art & letters by Kallista Meyers.

Published by Renegade Arts Canmore Ltd trading as Renegade Arts Entertainment

President: John Finbow - Publisher: Alexander Finbow
Business Development: Luisa Harkins - Marketing: Sean Tonelli
Reporting & Asset Management: Emily Pomeroy

Office of business:
Renegade Arts Canmore Ltd
25 Prospect Heights, Canmore Alberta T1W 2S2
email: contact@renegademail.com

Printed in Canada by Friesens

Supported by the Government of Alberta

# Foreword

Welcome to volume one of the collected Spine Chillers. In these pages you will discover the little known story about the time that some of the greatest horror writers of all time lived together in a grotty boarding house under the protection of the formidable Mrs Parkinson. You will discover the real inspiration for such classics as The Raven, A Christmas Carol and At The Mountains of Madness. Finally, the awful truth of what lurks in Mrs. Parkinson's the attic will be revealed, along with the mind-bending terror of The Werebadger! The Wicker Bloke! And... The Snowbeast! These comics were first published on the Renegade Arts Entertainment website. They are silly stories about a bunch of silly people doing silly things. I hope you enjoy them.

I was inspired by the sitcoms I loved as a kid, like Fawlty Towers, Dad's Army, Rising Damp, Last of The Summer Wine, and weekly comics like The Beano, Dandy, Whizzer and Chips, Topper, Buster, and The Beezer. Their daftness inspires me to this day.

This is my first published graphic novel so there are a few people I have to say thanks to for all their love and support over the years.

To Alexander Finbow and Doug Bradley for giving me the opportunity to do this, and to Sean Tonelli for the fab lettering.

Paul Scott and the Solar Wind crew, and the Paper Jam Comics Collective for all the help and advice over the years.

To my brother and sister for being my best friends. My Dad for filling my head with great music, my cousin Robert, who first inspired me to draw when I was a kid. My Mam and my Grandma for everything.

We had so much fun doing this comic-strip, and the boys have been away for far too long. So, I'm happy to reveal that they will be returning for a new series of adventures very soon.

Keep watching the pies,

Ben Clark
Durham
January 2019

For Dylan.

You are my world.

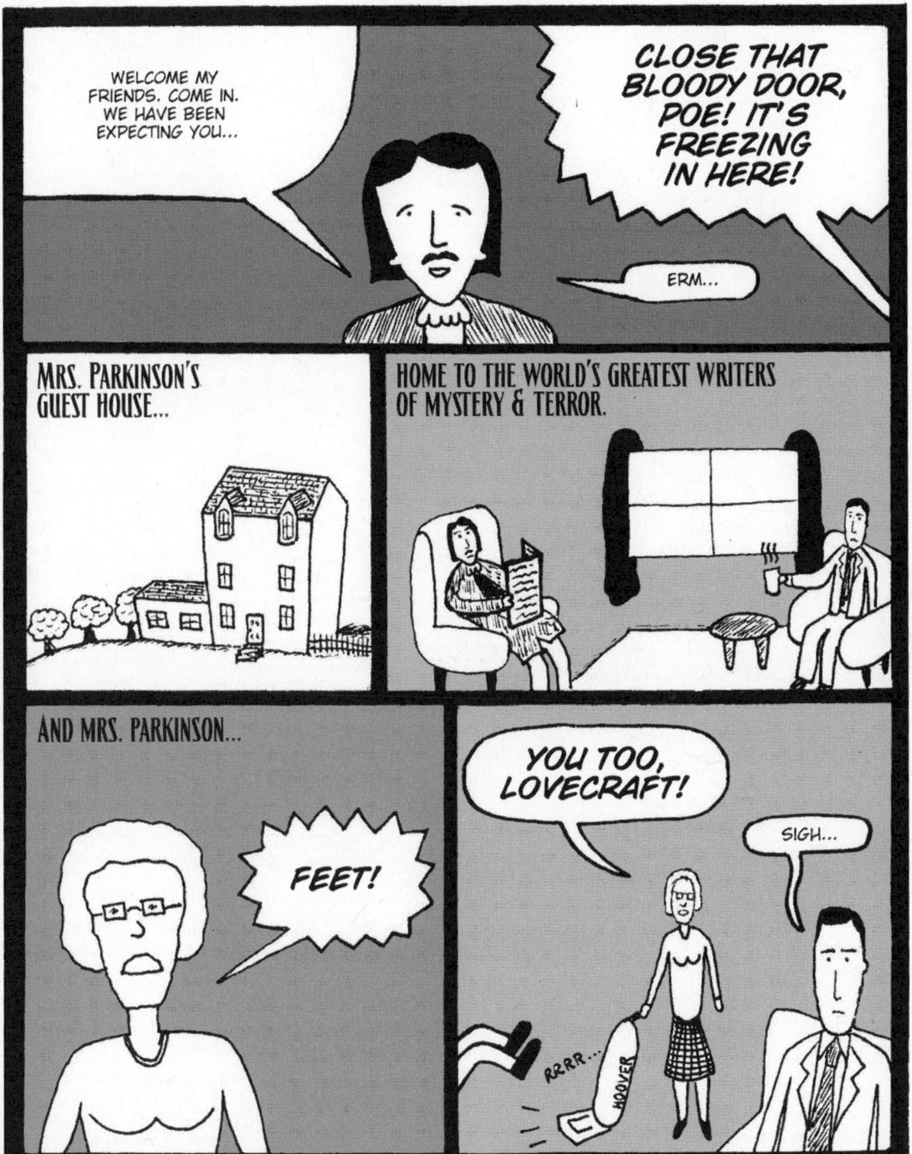
WELCOME MY FRIENDS. COME IN. WE HAVE BEEN EXPECTING YOU...
CLOSE THAT BLOODY DOOR, POE! IT'S FREEZING IN HERE!
ERM...
MRS. PARKINSON'S GUEST HOUSE...
HOME TO THE WORLD'S GREATEST WRITERS OF MYSTERY & TERROR.
AND MRS. PARKINSON...
FEET!
YOU TOO, LOVECRAFT!
SIGH...
RRRR...
HOOVER

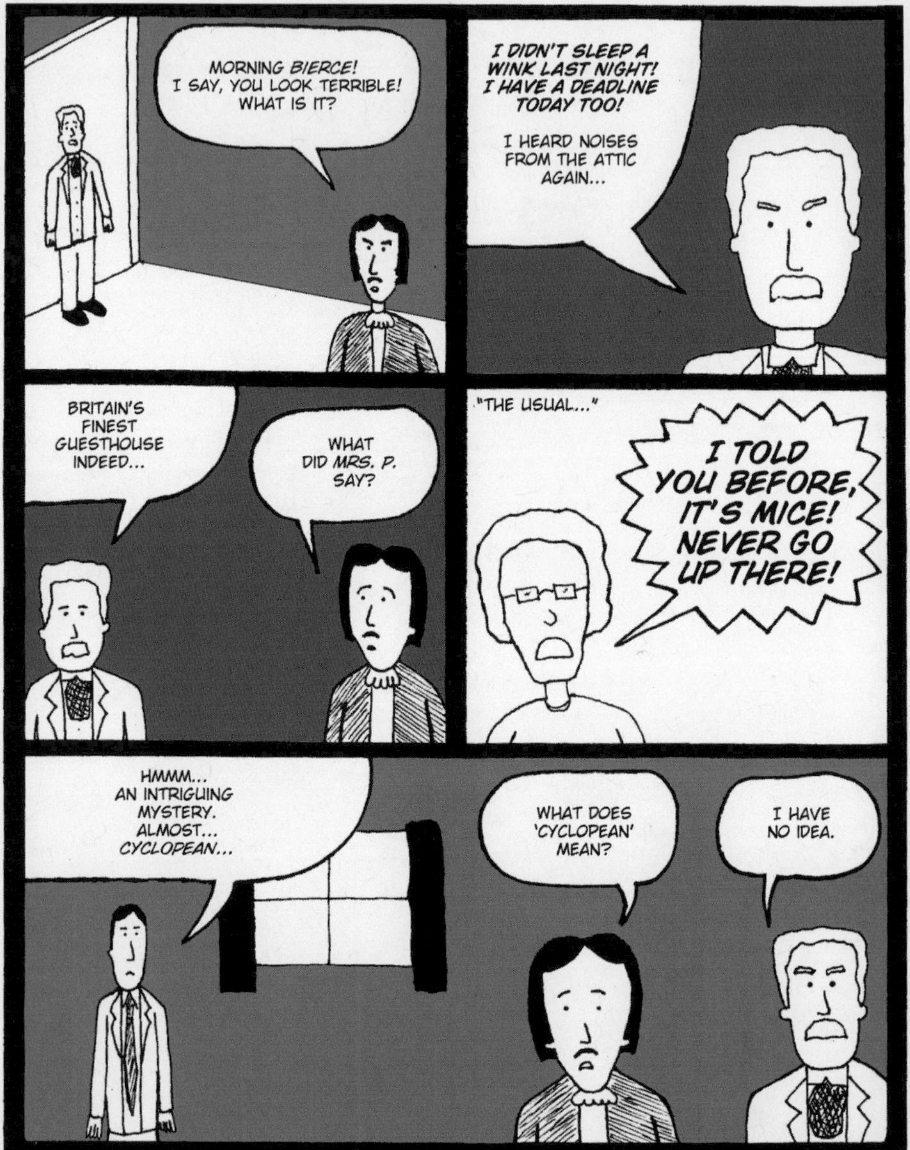
MORNING BIERCE! I SAY, YOU LOOK TERRIBLE! WHAT IS IT?
I DIDN'T SLEEP A WINK LAST NIGHT! I HAVE A DEADLINE TODAY TOO!
I HEARD NOISES FROM THE ATTIC AGAIN...
BRITAIN'S FINEST GUESTHOUSE INDEED...
WHAT DID MRS. P. SAY?
"THE USUAL..."
I TOLD YOU BEFORE, IT'S MICE! NEVER GO UP THERE!
HMMM... AN INTRIGUING MYSTERY. ALMOST... CYCLOPEAN...
WHAT DOES 'CYCLOPEAN' MEAN?
I HAVE NO IDEA.

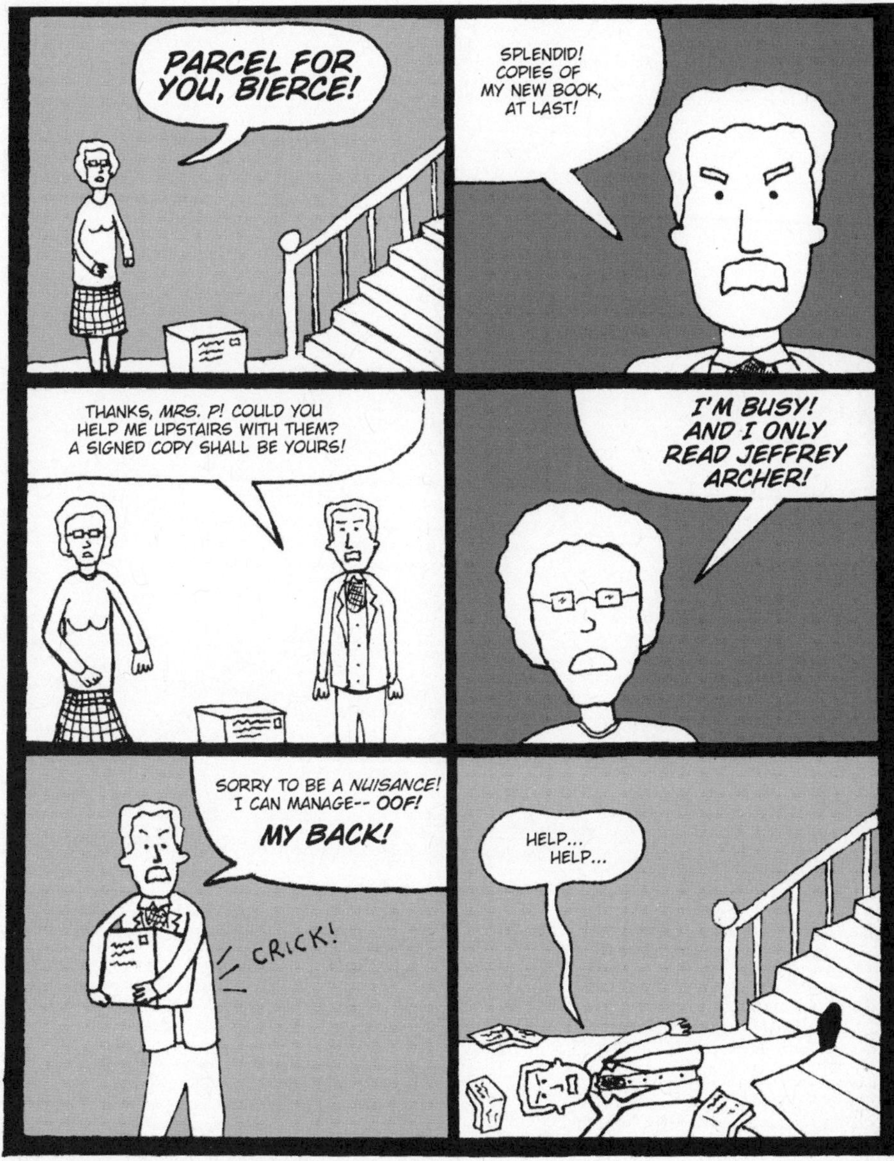
PARCEL FOR YOU, BIERCE!
SPLENDID! COPIES OF MY NEW BOOK, AT LAST!
THANKS, *MRS. P!* COULD YOU HELP ME UPSTAIRS WITH THEM? A SIGNED COPY SHALL BE YOURS!
I'M BUSY! AND I ONLY READ JEFFREY ARCHER!
SORRY TO BE A *NUISANCE!* I CAN MANAGE-- *OOF!*
**MY BACK!**
CRICK!
HELP... HELP...

It is altogether against my will that I tell my reasons for opposing this contemplated invasion of the Antartic...

It was a terrible, indescribable thing...

A shapeless congeries of protoplasmic bubbles, faintly self luminous, and with myriads of temporary eyes forming...

And still came that eldritch, mocking cry- 'Tekeli-Li! Tekeli-Li!'

ARE YOU GONNA EAT THAT OR WHAT?

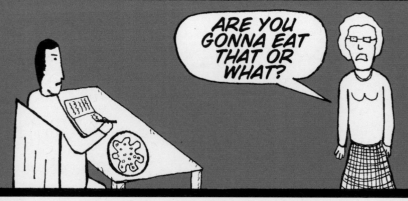

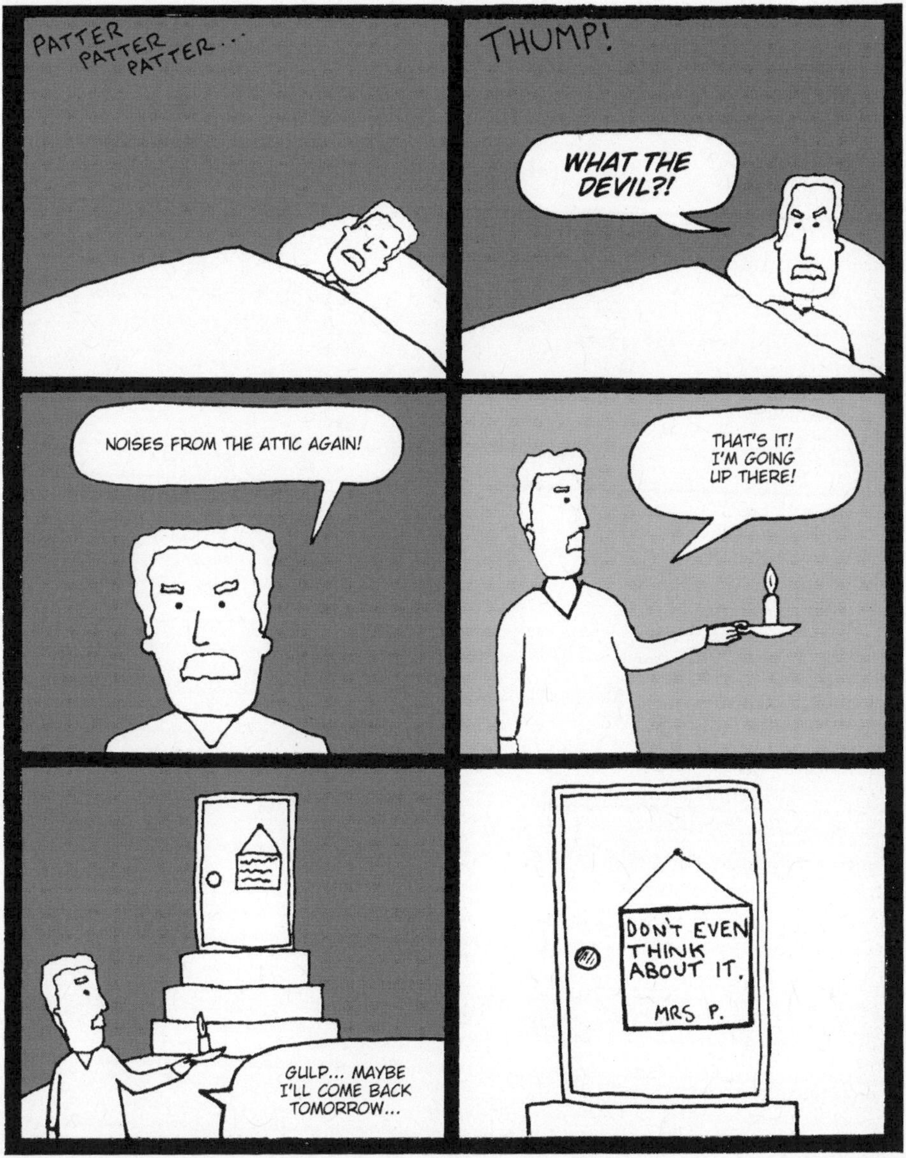
PATTER PATTER PATTER...
THUMP!
WHAT THE DEVIL?!
NOISES FROM THE ATTIC AGAIN!
THAT'S IT! I'M GOING UP THERE!
GULP... MAYBE I'LL COME BACK TOMORROW...
DON'T EVEN THINK ABOUT IT. MRS P.

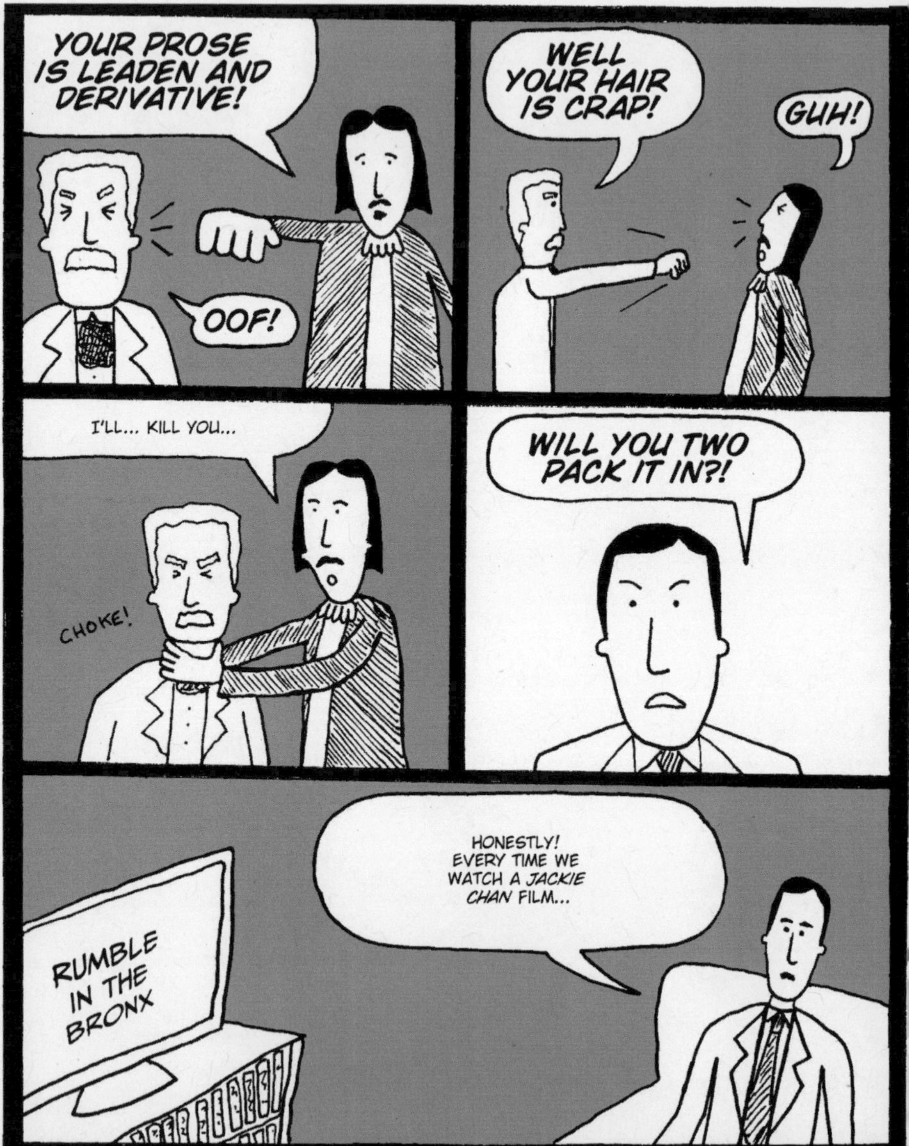
YOUR PROSE IS LEADEN AND DERIVATIVE!
OOF!
WELL YOUR HAIR IS CRAP!
GUH!
I'LL... KILL YOU...
CHOKE!
WILL YOU TWO PACK IT IN?!
RUMBLE IN THE BRONX
HONESTLY! EVERY TIME WE WATCH A *JACKIE CHAN* FILM...

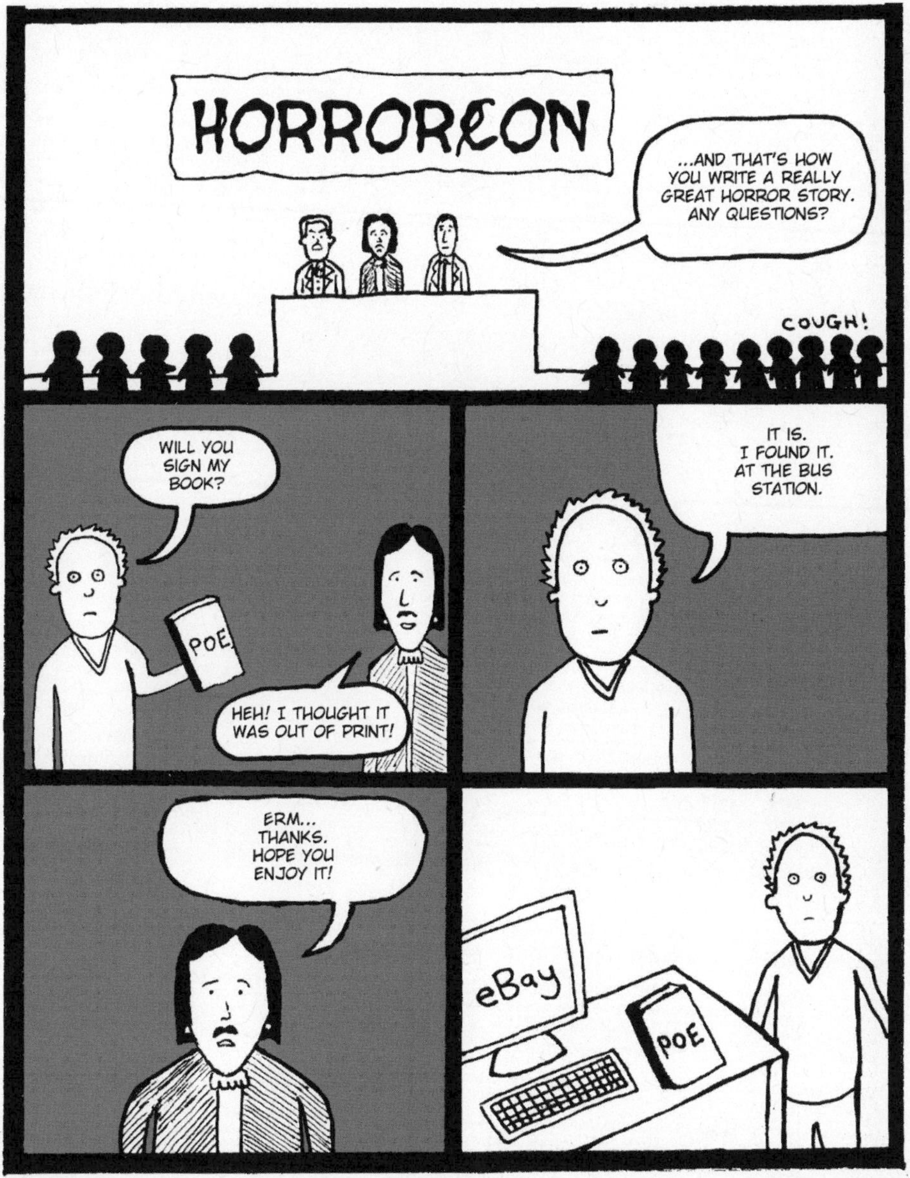
HORRORCON
...AND THAT'S HOW YOU WRITE A REALLY GREAT HORROR STORY. ANY QUESTIONS?
COUGH!
WILL YOU SIGN MY BOOK?
POE
HEH! I THOUGHT IT WAS OUT OF PRINT!
IT IS. I FOUND IT. AT THE BUS STATION.
ERM... THANKS. HOPE YOU ENJOY IT!
eBay
POE

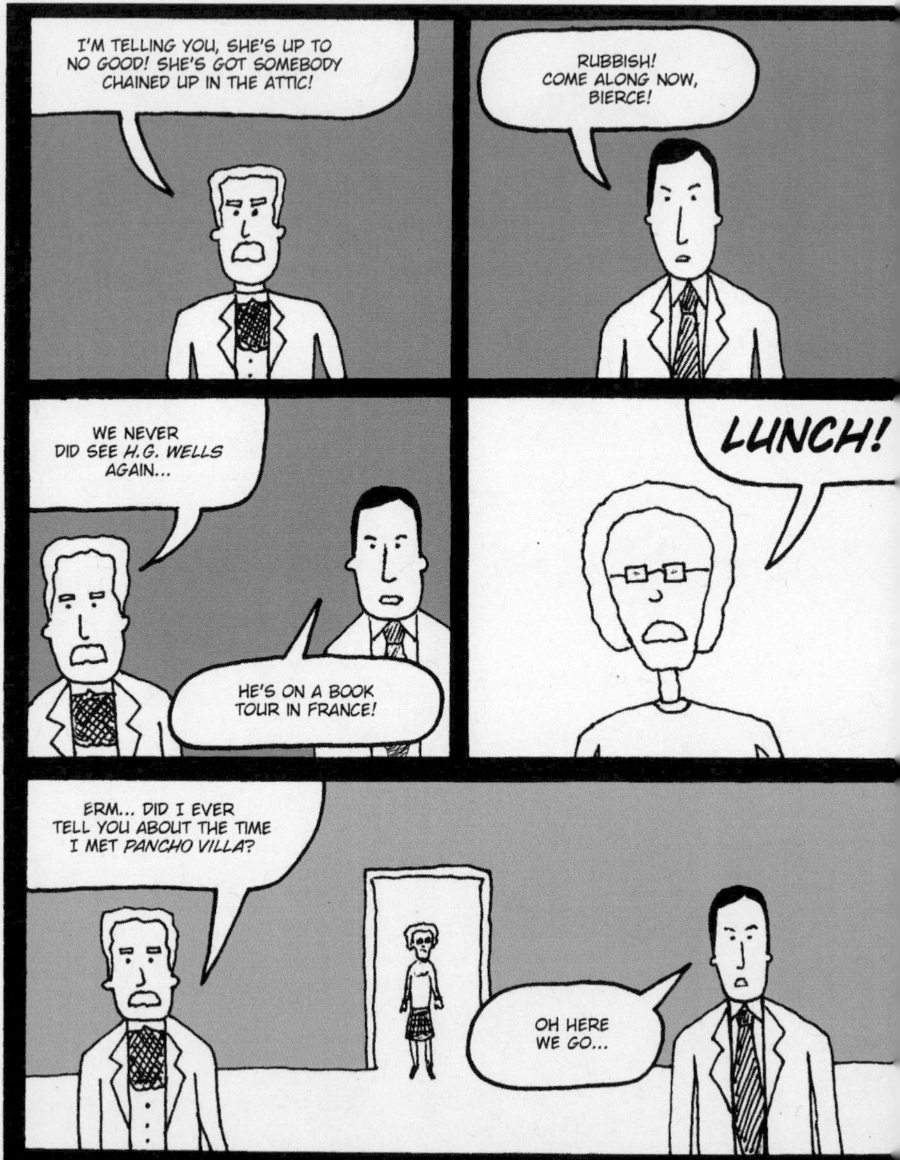
I'M TELLING YOU, SHE'S UP TO NO GOOD! SHE'S GOT SOMEBODY CHAINED UP IN THE ATTIC!
RUBBISH! COME ALONG NOW, BIERCE!
WE NEVER DID SEE *H.G. WELLS* AGAIN...
HE'S ON A BOOK TOUR IN FRANCE!
LUNCH!
ERM... DID I EVER TELL YOU ABOUT THE TIME I MET *PANCHO VILLA*?
OH HERE WE GO...

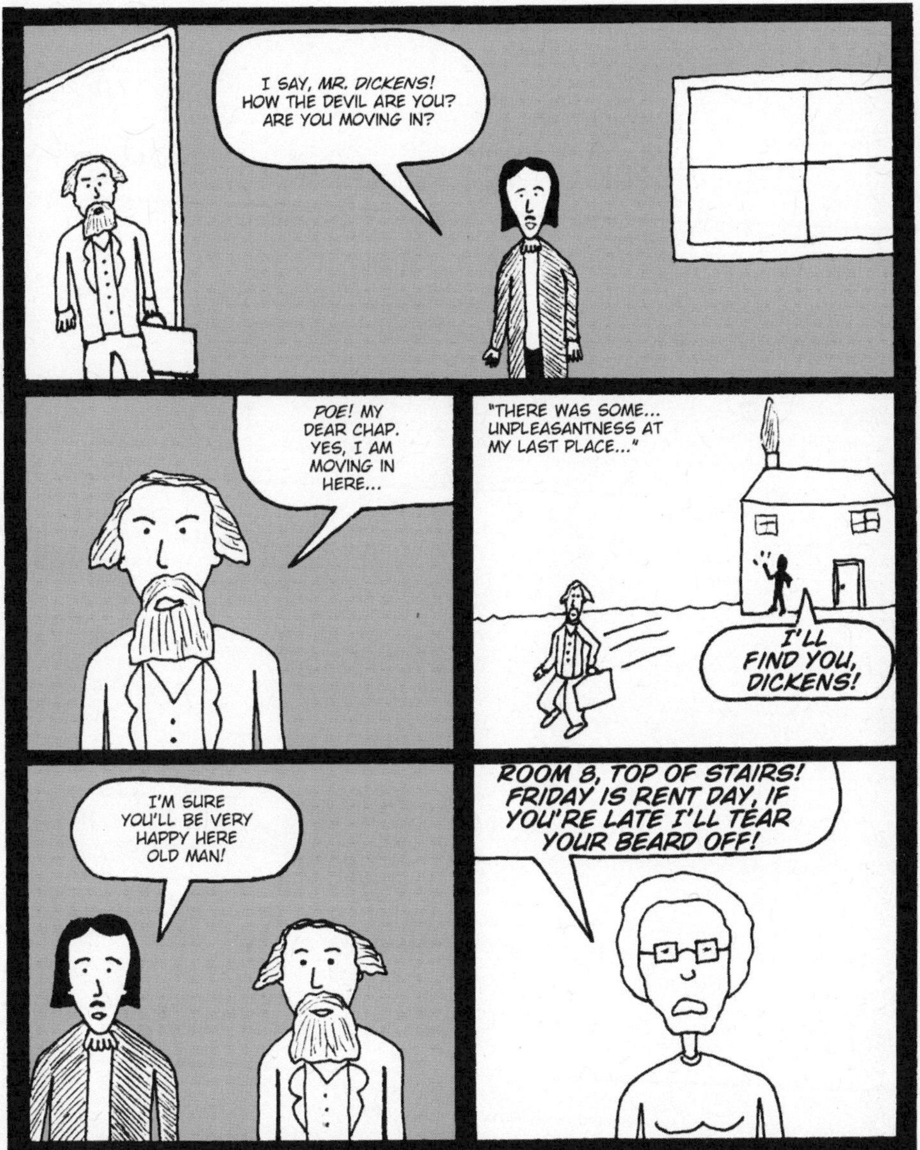
I SAY, MR. DICKENS! HOW THE DEVIL ARE YOU? ARE YOU MOVING IN?
POE! MY DEAR CHAP. YES, I AM MOVING IN HERE...
"THERE WAS SOME... UNPLEASANTNESS AT MY LAST PLACE..."
I'LL FIND YOU, DICKENS!
I'M SURE YOU'LL BE VERY HAPPY HERE OLD MAN!
ROOM 8, TOP OF STAIRS! FRIDAY IS RENT DAY, IF YOU'RE LATE I'LL TEAR YOUR BEARD OFF!

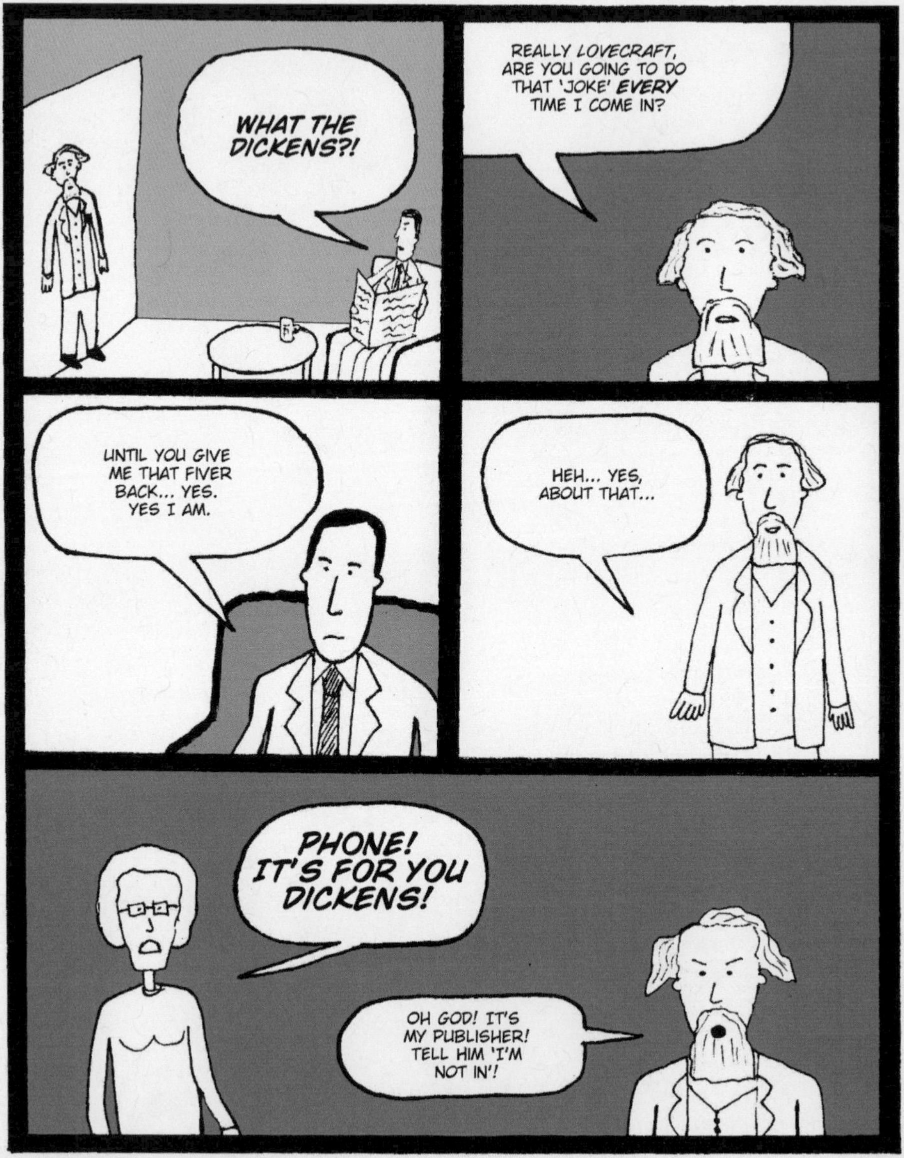
WHAT THE DICKENS?!
REALLY LOVECRAFT, ARE YOU GOING TO DO THAT 'JOKE' EVERY TIME I COME IN?
UNTIL YOU GIVE ME THAT FIVER BACK... YES. YES I AM.
HEH... YES, ABOUT THAT...
PHONE! IT'S FOR YOU DICKENS!
OH GOD! IT'S MY PUBLISHER! TELL HIM 'I'M NOT IN'!

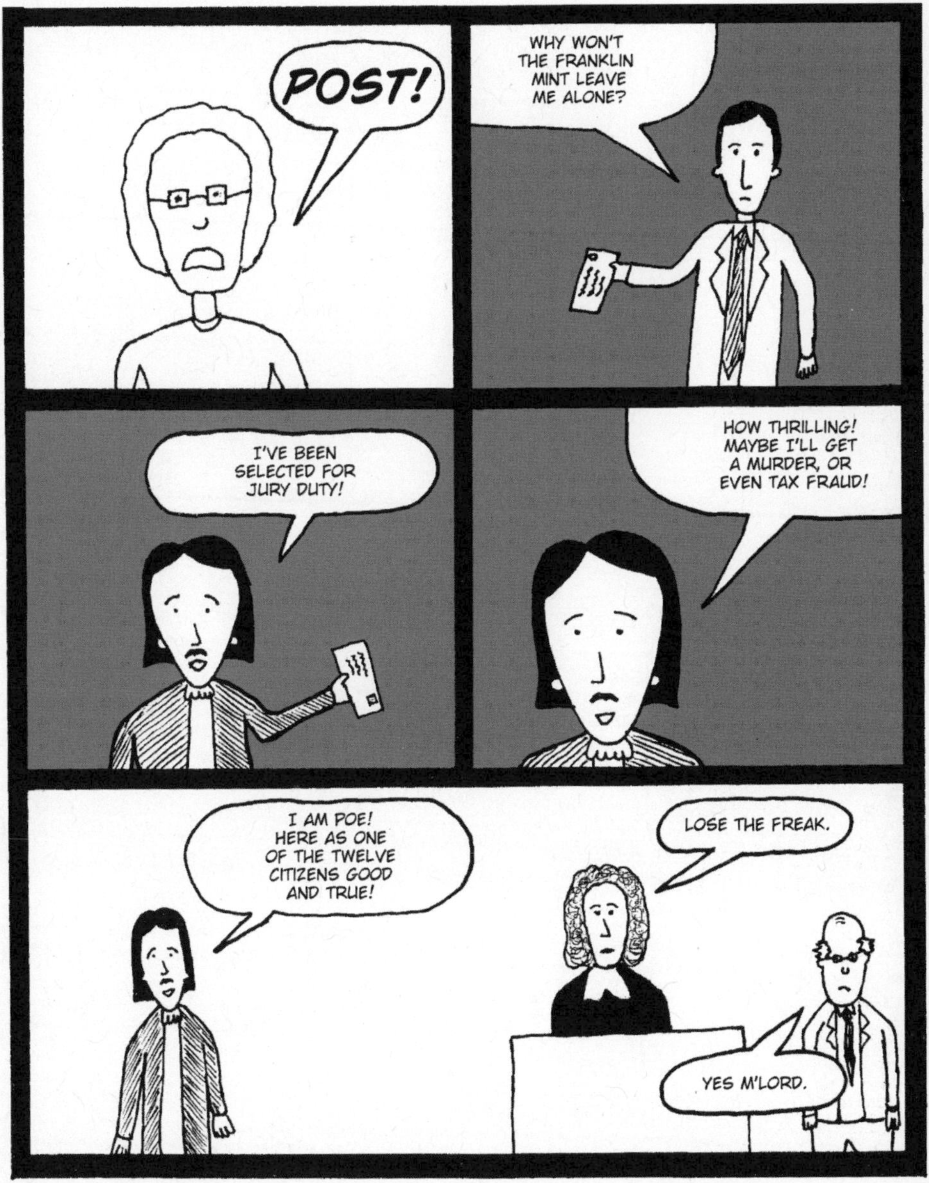
POST!
WHY WON'T THE FRANKLIN MINT LEAVE ME ALONE?
I'VE BEEN SELECTED FOR JURY DUTY!
HOW THRILLING! MAYBE I'LL GET A MURDER, OR EVEN TAX FRAUD!
I AM POE! HERE AS ONE OF THE TWELVE CITIZENS GOOD AND TRUE!
LOSE THE FREAK.
YES M'LORD.

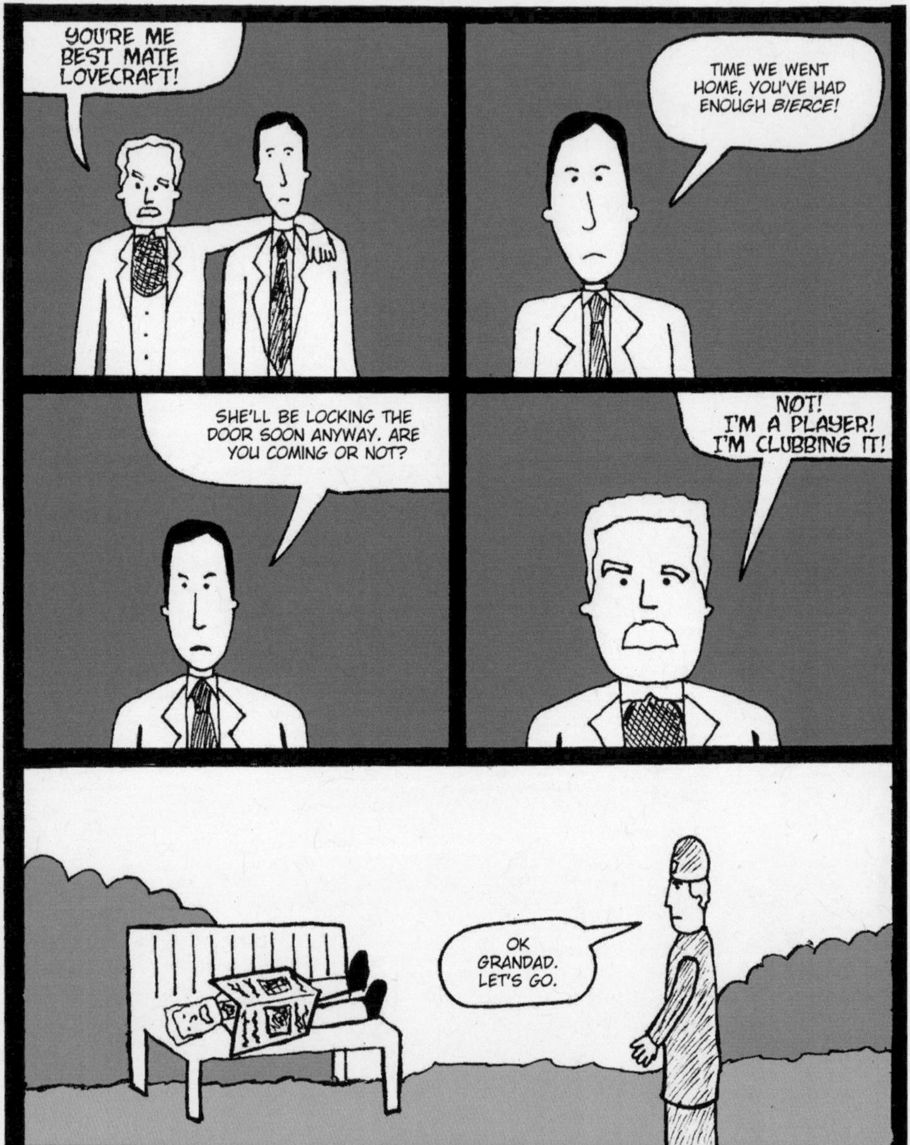
YOU'RE ME BEST MATE LOVECRAFT!
TIME WE WENT HOME, YOU'VE HAD ENOUGH *BIERCE*!
SHE'LL BE LOCKING THE DOOR SOON ANYWAY. ARE YOU COMING OR NOT?
NØT! I'M A PLAYER! I'M CLUBBING IT!
OK GRANDAD. LET'S GO.

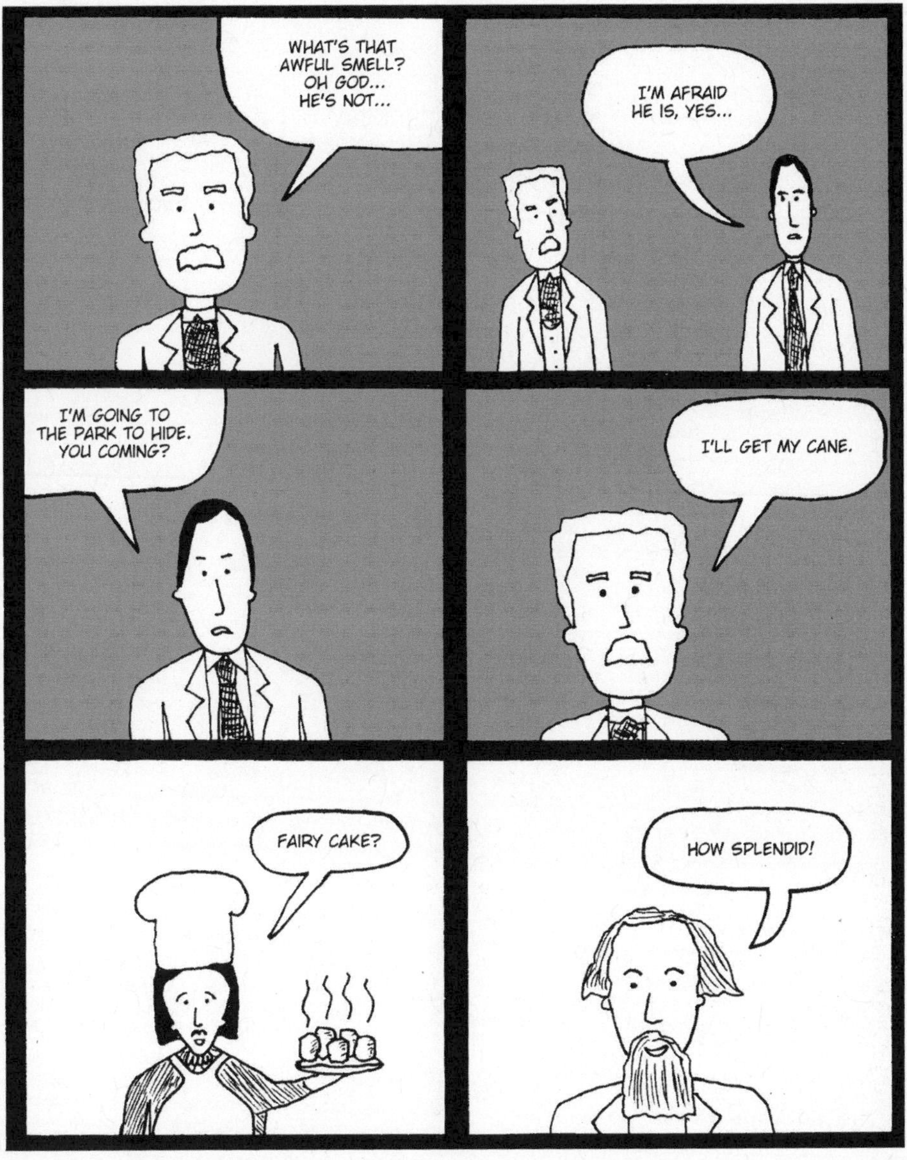
WHAT'S THAT AWFUL SMELL? OH GOD... HE'S NOT...
I'M AFRAID HE IS, YES...
I'M GOING TO THE PARK TO HIDE. YOU COMING?
I'LL GET MY CANE.
FAIRY CAKE?
HOW SPLENDID!

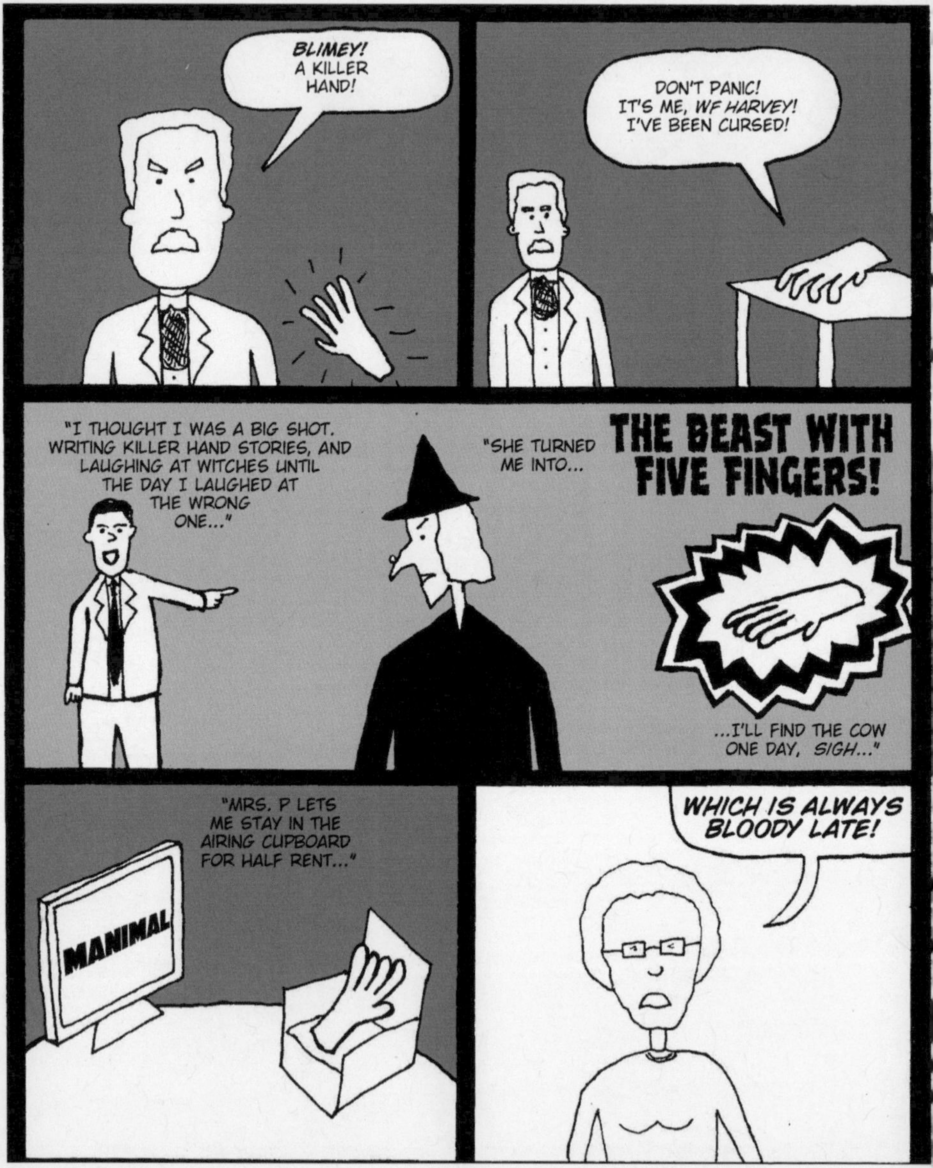

BLIMEY! A KILLER HAND!
DON'T PANIC! IT'S ME, WF HARVEY! I'VE BEEN CURSED!
"I THOUGHT I WAS A BIG SHOT. WRITING KILLER HAND STORIES, AND LAUGHING AT WITCHES UNTIL THE DAY I LAUGHED AT THE WRONG ONE..."
"SHE TURNED ME INTO...
THE BEAST WITH FIVE FINGERS!
...I'LL FIND THE COW ONE DAY, SIGH..."
"MRS. P LETS ME STAY IN THE AIRING CUPBOARD FOR HALF RENT..."
MANIMAL
WHICH IS ALWAYS BLOODY LATE!

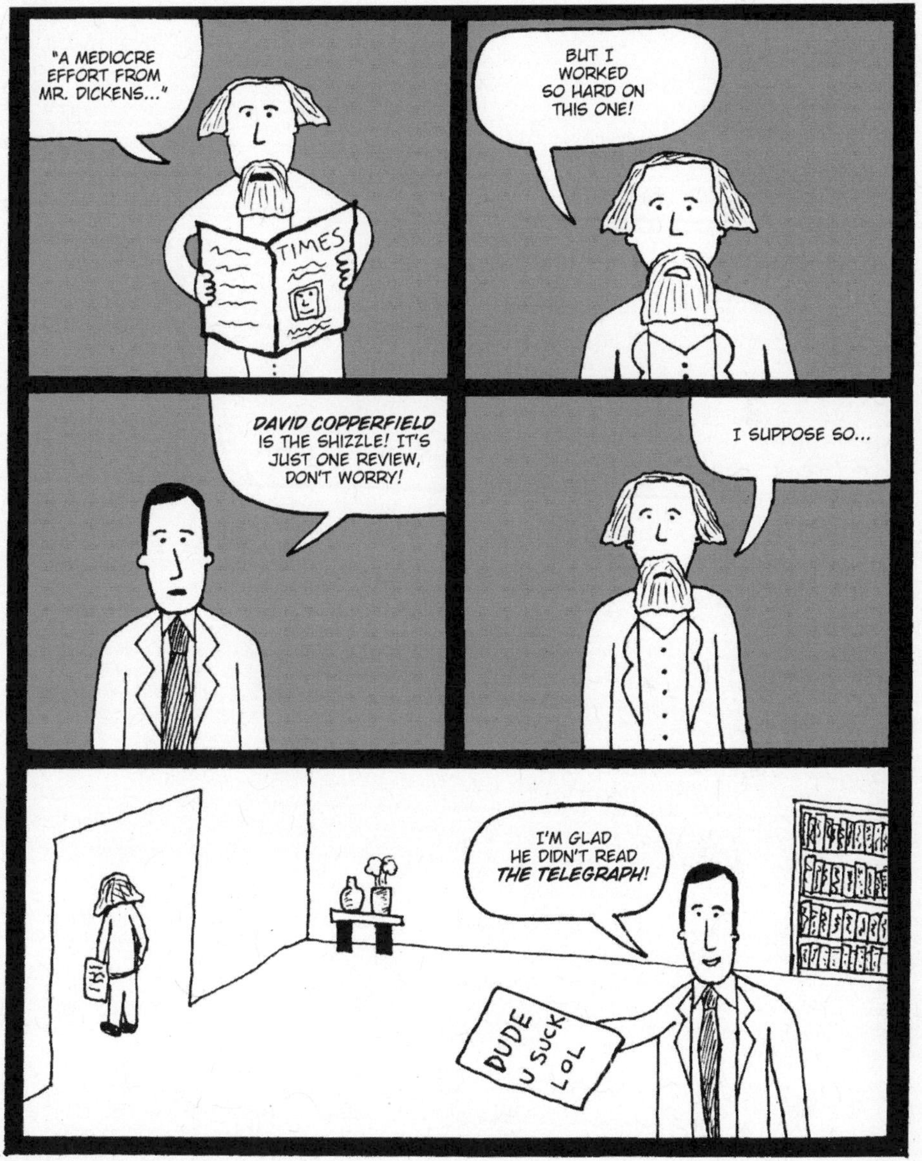
"A MEDIOCRE EFFORT FROM MR. DICKENS..."
TIMES
BUT I WORKED SO HARD ON THIS ONE!
DAVID COPPERFIELD IS THE SHIZZLE! IT'S JUST ONE REVIEW, DON'T WORRY!
I SUPPOSE SO...
I'M GLAD HE DIDN'T READ THE TELEGRAPH!
DUDE U SUCK LOL

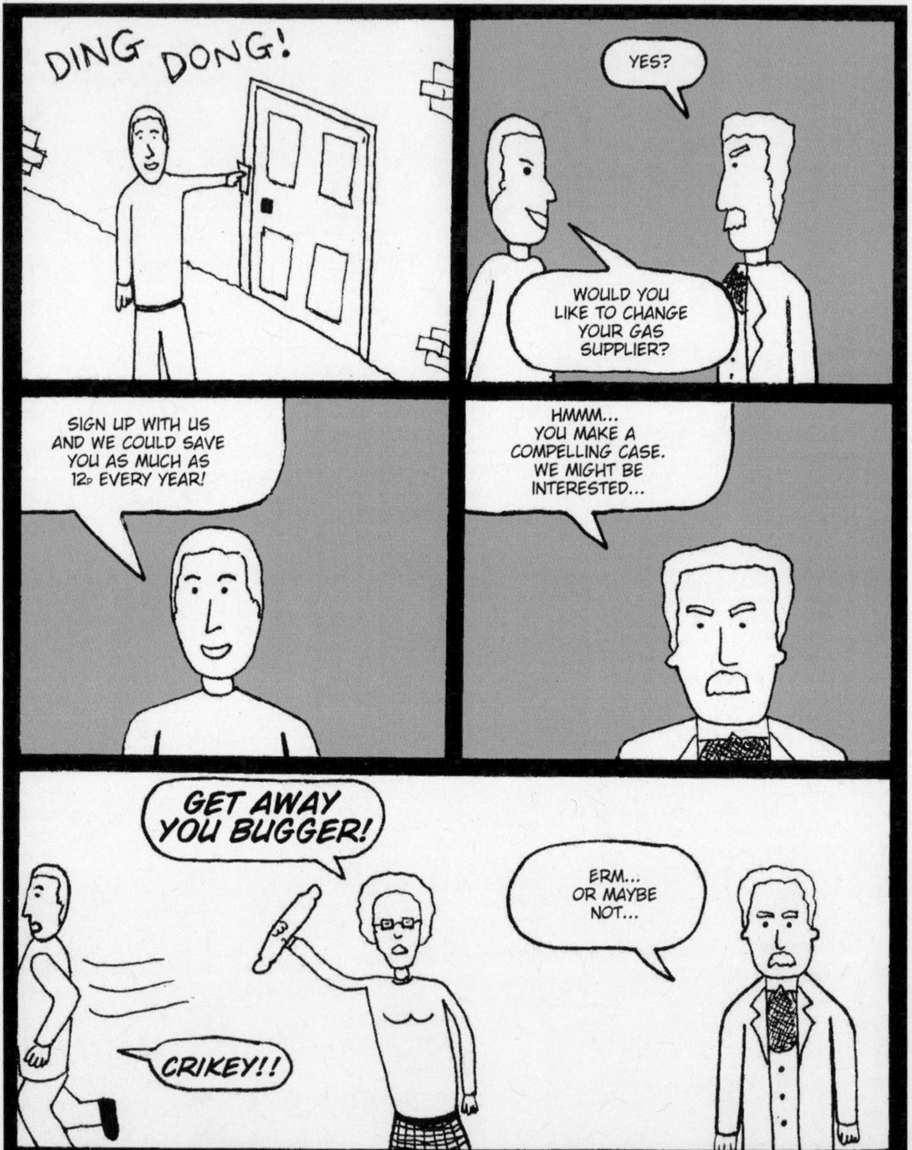
DING DONG!
YES?
WOULD YOU LIKE TO CHANGE YOUR GAS SUPPLIER?
SIGN UP WITH US AND WE COULD SAVE YOU AS MUCH AS 12P EVERY YEAR!
HMMM... YOU MAKE A COMPELLING CASE. WE MIGHT BE INTERESTED...
GET AWAY YOU BUGGER!
CRIKEY!!
ERM... OR MAYBE NOT...

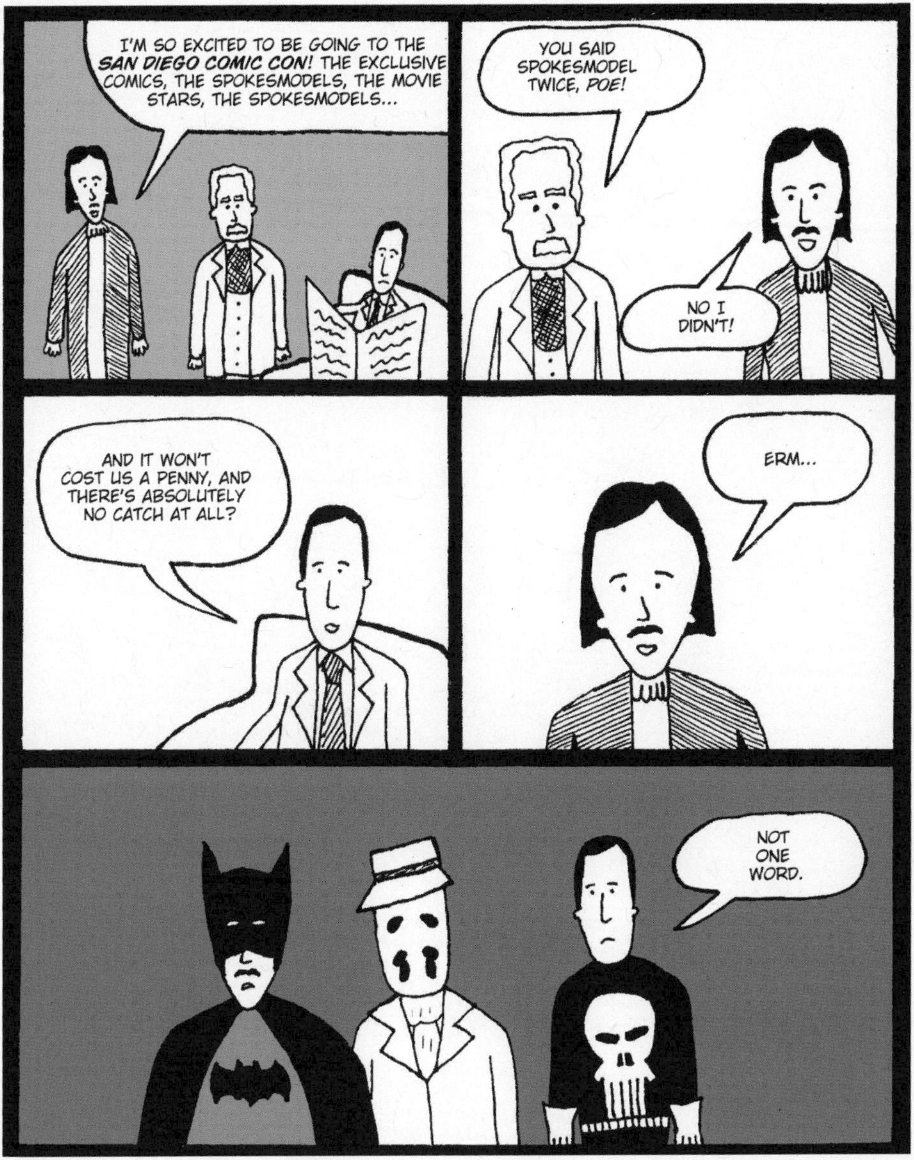
I'M SO EXCITED TO BE GOING TO THE SAN DIEGO COMIC CON! THE EXCLUSIVE COMICS, THE SPOKESMODELS, THE MOVIE STARS, THE SPOKESMODELS...
YOU SAID SPOKESMODEL TWICE, POE!
NO I DIDN'T!
AND IT WON'T COST US A PENNY, AND THERE'S ABSOLUTELY NO CATCH AT ALL?
ERM...
NOT ONE WORD.

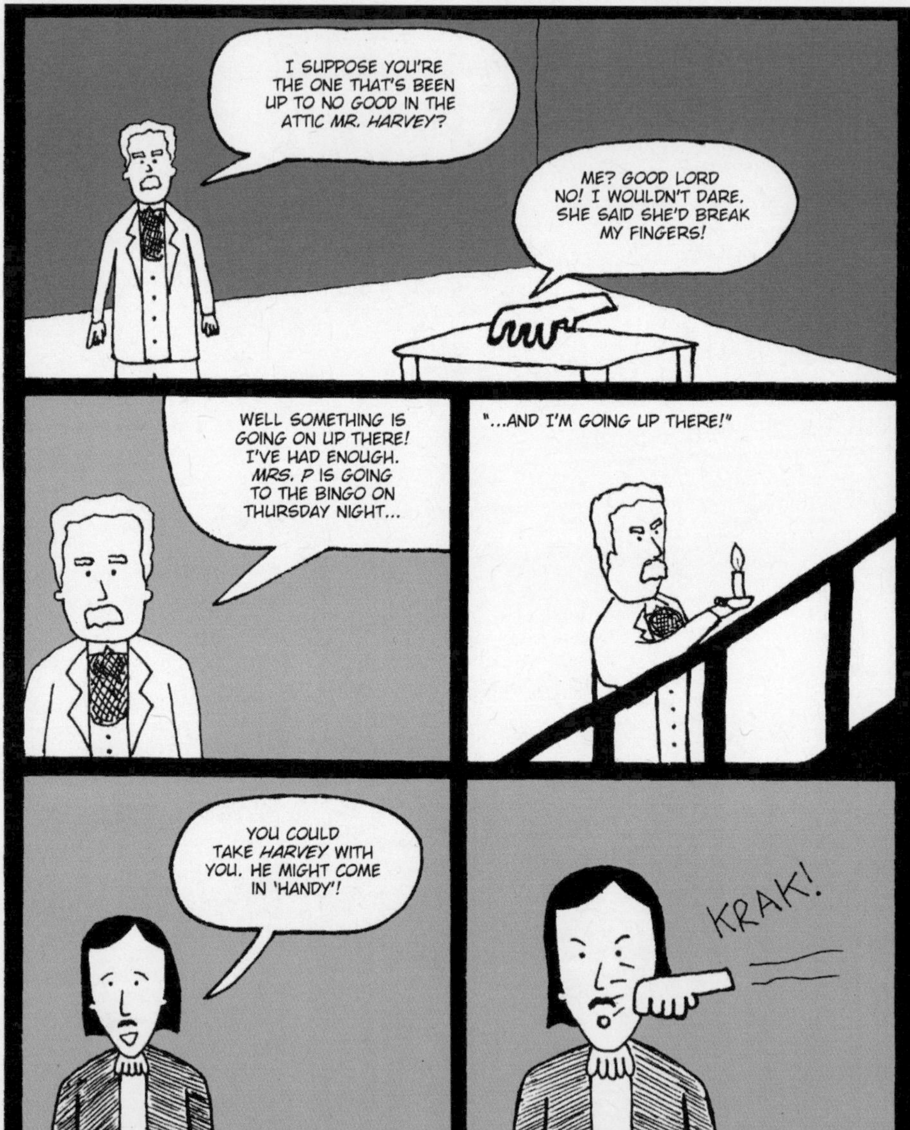
I SUPPOSE YOU'RE THE ONE THAT'S BEEN UP TO NO GOOD IN THE ATTIC MR. HARVEY?
ME? GOOD LORD NO! I WOULDN'T DARE. SHE SAID SHE'D BREAK MY FINGERS!
WELL SOMETHING IS GOING ON UP THERE! I'VE HAD ENOUGH. MRS. P IS GOING TO THE BINGO ON THURSDAY NIGHT...
"...AND I'M GOING UP THERE!"
YOU COULD TAKE HARVEY WITH YOU. HE MIGHT COME IN 'HANDY'!
KRAK!

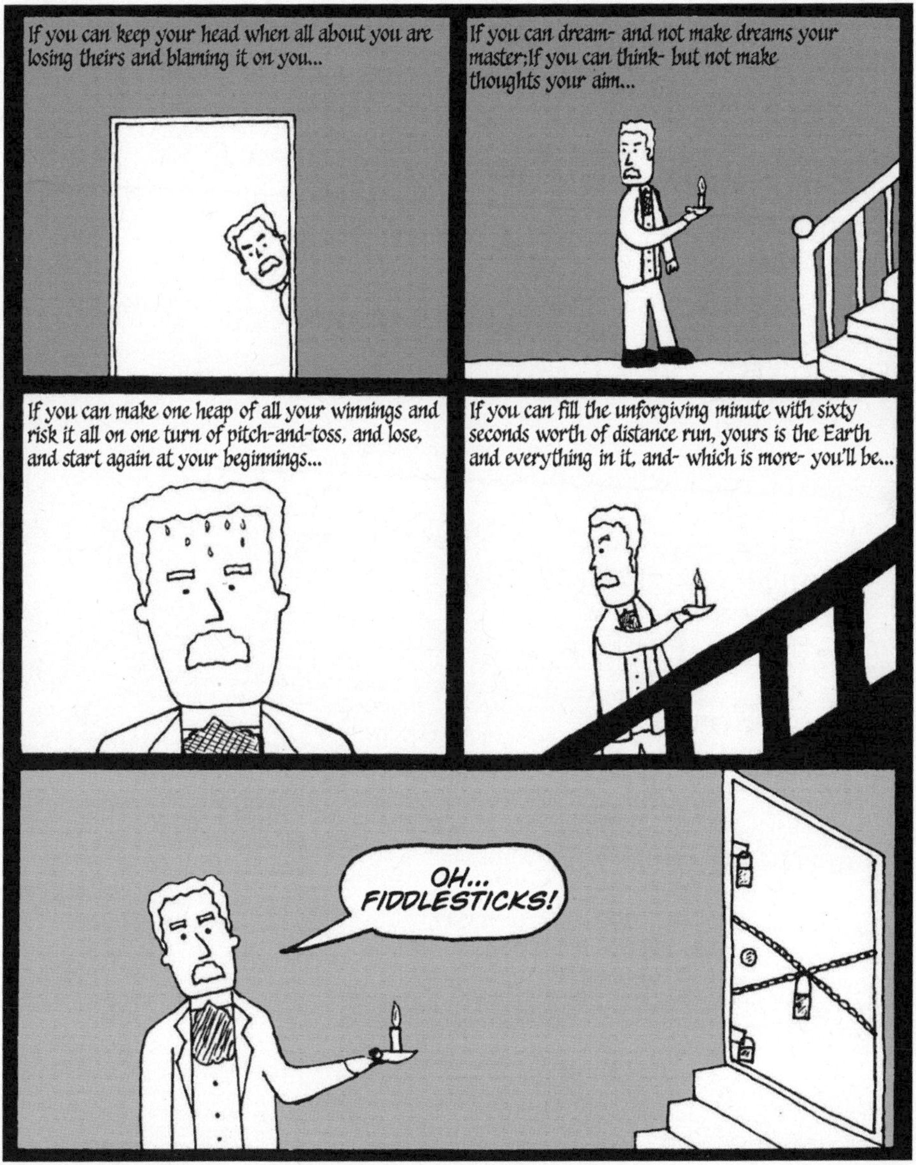
If you can keep your head when all about you are losing theirs and blaming it on you...
If you can dream- and not make dreams your master;If you can think- but not make thoughts your aim...
If you can make one heap of all your winnings and risk it all on one turn of pitch-and-toss, and lose, and start again at your beginnings...
If you can fill the unforgiving minute with sixty seconds worth of distance run, yours is the Earth and everything in it, and- which is more- you'll be...
OH... FIDDLESTICKS!

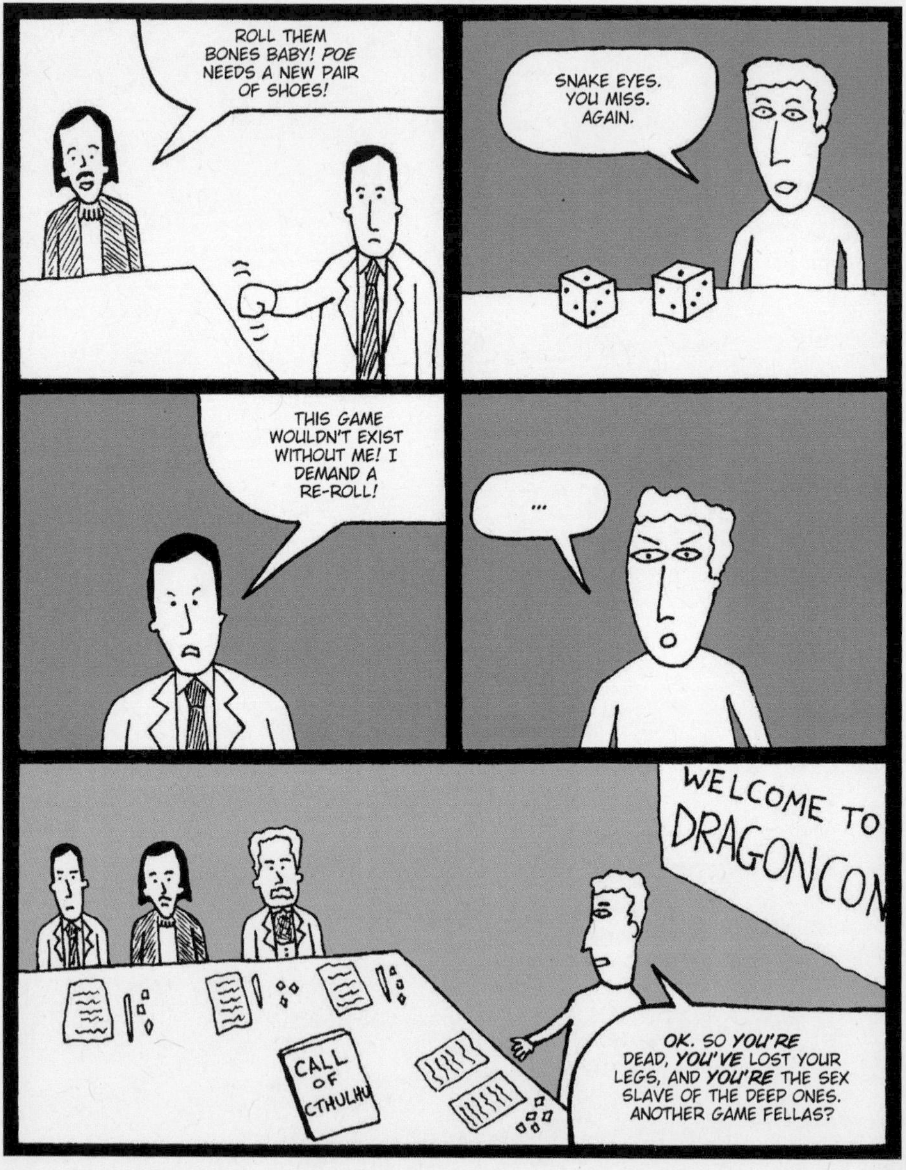
ROLL THEM BONES BABY! POE NEEDS A NEW PAIR OF SHOES!
SNAKE EYES. YOU MISS. AGAIN.
THIS GAME WOULDN'T EXIST WITHOUT ME! I DEMAND A RE-ROLL!
...
WELCOME TO DRAGONCON
CALL OF CTHULHU
OK. SO YOU'RE DEAD, YOU'VE LOST YOUR LEGS, AND YOU'RE THE SEX SLAVE OF THE DEEP ONES. ANOTHER GAME FELLAS?

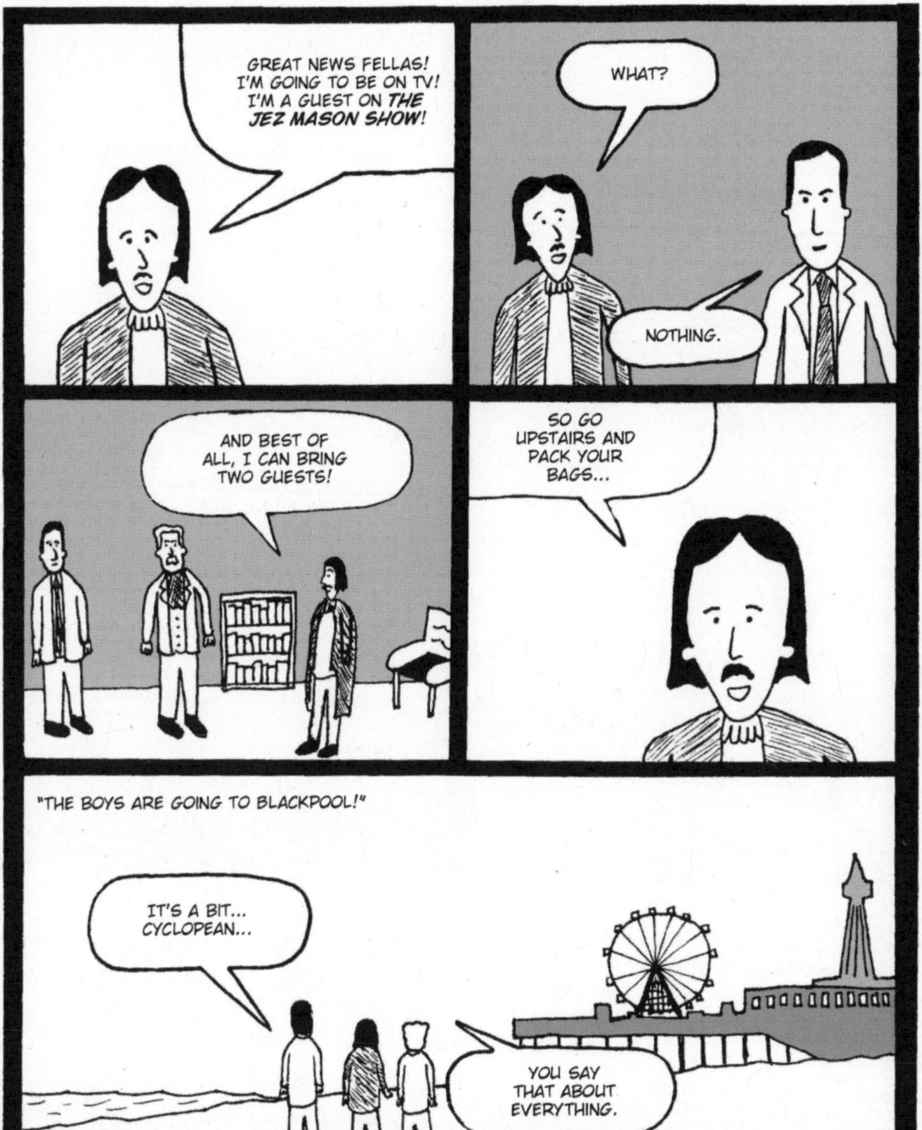
GREAT NEWS FELLAS! I'M GOING TO BE ON TV! I'M A GUEST ON *THE JEZ MASON SHOW*!
WHAT?
NOTHING.
AND BEST OF ALL, I CAN BRING TWO GUESTS!
SO GO UPSTAIRS AND PACK YOUR BAGS...
"THE BOYS ARE GOING TO BLACKPOOL!"
IT'S A BIT... CYCLOPEAN...
YOU SAY THAT ABOUT EVERYTHING.

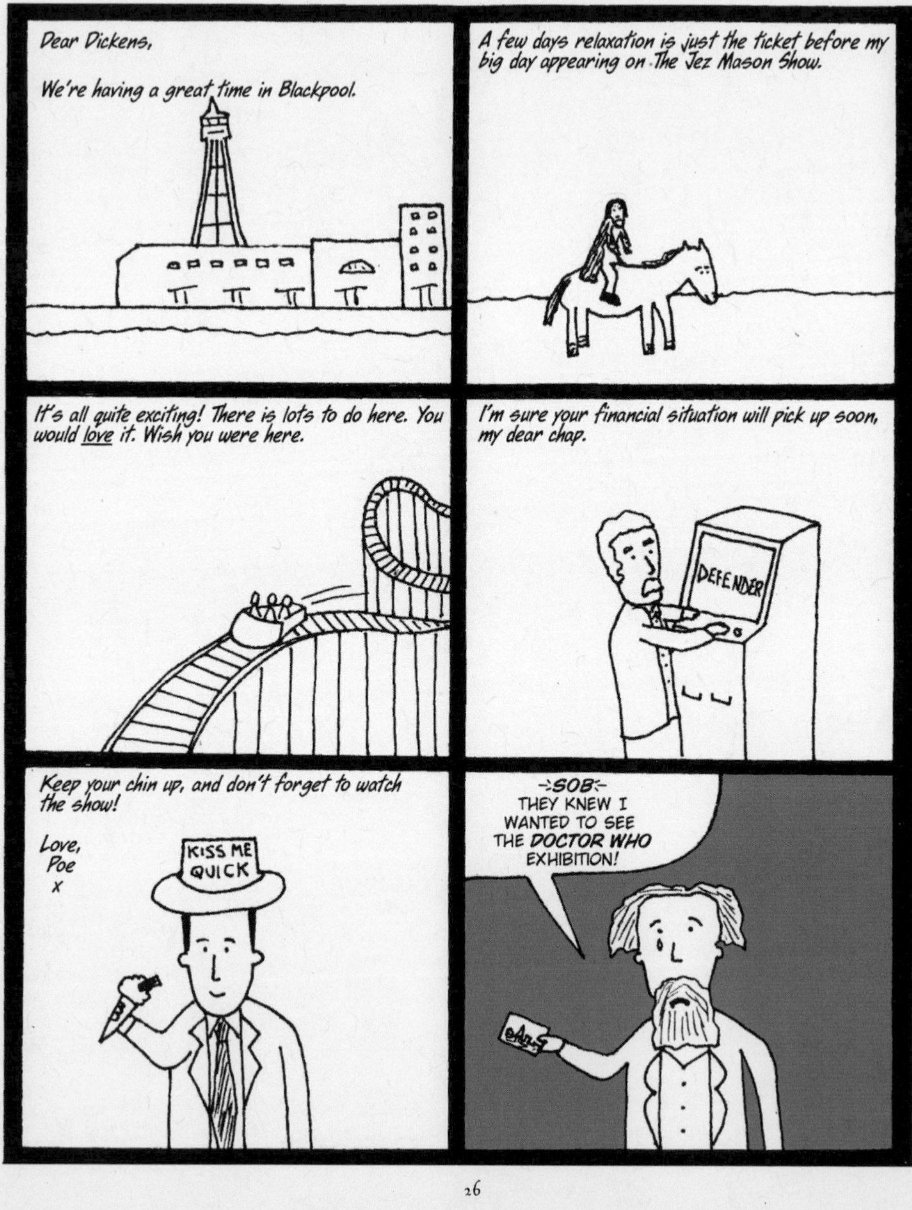
Dear Dickens,
We're having a great time in Blackpool.
A few days relaxation is just the ticket before my big day appearing on The Jez Mason Show.
It's all quite exciting! There is lots to do here. You would love it. Wish you were here.
I'm sure your financial situation will pick up soon, my dear chap.
DEFENDER
Keep your chin up, and don't forget to watch the show!
Love,
Poe
x
KISS ME QUICK
SOB
THEY KNEW I WANTED TO SEE THE DOCTOR WHO EXHIBITION!

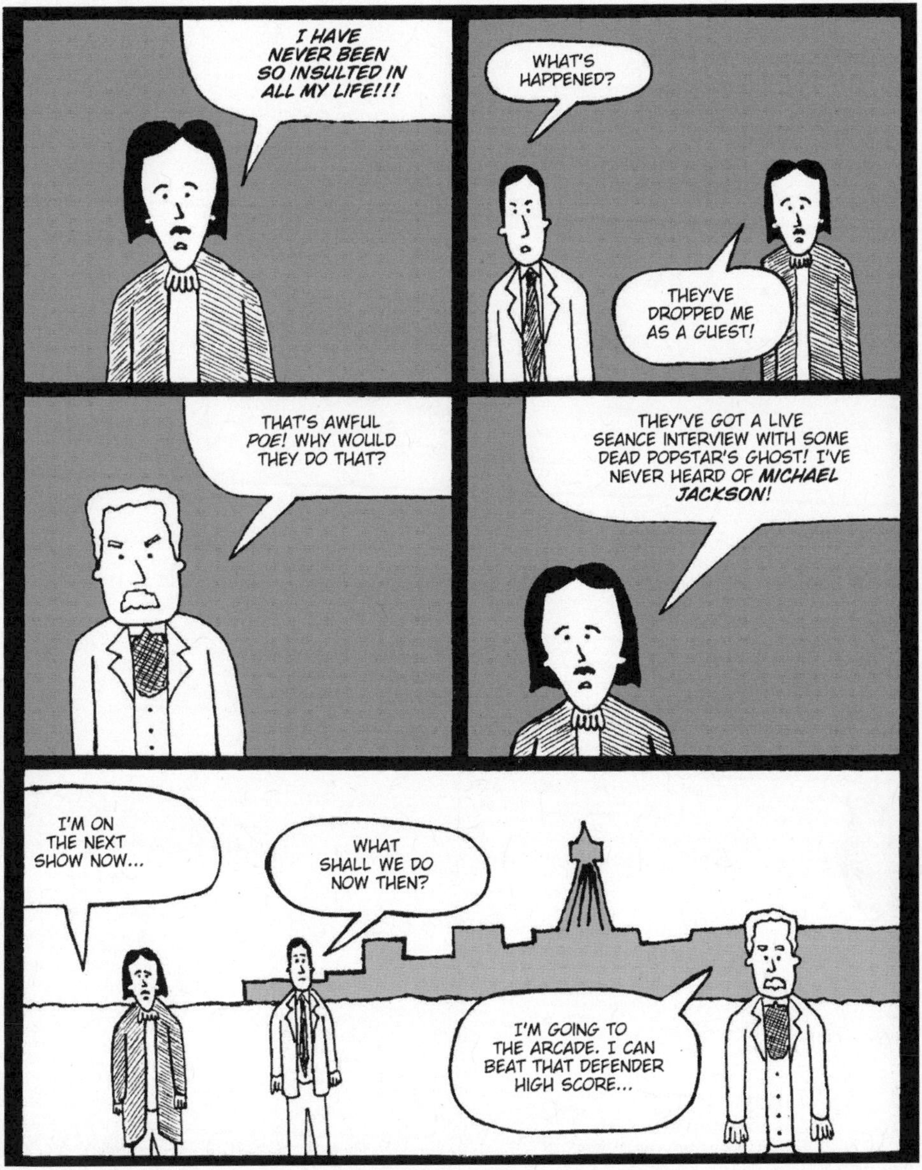
I HAVE NEVER BEEN SO INSULTED IN ALL MY LIFE!!!
WHAT'S HAPPENED?
THEY'VE DROPPED ME AS A GUEST!
THAT'S AWFUL POE! WHY WOULD THEY DO THAT?
THEY'VE GOT A LIVE SEANCE INTERVIEW WITH SOME DEAD POPSTAR'S GHOST! I'VE NEVER HEARD OF MICHAEL JACKSON!
I'M ON THE NEXT SHOW NOW...
WHAT SHALL WE DO NOW THEN?
I'M GOING TO THE ARCADE. I CAN BEAT THAT DEFENDER HIGH SCORE...

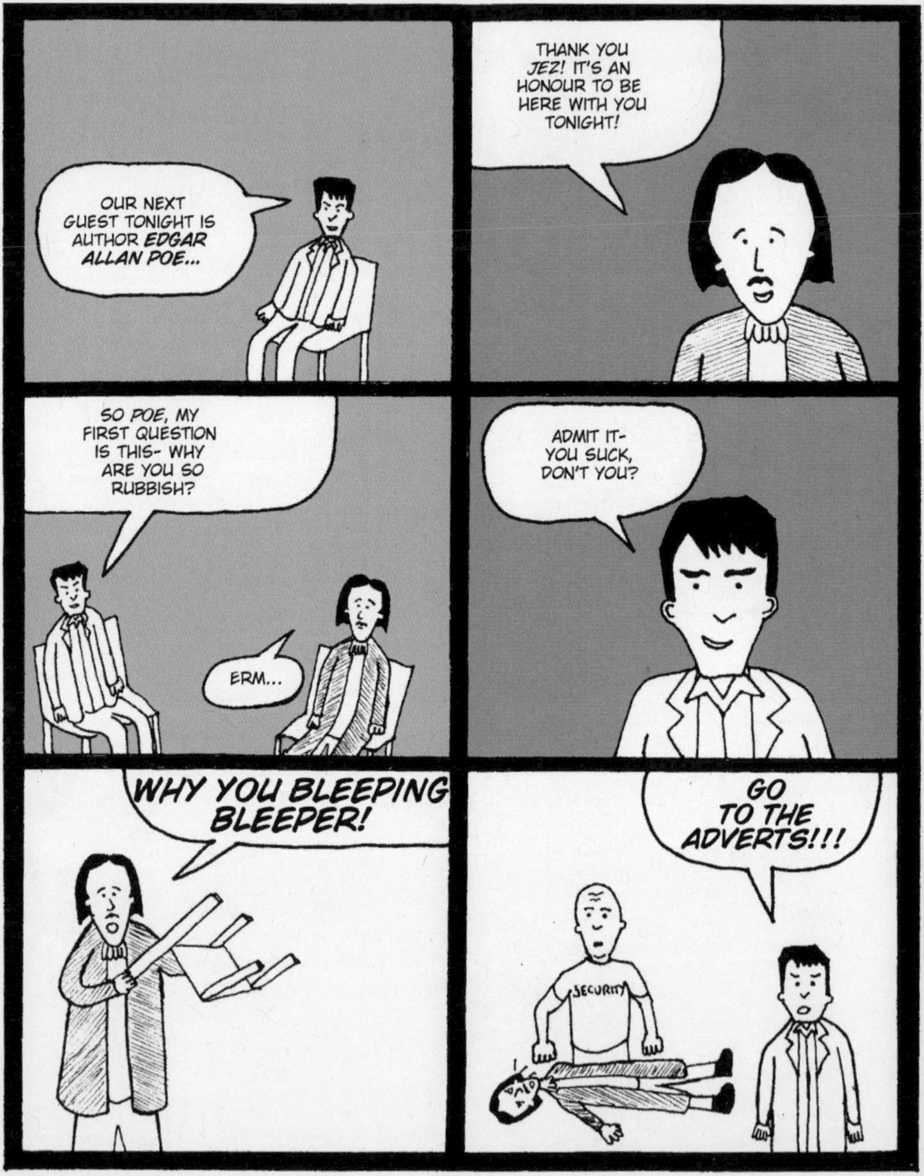
OUR NEXT GUEST TONIGHT IS AUTHOR EDGAR ALLAN POE...
THANK YOU JEZ! IT'S AN HONOUR TO BE HERE WITH YOU TONIGHT!
SO POE, MY FIRST QUESTION IS THIS- WHY ARE YOU SO RUBBISH?
ERM...
ADMIT IT- YOU SUCK, DON'T YOU?
WHY YOU BLEEPING BLEEPER!
GO TO THE ADVERTS!!!
SECURITY

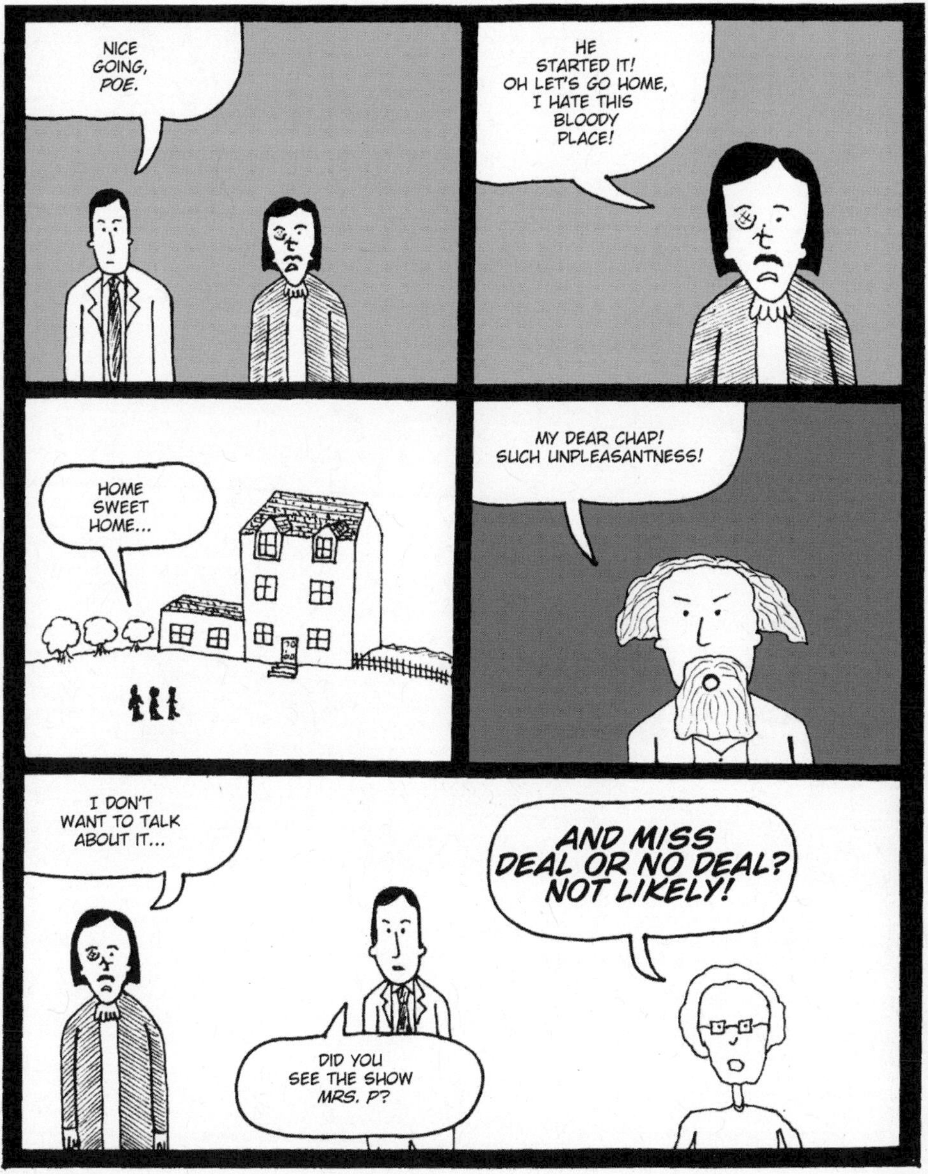
NICE GOING, POE.
HE STARTED IT! OH LET'S GO HOME, I HATE THIS BLOODY PLACE!
HOME SWEET HOME...
MY DEAR CHAP! SUCH UNPLEASANTNESS!
I DON'T WANT TO TALK ABOUT IT...
DID YOU SEE THE SHOW MRS. P?
AND MISS DEAL OR NO DEAL? NOT LIKELY!

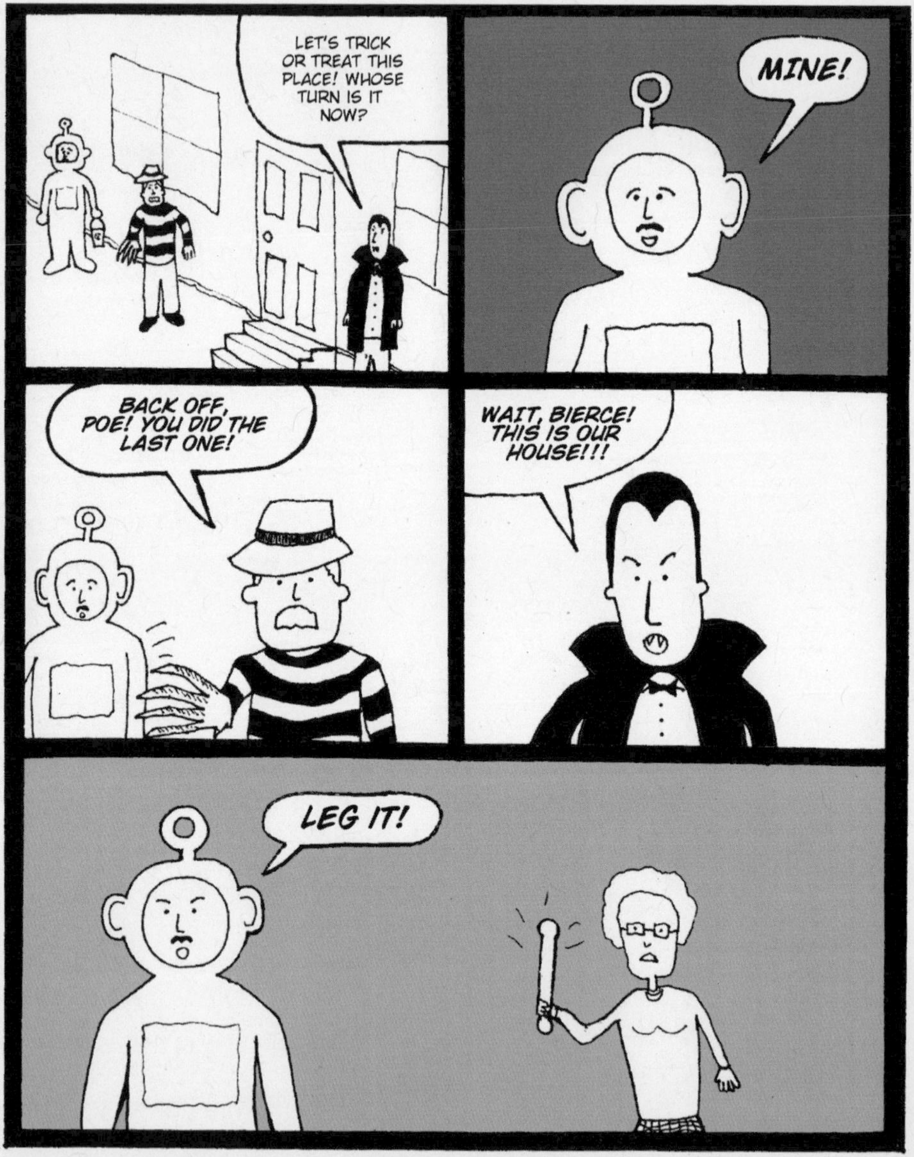
LET'S TRICK OR TREAT THIS PLACE! WHOSE TURN IS IT NOW?
MINE!
BACK OFF, POE! YOU DID THE LAST ONE!
WAIT, BIERCE! THIS IS OUR HOUSE!!!
LEG IT!

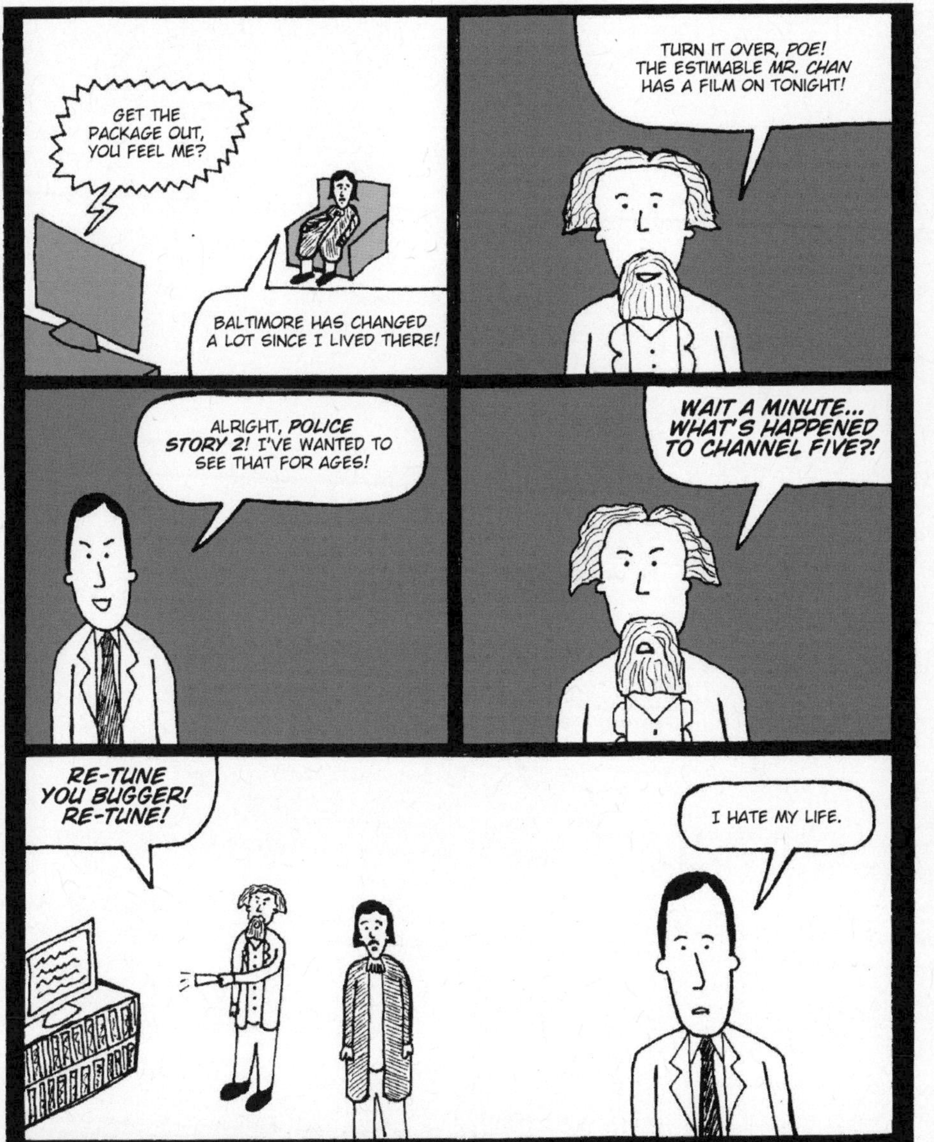
GET THE PACKAGE OUT, YOU FEEL ME?
BALTIMORE HAS CHANGED A LOT SINCE I LIVED THERE!
TURN IT OVER, *POE!* THE ESTIMABLE *MR. CHAN* HAS A FILM ON TONIGHT!
ALRIGHT, *POLICE STORY 2!* I'VE WANTED TO SEE THAT FOR AGES!
*WAIT A MINUTE... WHAT'S HAPPENED TO CHANNEL FIVE?!*
*RE-TUNE YOU BUGGER! RE-TUNE!*
I HATE MY LIFE.

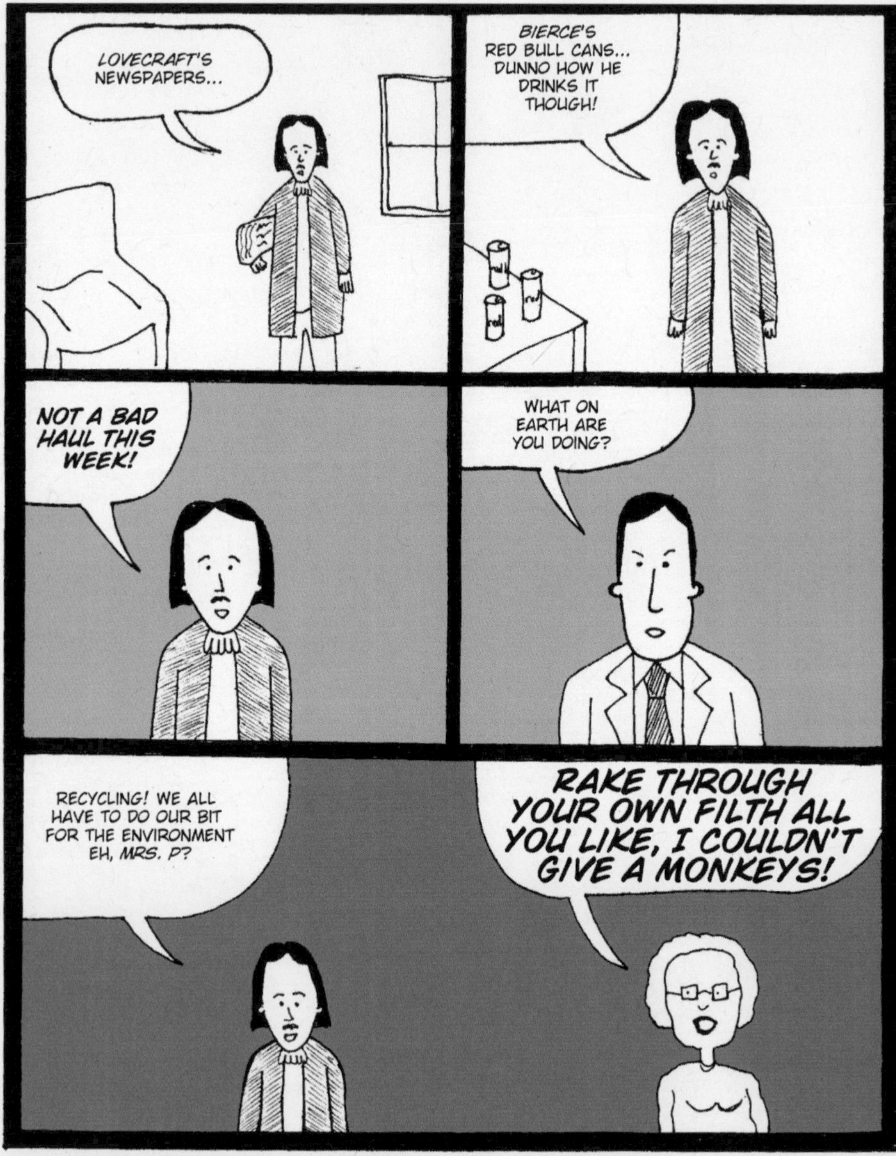
LOVECRAFT'S NEWSPAPERS...
BIERCE'S RED BULL CANS... DUNNO HOW HE DRINKS IT THOUGH!
NOT A BAD HAUL THIS WEEK!
WHAT ON EARTH ARE YOU DOING?
RECYCLING! WE ALL HAVE TO DO OUR BIT FOR THE ENVIRONMENT EH, MRS. P?
RAKE THROUGH YOUR OWN FILTH ALL YOU LIKE, I COULDN'T GIVE A MONKEYS!

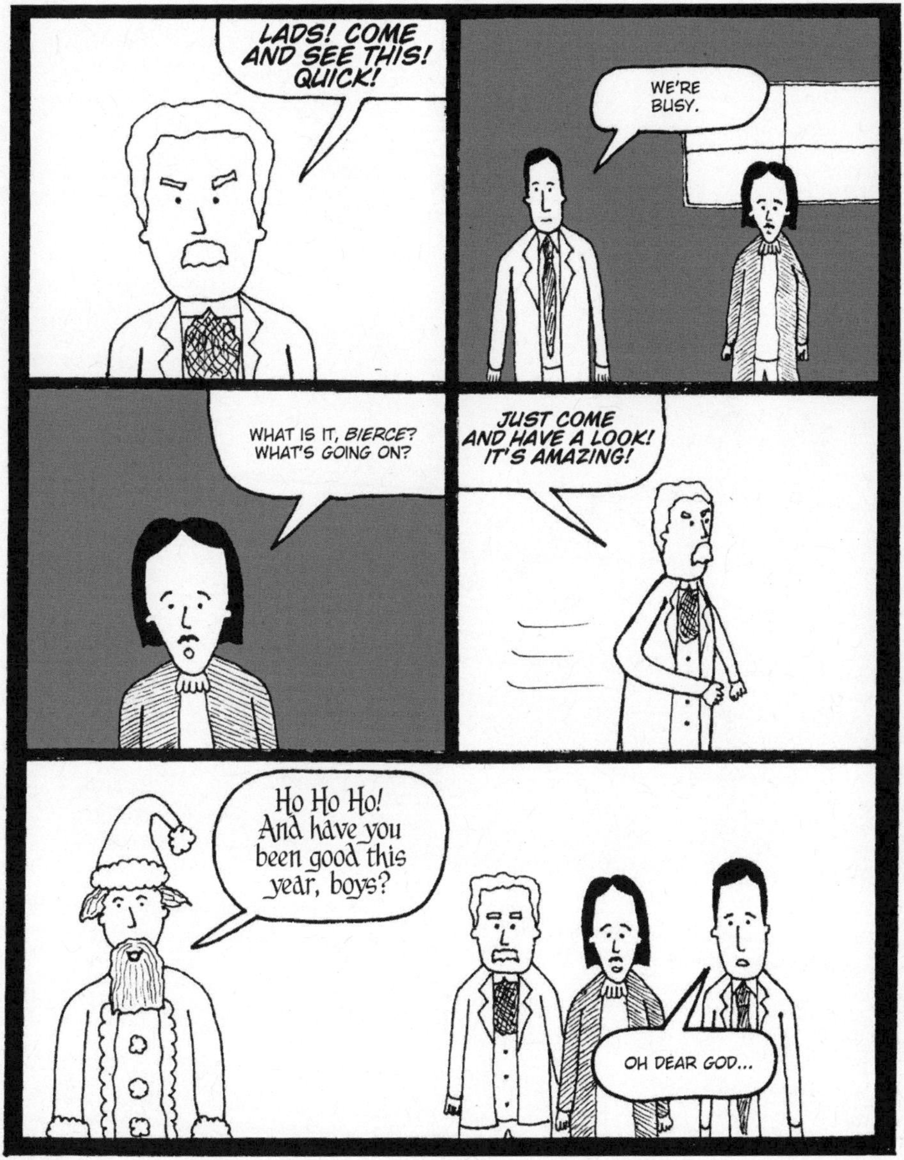
LADS! COME AND SEE THIS! QUICK!
WE'RE BUSY.
WHAT IS IT, BIERCE? WHAT'S GOING ON?
JUST COME AND HAVE A LOOK! IT'S AMAZING!
Ho Ho Ho! And have you been good this year, boys?
OH DEAR GOD...

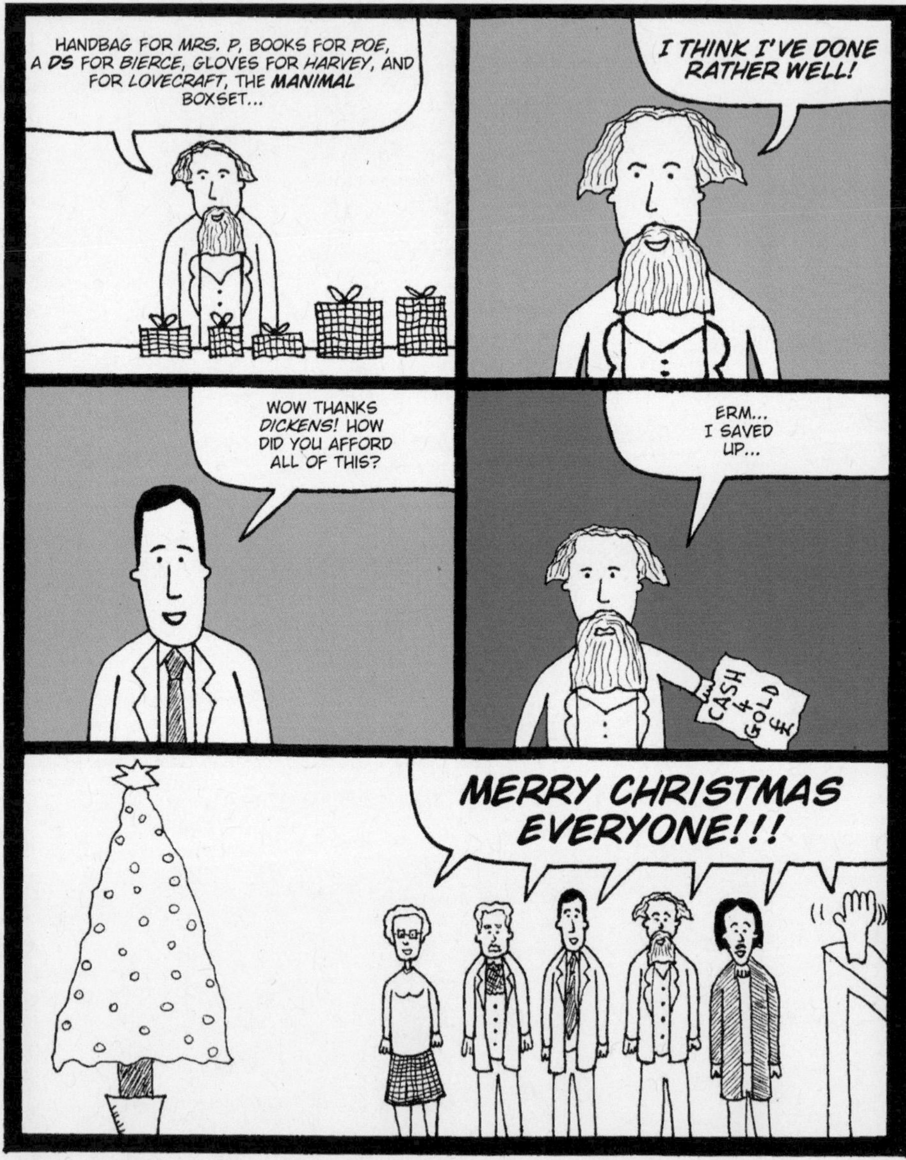
HANDBAG FOR MRS. P, BOOKS FOR POE, A DS FOR BIERCE, GLOVES FOR HARVEY, AND FOR LOVECRAFT, THE MANIMAL BOXSET...
I THINK I'VE DONE RATHER WELL!
WOW THANKS DICKENS! HOW DID YOU AFFORD ALL OF THIS?
ERM... I SAVED UP...
CASH 4 GOLD £
MERRY CHRISTMAS EVERYONE!!!

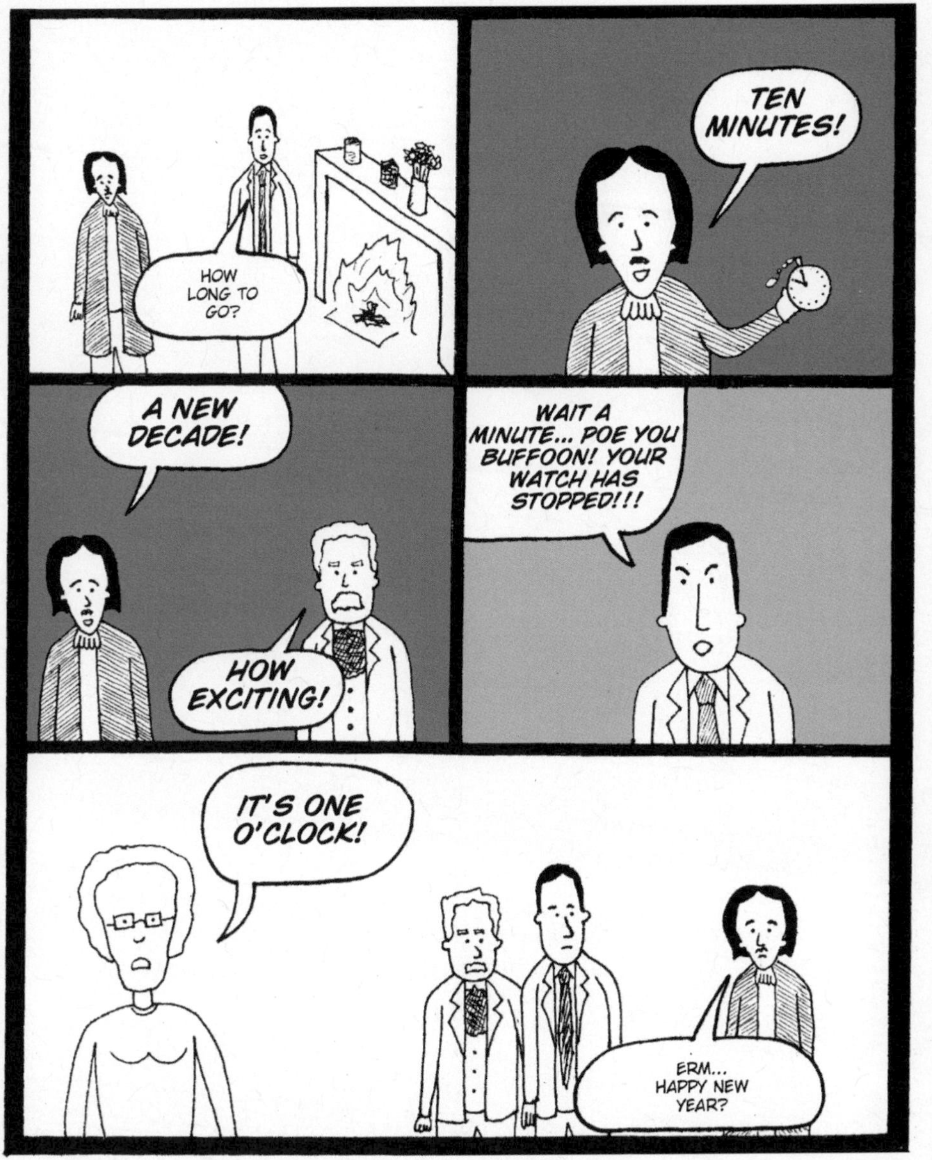
HOW LONG TO GO?
TEN MINUTES!
A NEW DECADE!
HOW EXCITING!
WAIT A MINUTE... POE YOU BUFFOON! YOUR WATCH HAS STOPPED!!!
IT'S ONE O'CLOCK!
ERM... HAPPY NEW YEAR?

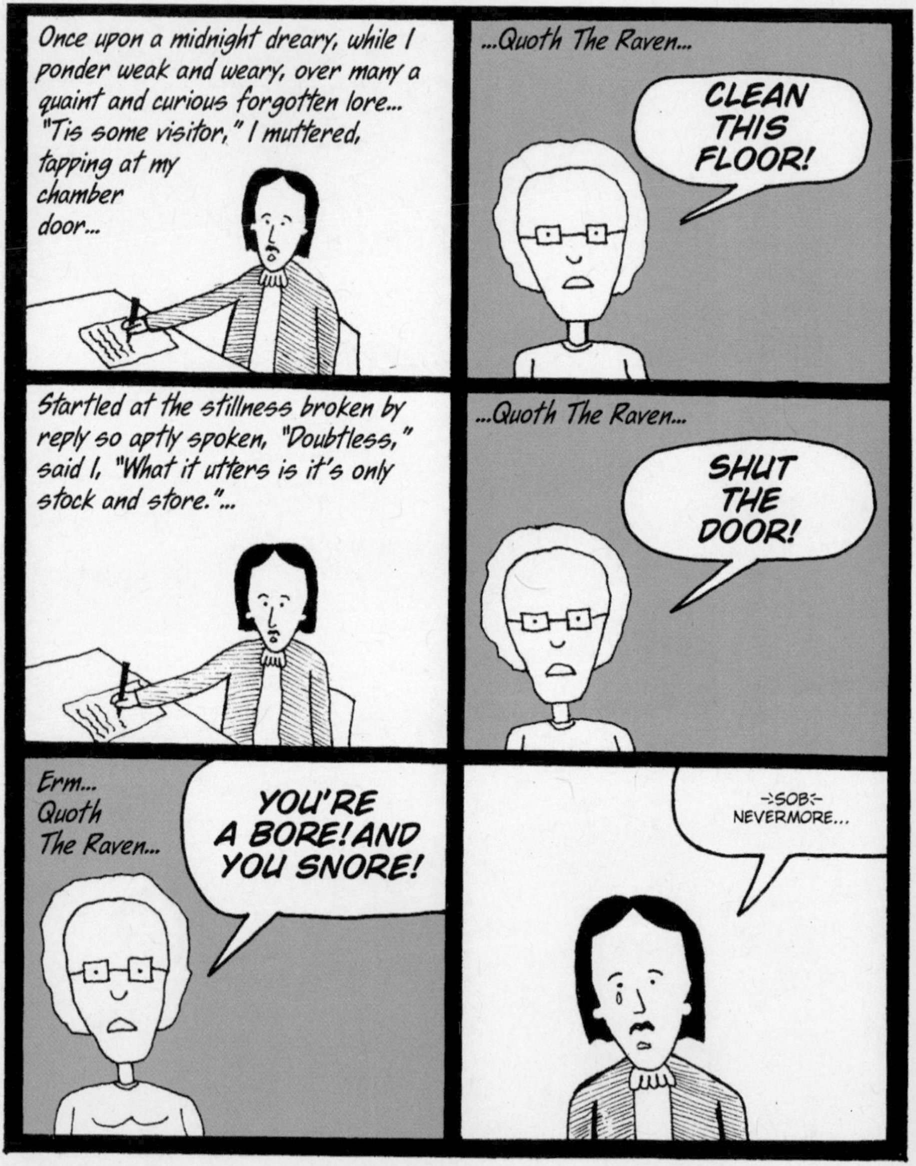

Once upon a midnight dreary, while I ponder weak and weary, over many a quaint and curious forgotten lore... "Tis some visitor," I muttered, tapping at my chamber door...
...Quoth The Raven...
CLEAN THIS FLOOR!
Startled at the stillness broken by reply so aptly spoken, "Doubtless," said I, "What it utters is it's only stock and store."...
...Quoth The Raven...
SHUT THE DOOR!
Erm... Quoth The Raven...
YOU'RE A BORE! AND YOU SNORE!
SOB
NEVERMORE...

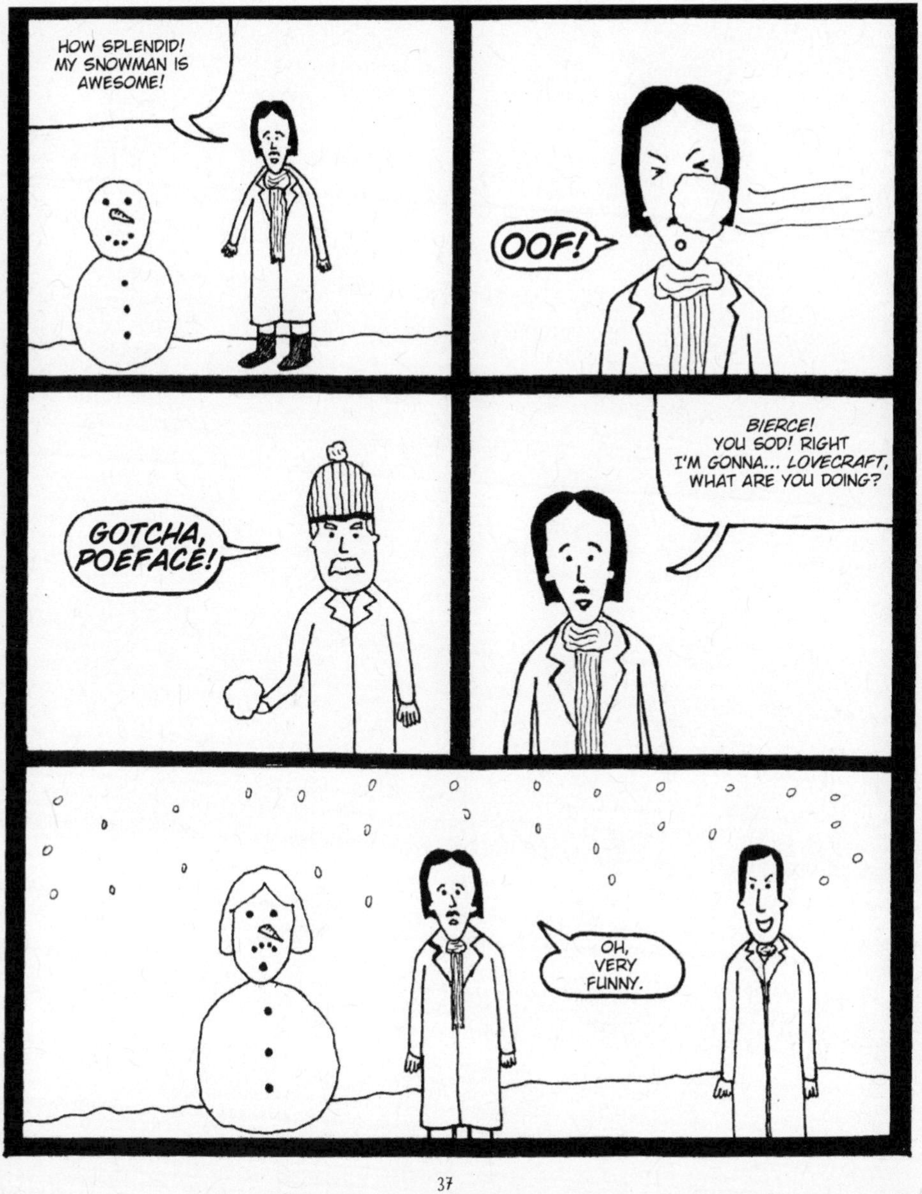
HOW SPLENDID! MY SNOWMAN IS AWESOME!
OOF!
GOTCHA, POEFACE!
BIERCE! YOU SOD! RIGHT I'M GONNA... LOVECRAFT, WHAT ARE YOU DOING?
OH, VERY FUNNY.

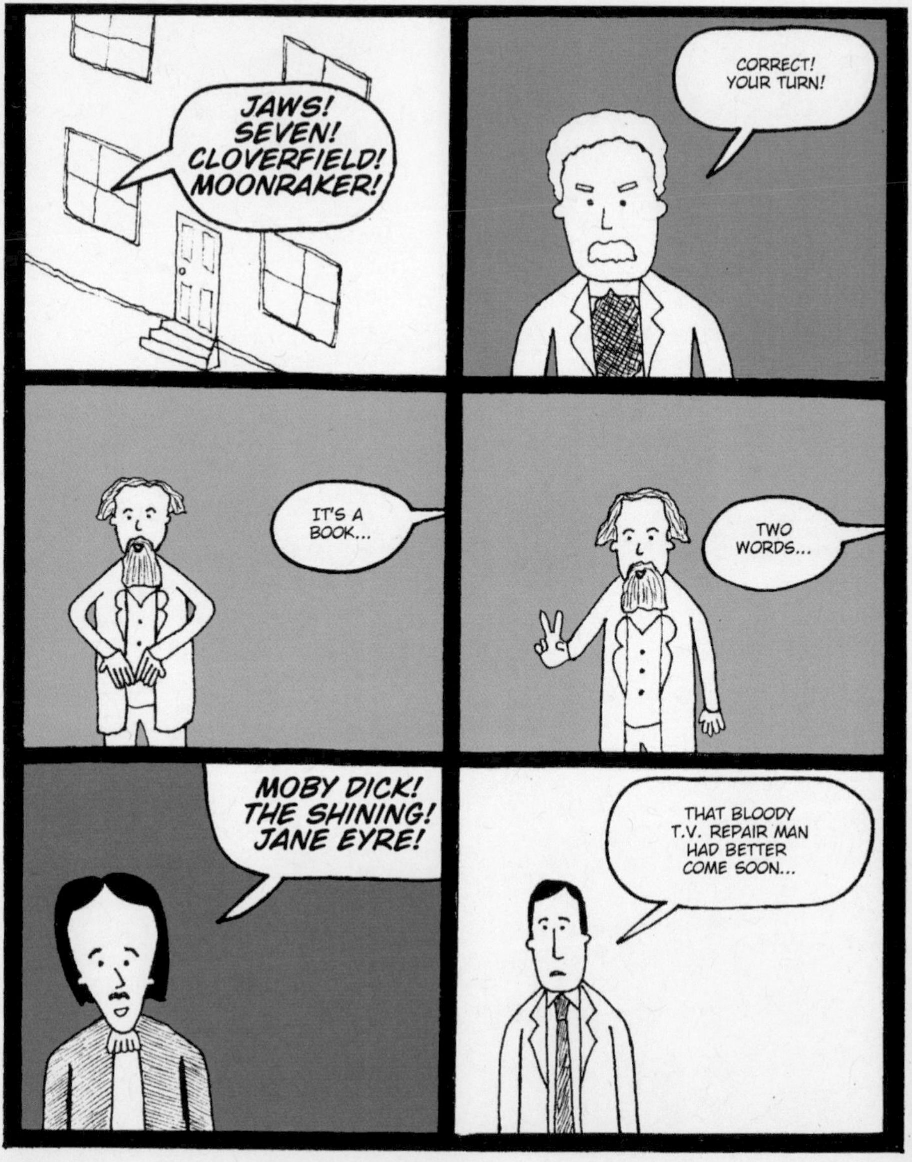
JAWS! SEVEN! CLOVERFIELD! MOONRAKER!
CORRECT! YOUR TURN!
IT'S A BOOK...
TWO WORDS...
MOBY DICK! THE SHINING! JANE EYRE!
THAT BLOODY T.V. REPAIR MAN HAD BETTER COME SOON...

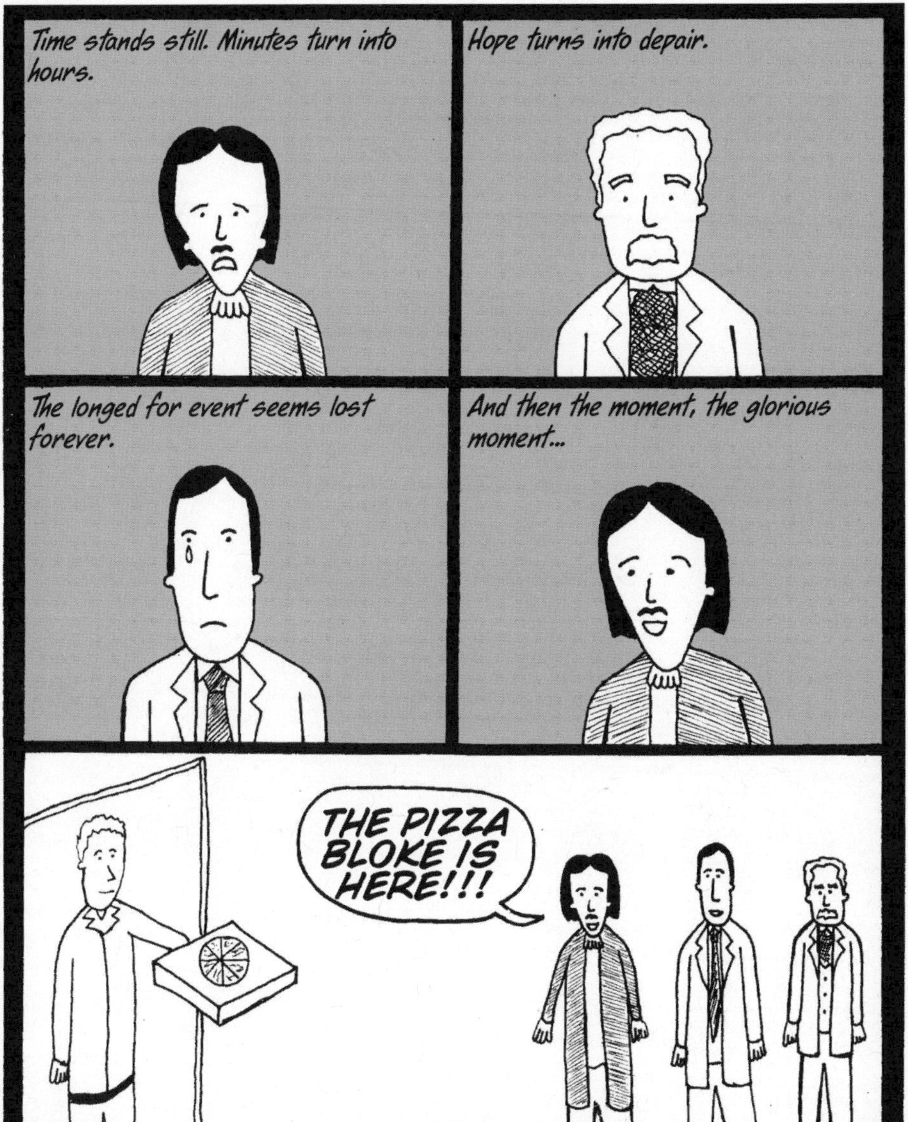
Time stands still. Minutes turn into hours.
Hope turns into depair.
The longed for event seems lost forever.
And then the moment, the glorious moment...
THE PIZZA BLOKE IS HERE!!!

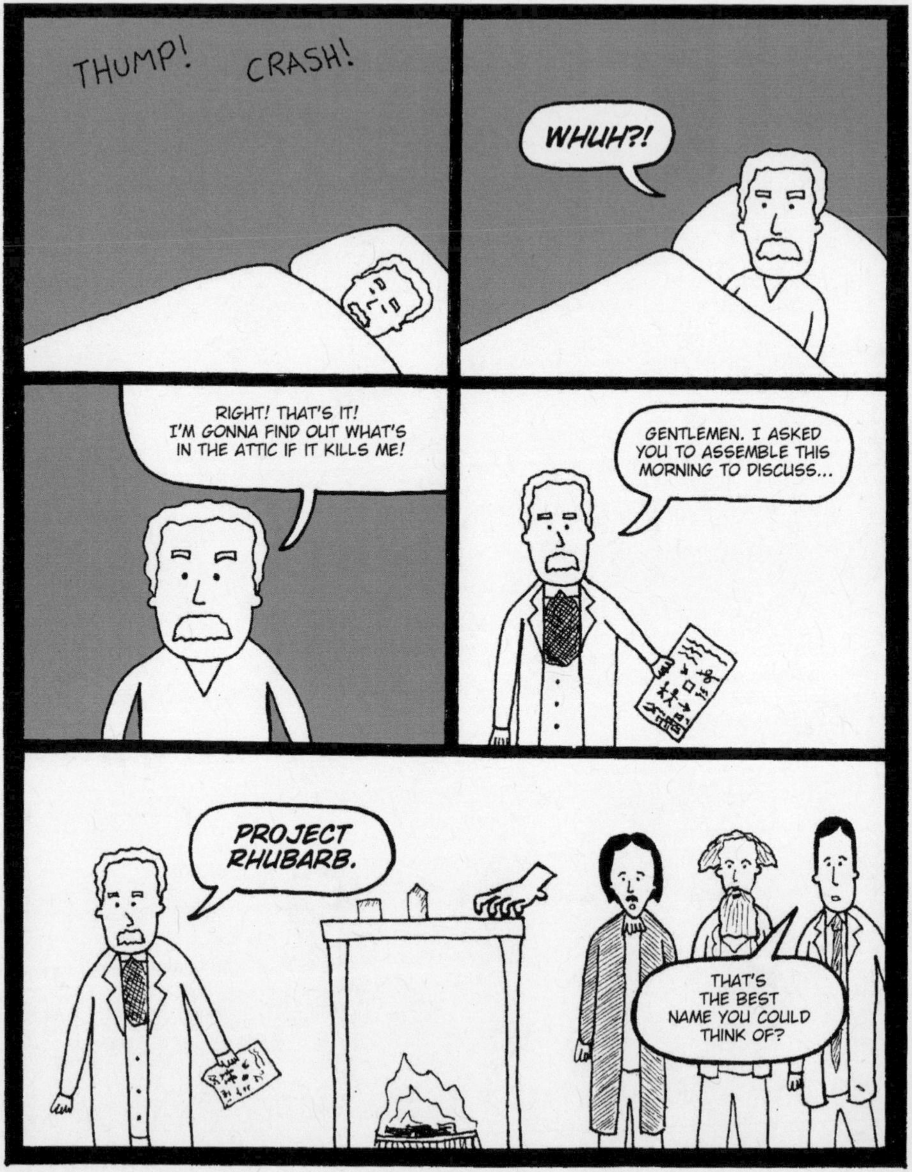
THUMP! CRASH!
WHUH?!
RIGHT! THAT'S IT! I'M GONNA FIND OUT WHAT'S IN THE ATTIC IF IT KILLS ME!
GENTLEMEN. I ASKED YOU TO ASSEMBLE THIS MORNING TO DISCUSS...
PROJECT RHUBARB.
THAT'S THE BEST NAME YOU COULD THINK OF?

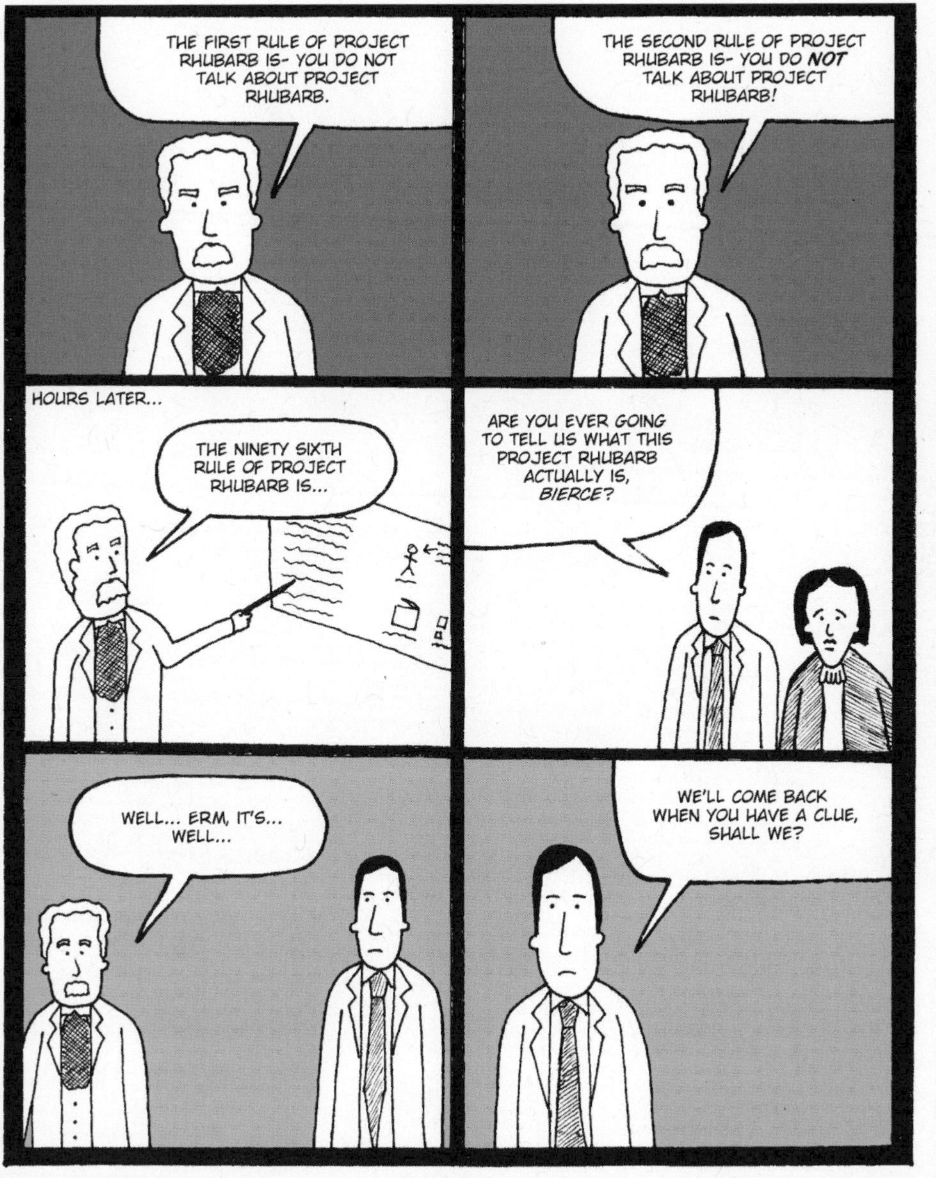
THE FIRST RULE OF PROJECT RHUBARB IS- YOU DO NOT TALK ABOUT PROJECT RHUBARB.
THE SECOND RULE OF PROJECT RHUBARB IS- YOU DO **NOT** TALK ABOUT PROJECT RHUBARB!
HOURS LATER...
THE NINETY SIXTH RULE OF PROJECT RHUBARB IS...
ARE YOU EVER GOING TO TELL US WHAT THIS PROJECT RHUBARB ACTUALLY IS, *BIERCE*?
WELL... ERM, IT'S... WELL...
WE'LL COME BACK WHEN YOU HAVE A CLUE, SHALL WE?

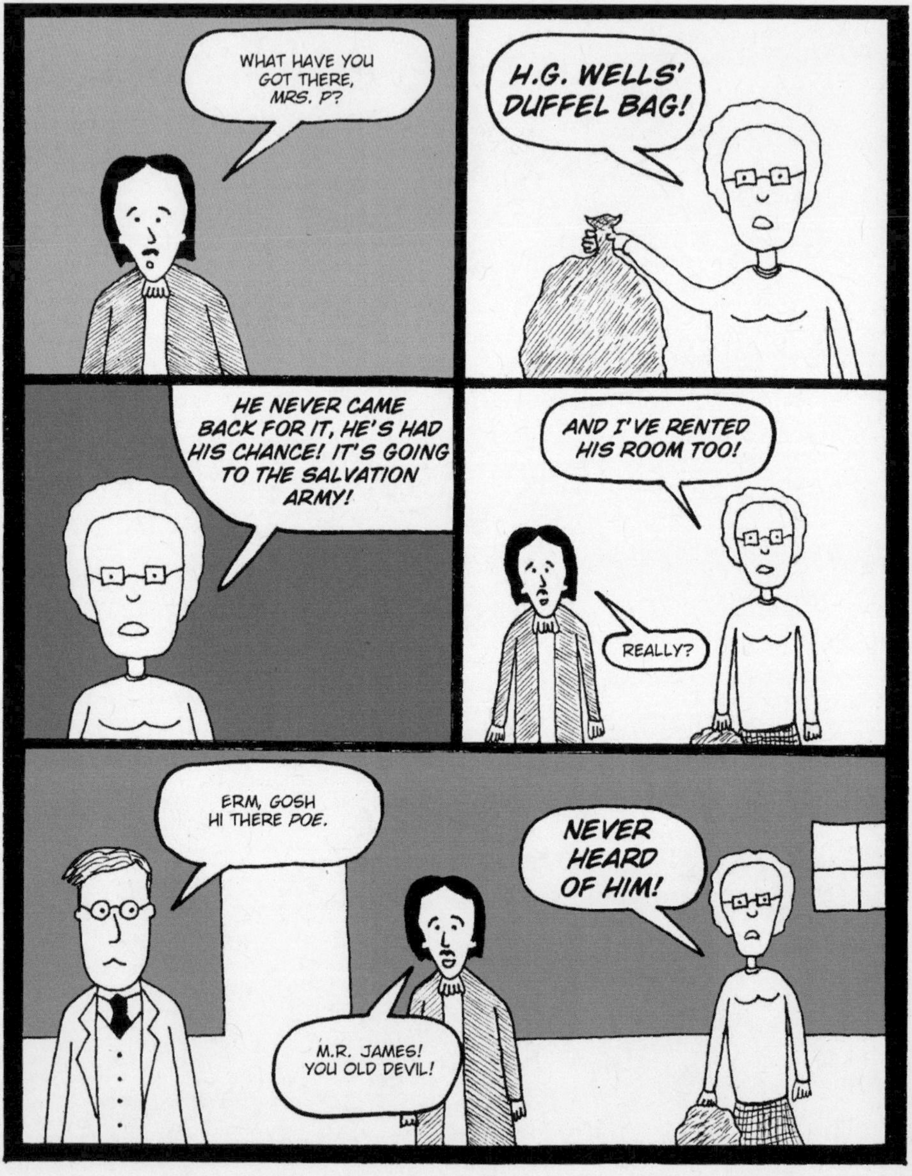
WHAT HAVE YOU GOT THERE, MRS. P?
H.G. WELLS' DUFFEL BAG!
HE NEVER CAME BACK FOR IT, HE'S HAD HIS CHANCE! IT'S GOING TO THE SALVATION ARMY!
AND I'VE RENTED HIS ROOM TOO!
REALLY?
ERM, GOSH HI THERE POE.
M.R. JAMES! YOU OLD DEVIL!
NEVER HEARD OF HIM!

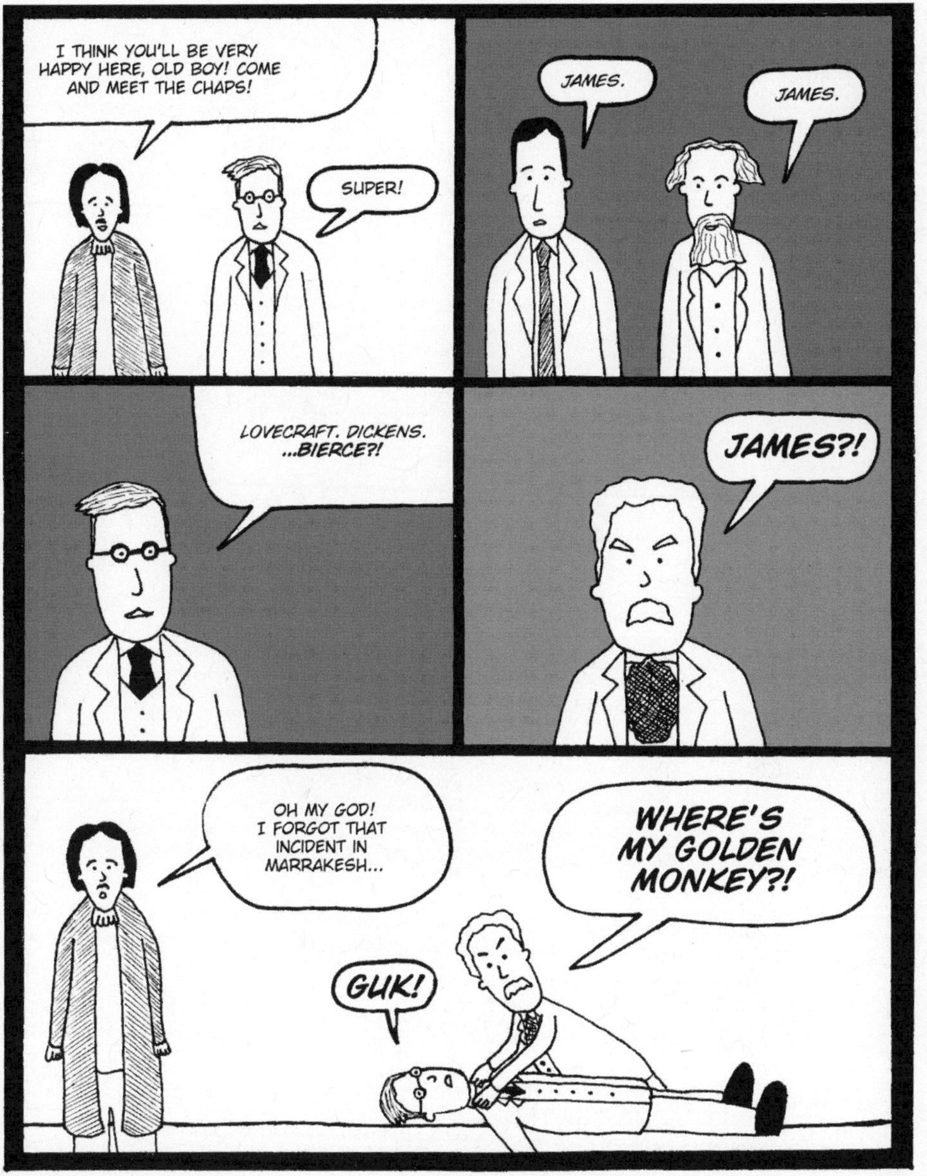
I THINK YOU'LL BE VERY HAPPY HERE, OLD BOY! COME AND MEET THE CHAPS!
SUPER!
JAMES.
JAMES.
LOVECRAFT. DICKENS. ...BIERCE?!
JAMES?!
OH MY GOD! I FORGOT THAT INCIDENT IN MARRAKESH...
WHERE'S MY GOLDEN MONKEY?!
GUK!

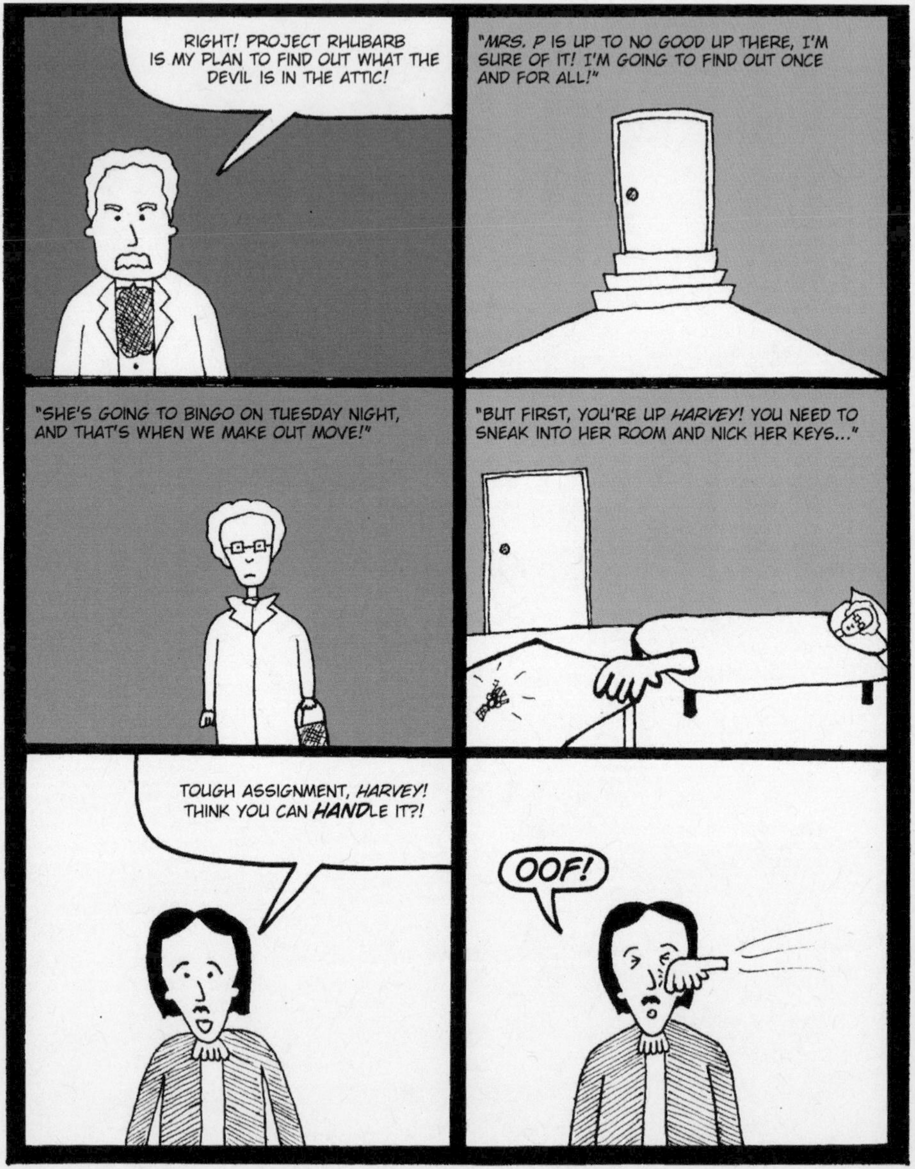
RIGHT! PROJECT RHUBARB IS MY PLAN TO FIND OUT WHAT THE DEVIL IS IN THE ATTIC!
"MRS. P IS UP TO NO GOOD UP THERE, I'M SURE OF IT! I'M GOING TO FIND OUT ONCE AND FOR ALL!"
"SHE'S GOING TO BINGO ON TUESDAY NIGHT, AND THAT'S WHEN WE MAKE OUT MOVE!"
"BUT FIRST, YOU'RE UP HARVEY! YOU NEED TO SNEAK INTO HER ROOM AND NICK HER KEYS..."
TOUGH ASSIGNMENT, HARVEY! THINK YOU CAN HANDLE IT?!
OOF!

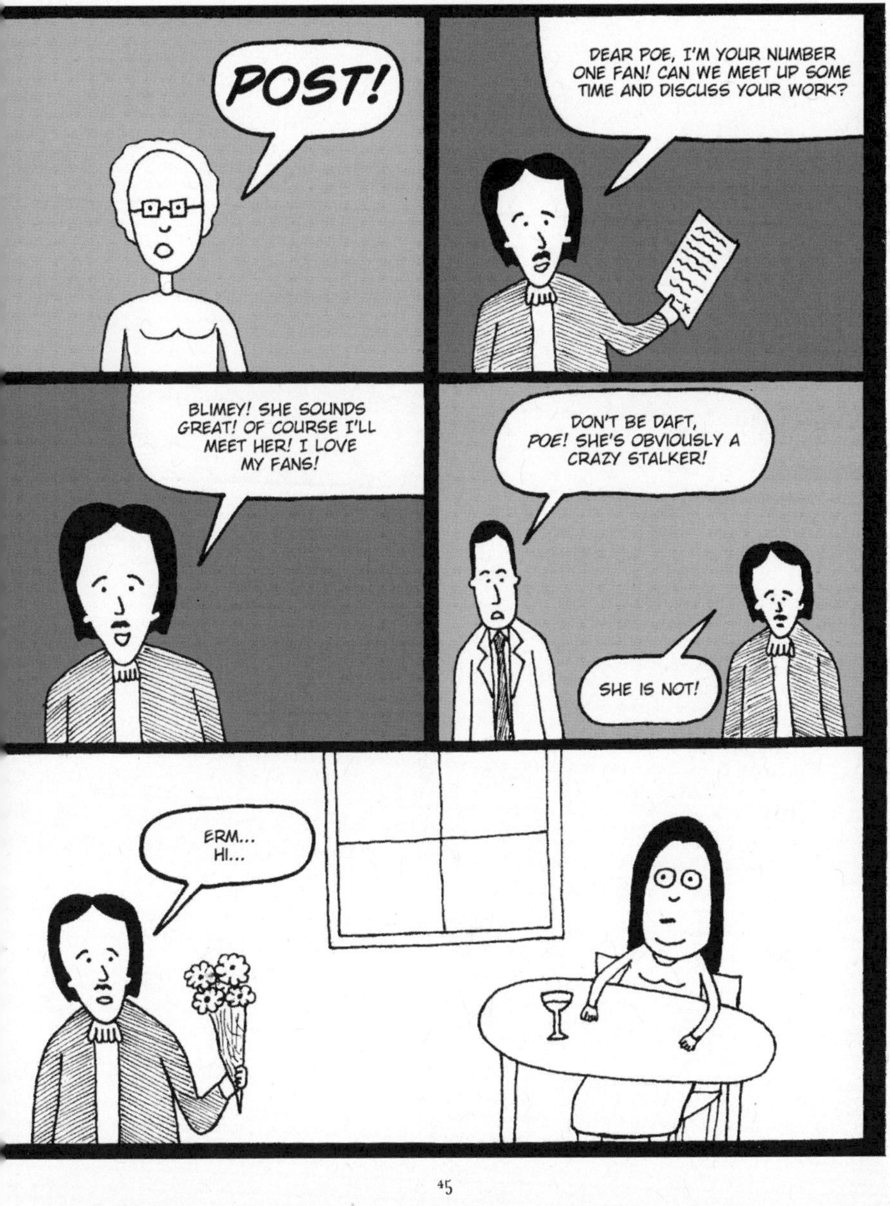
POST!
DEAR POE, I'M YOUR NUMBER ONE FAN! CAN WE MEET UP SOME TIME AND DISCUSS YOUR WORK?
BLIMEY! SHE SOUNDS GREAT! OF COURSE I'LL MEET HER! I LOVE MY FANS!
DON'T BE DAFT, POE! SHE'S OBVIOUSLY A CRAZY STALKER!
SHE IS NOT!
ERM... HI...

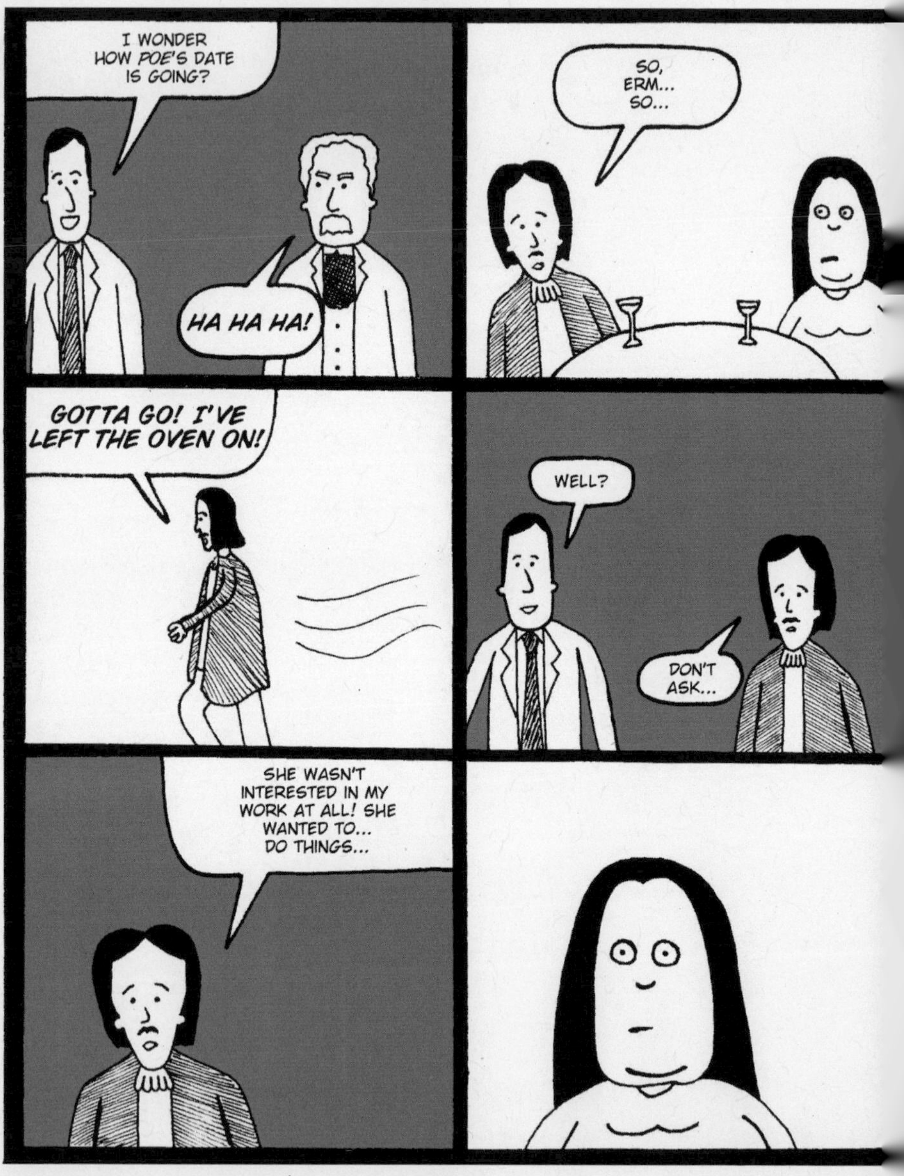
I WONDER HOW POE'S DATE IS GOING?
HA HA HA!
SO, ERM... SO...
GOTTA GO! I'VE LEFT THE OVEN ON!
WELL?
DON'T ASK...
SHE WASN'T INTERESTED IN MY WORK AT ALL! SHE WANTED TO... DO THINGS...

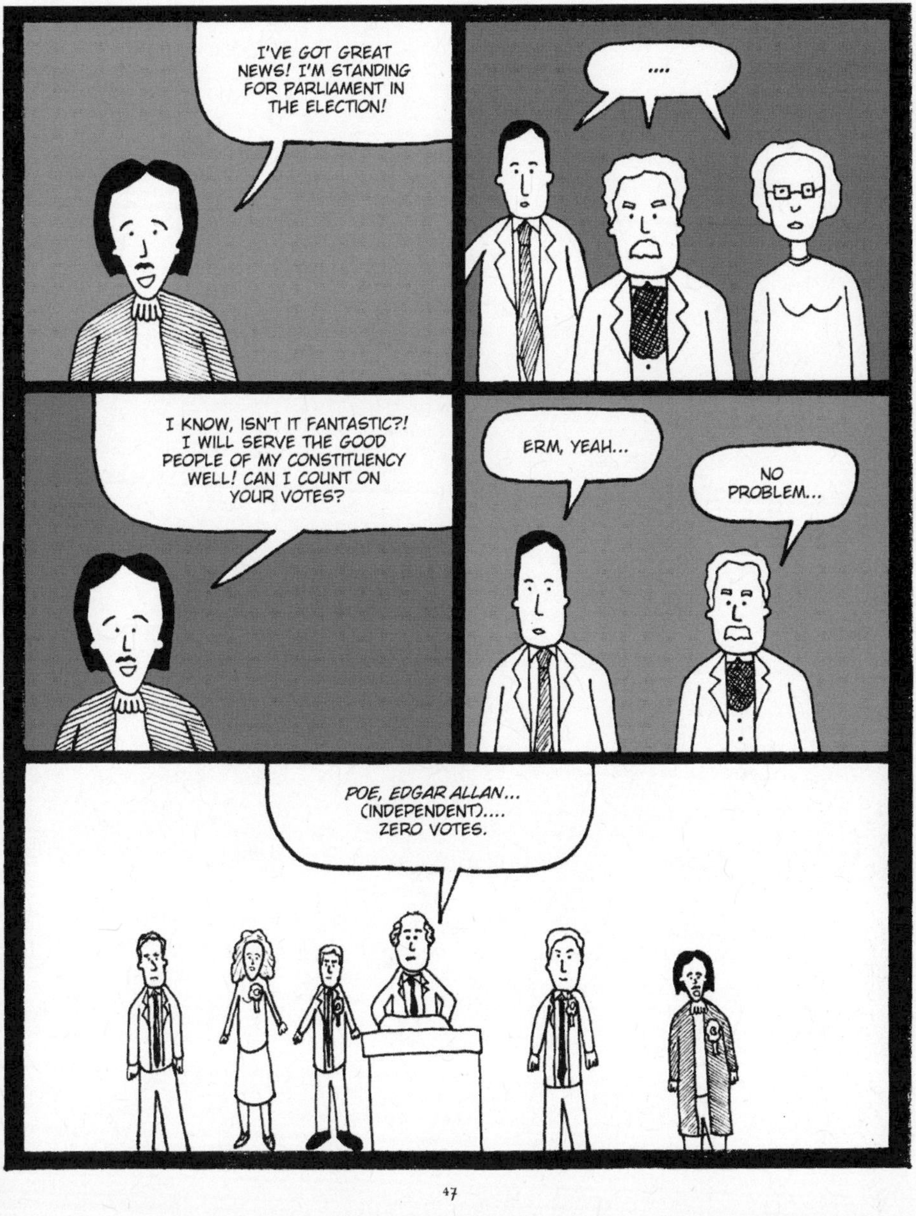
I'VE GOT GREAT NEWS! I'M STANDING FOR PARLIAMENT IN THE ELECTION!
....
I KNOW, ISN'T IT FANTASTIC?! I WILL SERVE THE GOOD PEOPLE OF MY CONSTITUENCY WELL! CAN I COUNT ON YOUR VOTES?
ERM, YEAH...
NO PROBLEM...
POE, EDGAR ALLAN... (INDEPENDENT).... ZERO VOTES.

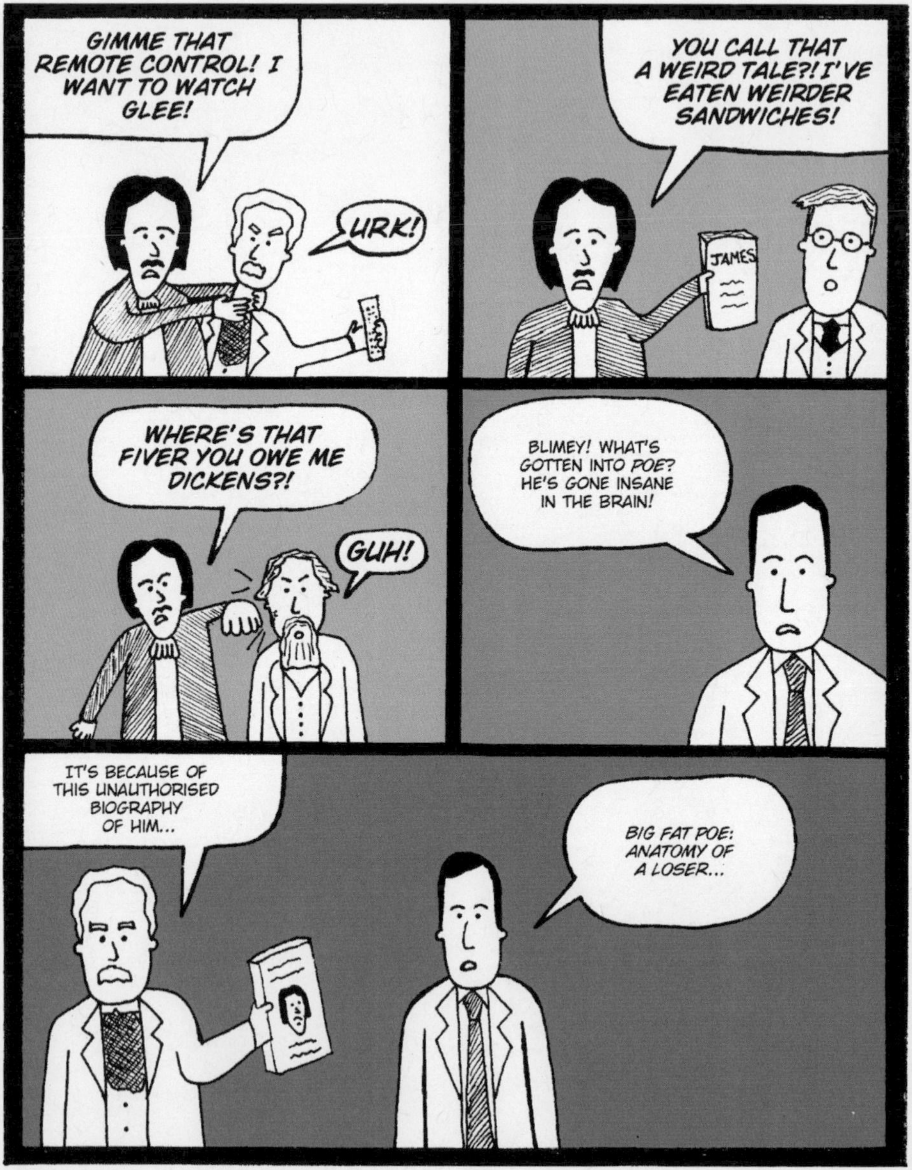
GIMME THAT REMOTE CONTROL! I WANT TO WATCH GLEE!
URK!
YOU CALL THAT A WEIRD TALE?! I'VE EATEN WEIRDER SANDWICHES!
JAMES
WHERE'S THAT FIVER YOU OWE ME DICKENS?!
GUH!
BLIMEY! WHAT'S GOTTEN INTO POE? HE'S GONE INSANE IN THE BRAIN!
IT'S BECAUSE OF THIS UNAUTHORISED BIOGRAPHY OF HIM...
BIG FAT POE: ANATOMY OF A LOSER...

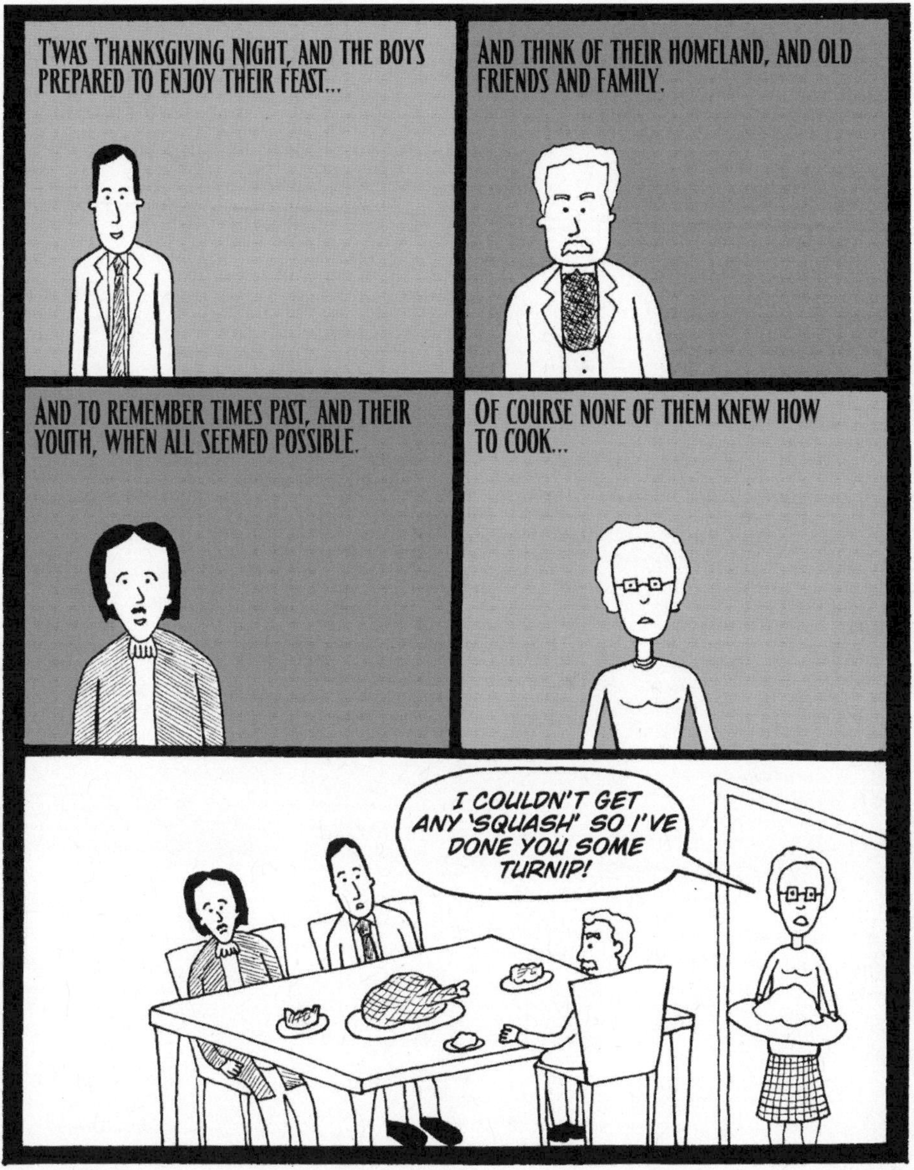
TWAS THANKSGIVING NIGHT, AND THE BOYS PREPARED TO ENJOY THEIR FEAST...
AND THINK OF THEIR HOMELAND, AND OLD FRIENDS AND FAMILY.
AND TO REMEMBER TIMES PAST, AND THEIR YOUTH, WHEN ALL SEEMED POSSIBLE.
OF COURSE NONE OF THEM KNEW HOW TO COOK...
I COULDN'T GET ANY 'SQUASH' SO I'VE DONE YOU SOME TURNIP!

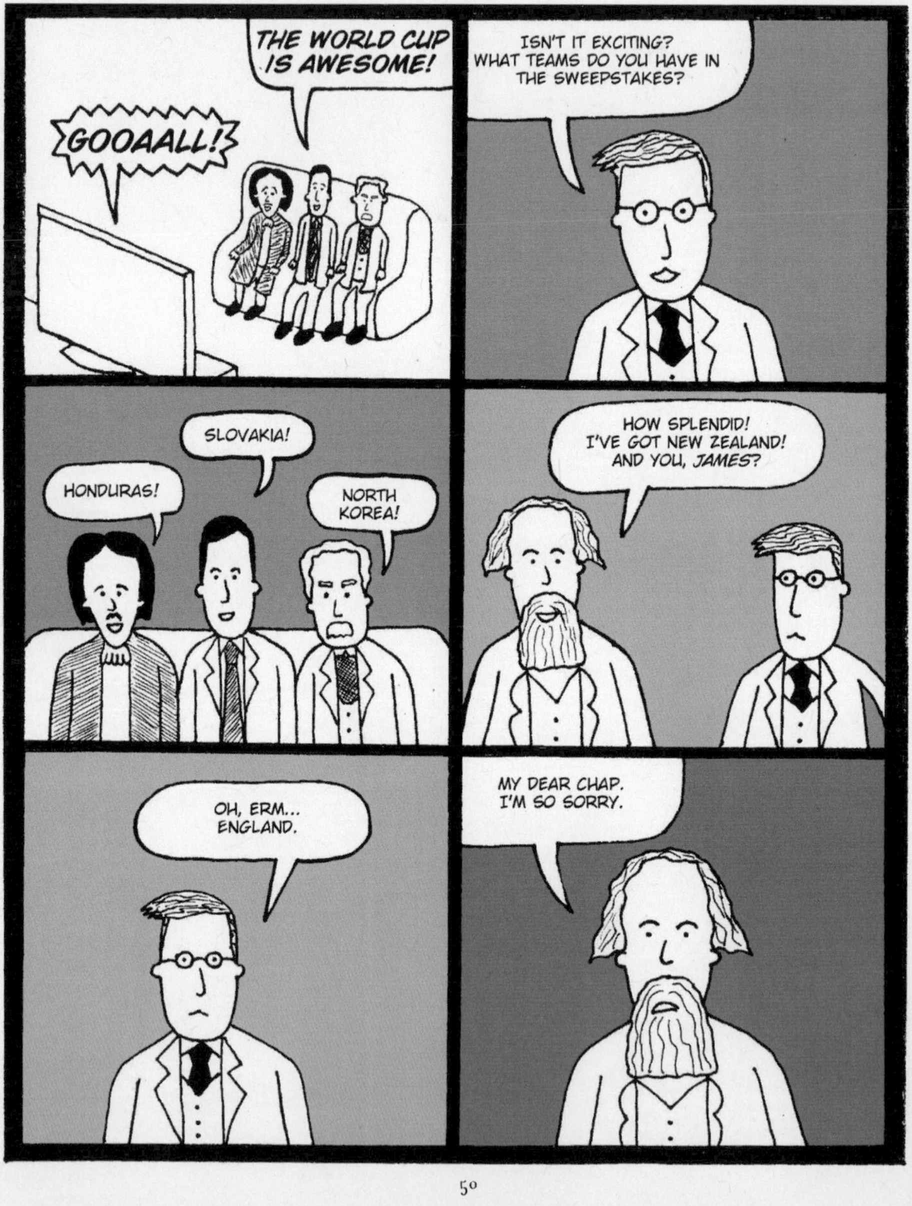
THE WORLD CUP IS AWESOME!
GOOAALL!
ISN'T IT EXCITING? WHAT TEAMS DO YOU HAVE IN THE SWEEPSTAKES?
HONDURAS!
SLOVAKIA!
NORTH KOREA!
HOW SPLENDID! I'VE GOT NEW ZEALAND! AND YOU, JAMES?
OH, ERM... ENGLAND.
MY DEAR CHAP. I'M SO SORRY.

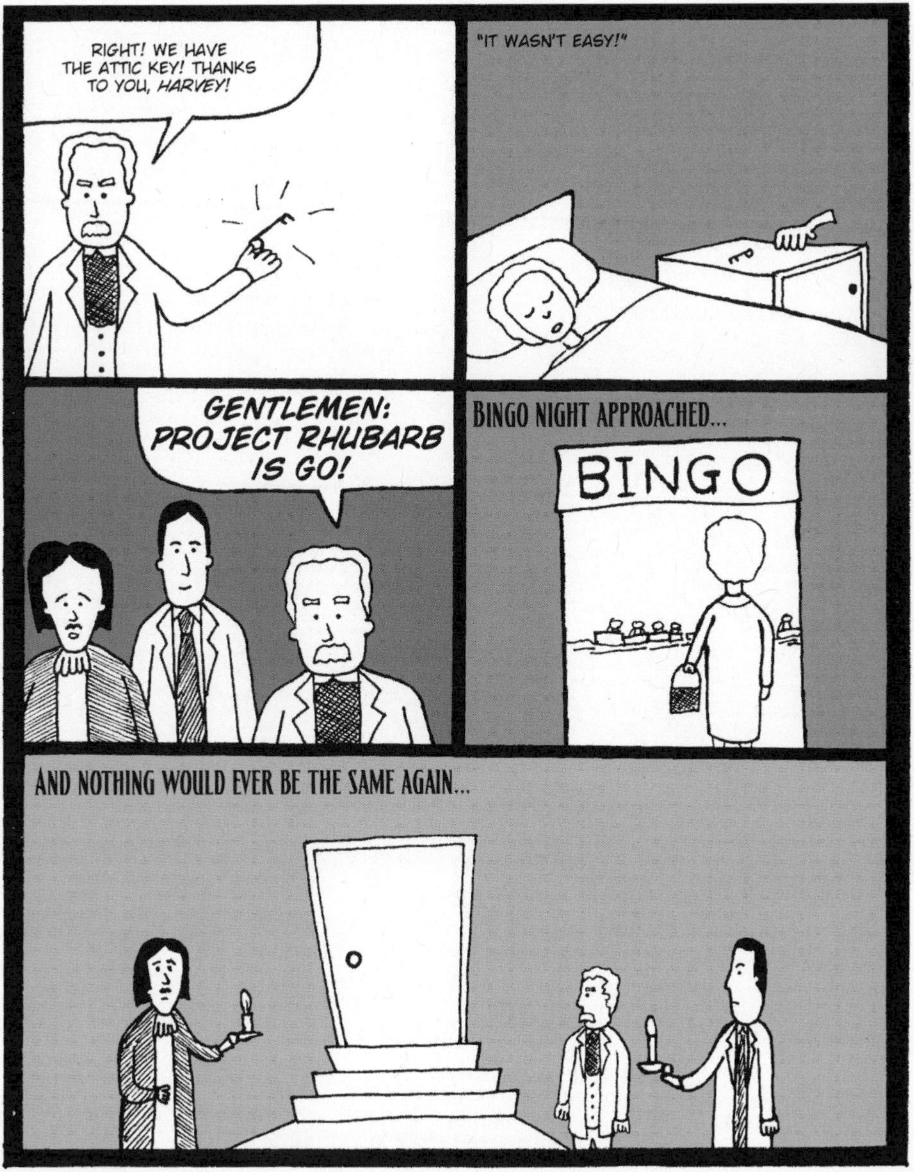
RIGHT! WE HAVE THE ATTIC KEY! THANKS TO YOU, HARVEY!
"IT WASN'T EASY!"
GENTLEMEN: PROJECT RHUBARB IS GO!
BINGO NIGHT APPROACHED...
BINGO
AND NOTHING WOULD EVER BE THE SAME AGAIN...

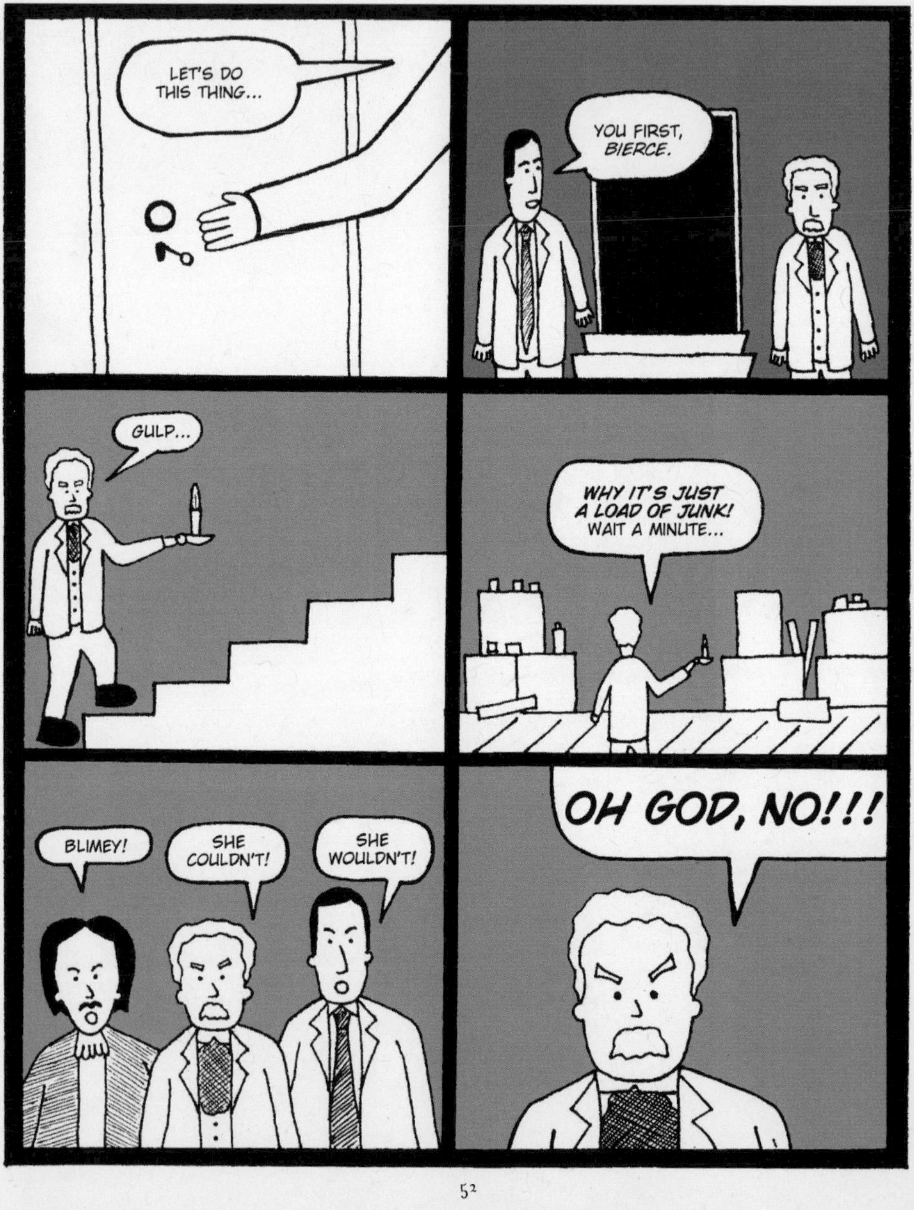
LET'S DO THIS THING...
YOU FIRST, BIERCE.
GULP...
WHY IT'S JUST A LOAD OF JUNK! WAIT A MINUTE...
BLIMEY!
SHE COULDN'T!
SHE WOULDN'T!
OH GOD, NO!!!

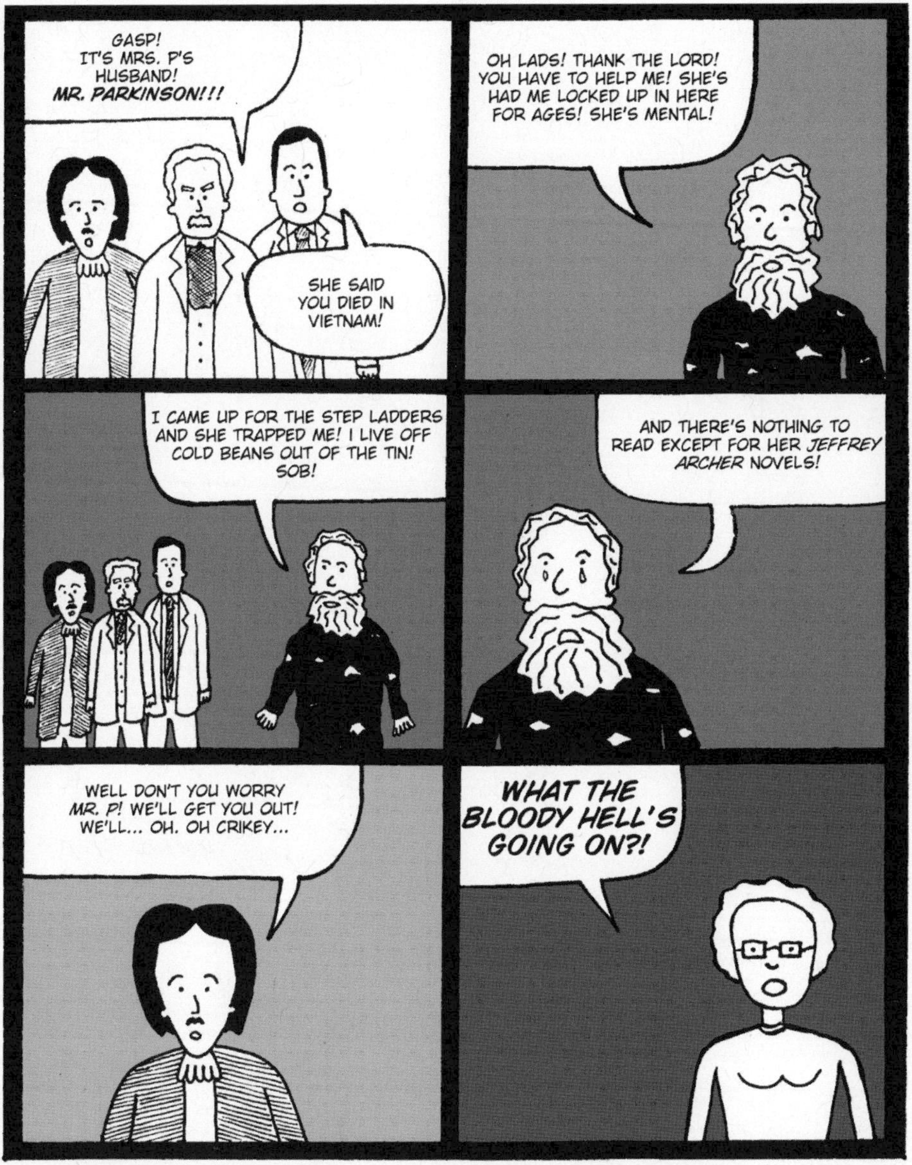
GASP! IT'S MRS. P'S HUSBAND! **MR. PARKINSON!!!**
SHE SAID YOU DIED IN VIETNAM!
OH LADS! THANK THE LORD! YOU HAVE TO HELP ME! SHE'S HAD ME LOCKED UP IN HERE FOR AGES! SHE'S MENTAL!
I CAME UP FOR THE STEP LADDERS AND SHE TRAPPED ME! I LIVE OFF COLD BEANS OUT OF THE TIN! SOB!
AND THERE'S NOTHING TO READ EXCEPT FOR HER *JEFFREY ARCHER* NOVELS!
WELL DON'T YOU WORRY *MR. P!* WE'LL GET YOU OUT! WE'LL... OH. OH CRIKEY...
***WHAT THE BLOODY HELL'S GOING ON?!***

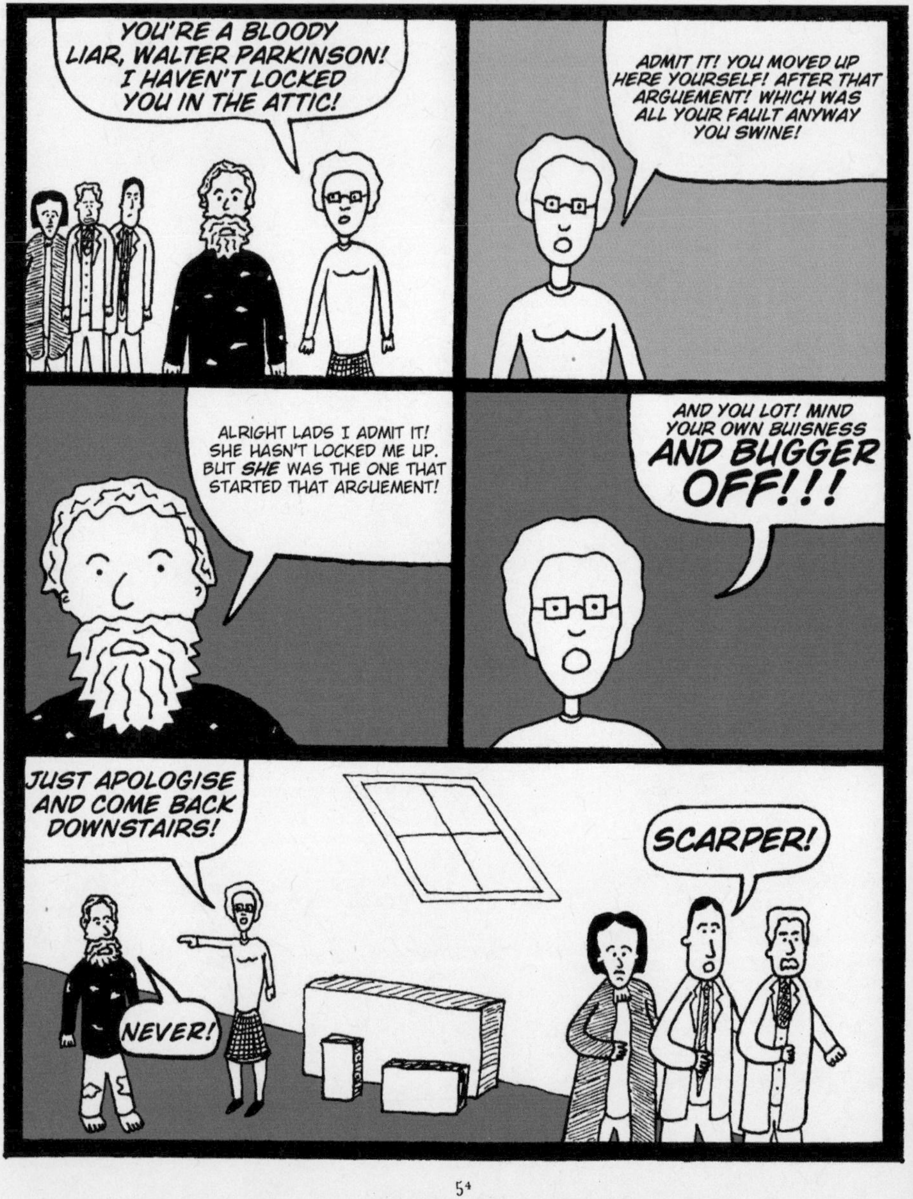
YOU'RE A BLOODY LIAR, WALTER PARKINSON! I HAVEN'T LOCKED YOU IN THE ATTIC!
ADMIT IT! YOU MOVED UP HERE YOURSELF! AFTER THAT ARGUEMENT! WHICH WAS ALL YOUR FAULT ANYWAY YOU SWINE!
ALRIGHT LADS I ADMIT IT! SHE HASN'T LOCKED ME UP. BUT SHE WAS THE ONE THAT STARTED THAT ARGUEMENT!
AND YOU LOT! MIND YOUR OWN BUISNESS AND BUGGER OFF!!!
JUST APOLOGISE AND COME BACK DOWNSTAIRS!
NEVER!
SCARPER!

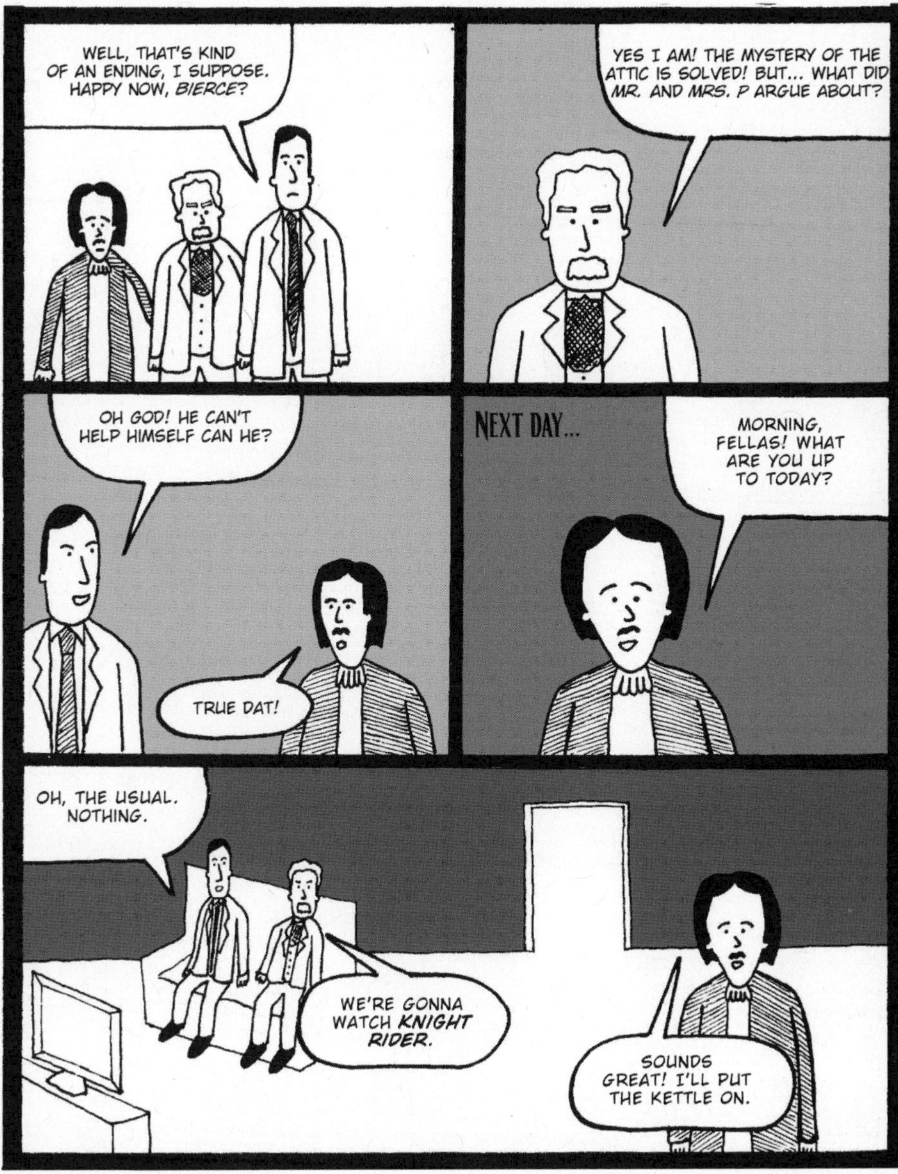
WELL, THAT'S KIND OF AN ENDING, I SUPPOSE. HAPPY NOW, BIERCE?
YES I AM! THE MYSTERY OF THE ATTIC IS SOLVED! BUT... WHAT DID MR. AND MRS. P ARGUE ABOUT?
OH GOD! HE CAN'T HELP HIMSELF CAN HE?
TRUE DAT!
NEXT DAY...
MORNING, FELLAS! WHAT ARE YOU UP TO TODAY?
OH, THE USUAL. NOTHING.
WE'RE GONNA WATCH KNIGHT RIDER.
SOUNDS GREAT! I'LL PUT THE KETTLE ON.

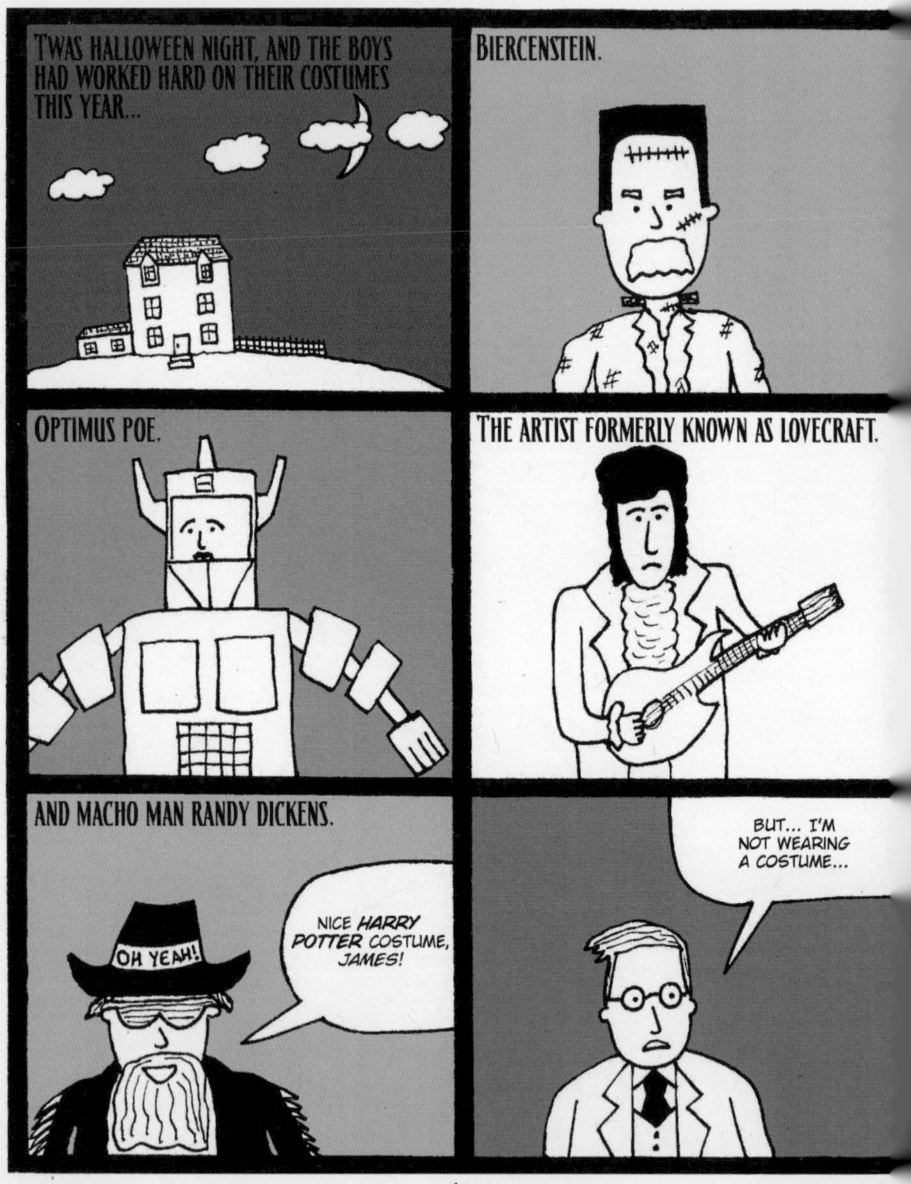
TWAS HALLOWEEN NIGHT, AND THE BOYS HAD WORKED HARD ON THEIR COSTUMES THIS YEAR...
BIERCENSTEIN.
OPTIMUS POE.
THE ARTIST FORMERLY KNOWN AS LOVECRAFT.
AND MACHO MAN RANDY DICKENS.
OH YEAH!
NICE HARRY POTTER COSTUME, JAMES!
BUT... I'M NOT WEARING A COSTUME...

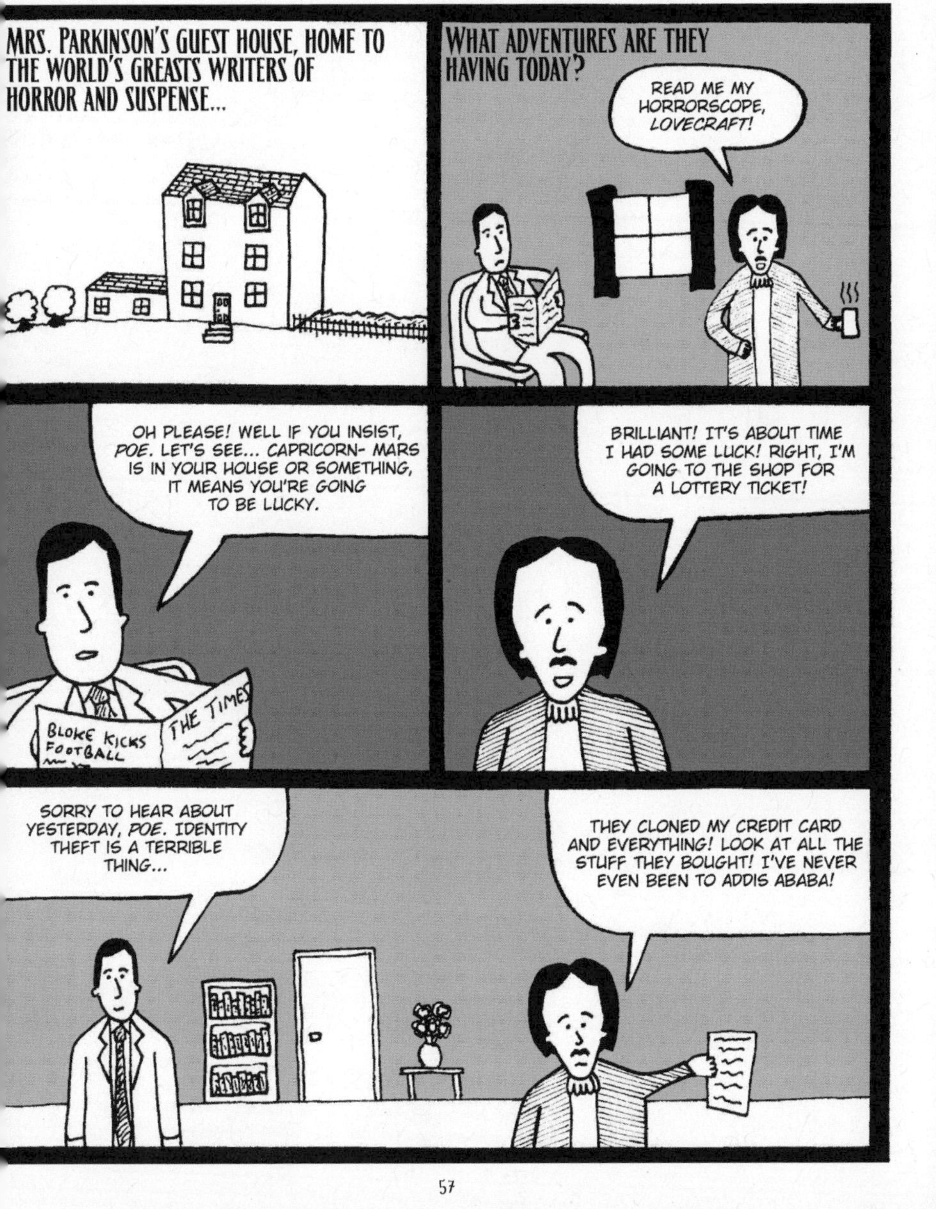
MRS. PARKINSON'S GUEST HOUSE, HOME TO THE WORLD'S GREASTS WRITERS OF HORROR AND SUSPENSE...
WHAT ADVENTURES ARE THEY HAVING TODAY?
READ ME MY HORRORSCOPE, LOVECRAFT!
OH PLEASE! WELL IF YOU INSIST, POE. LET'S SEE... CAPRICORN- MARS IS IN YOUR HOUSE OR SOMETHING, IT MEANS YOU'RE GOING TO BE LUCKY.
BLOKE KICKS FOOTBALL
THE TIMES
BRILLIANT! IT'S ABOUT TIME I HAD SOME LUCK! RIGHT, I'M GOING TO THE SHOP FOR A LOTTERY TICKET!
SORRY TO HEAR ABOUT YESTERDAY, POE. IDENTITY THEFT IS A TERRIBLE THING...
THEY CLONED MY CREDIT CARD AND EVERYTHING! LOOK AT ALL THE STUFF THEY BOUGHT! I'VE NEVER EVEN BEEN TO ADDIS ABABA!

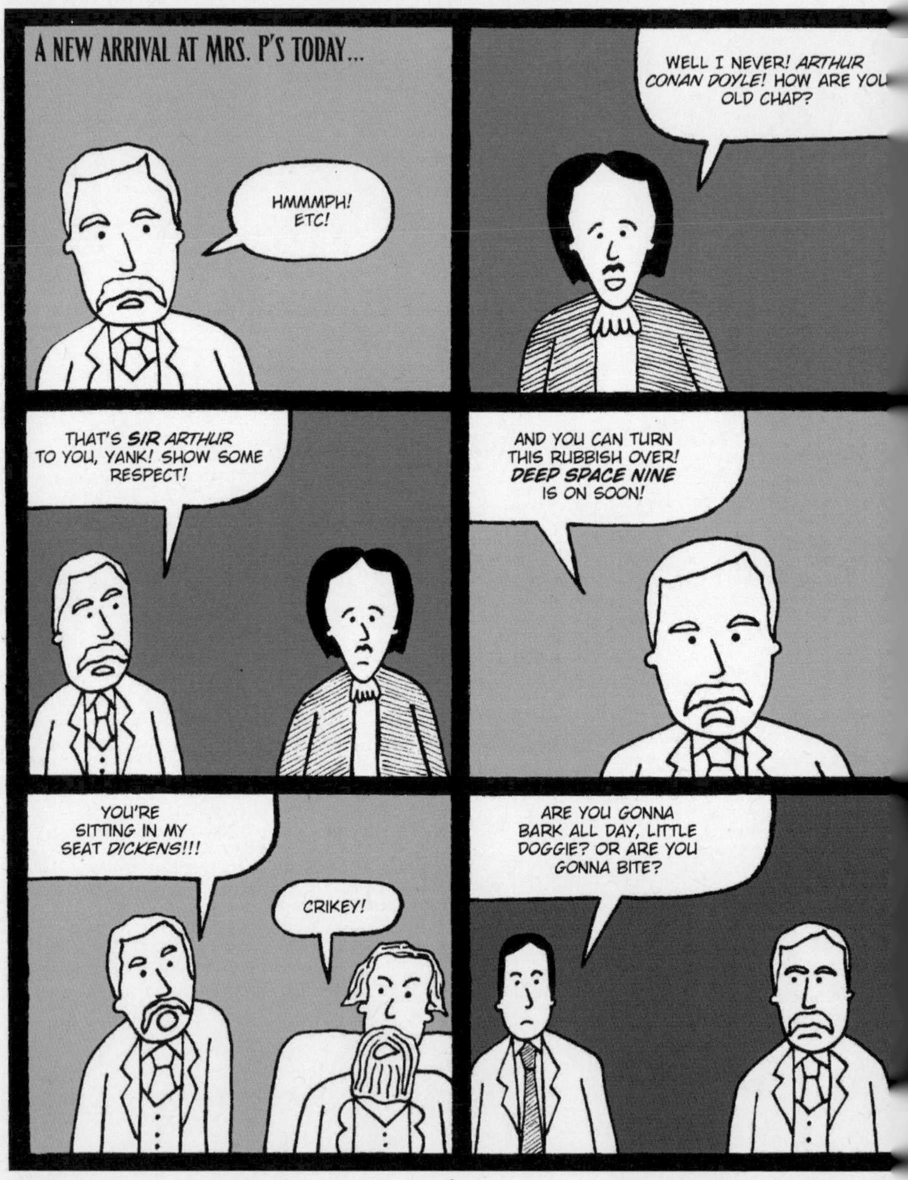
A NEW ARRIVAL AT MRS. P'S TODAY...
HMMMPH! ETC!
WELL I NEVER! ARTHUR CONAN DOYLE! HOW ARE YOU OLD CHAP?
THAT'S SIR ARTHUR TO YOU, YANK! SHOW SOME RESPECT!
AND YOU CAN TURN THIS RUBBISH OVER! DEEP SPACE NINE IS ON SOON!
YOU'RE SITTING IN MY SEAT DICKENS!!!
CRIKEY!
ARE YOU GONNA BARK ALL DAY, LITTLE DOGGIE? OR ARE YOU GONNA BITE?

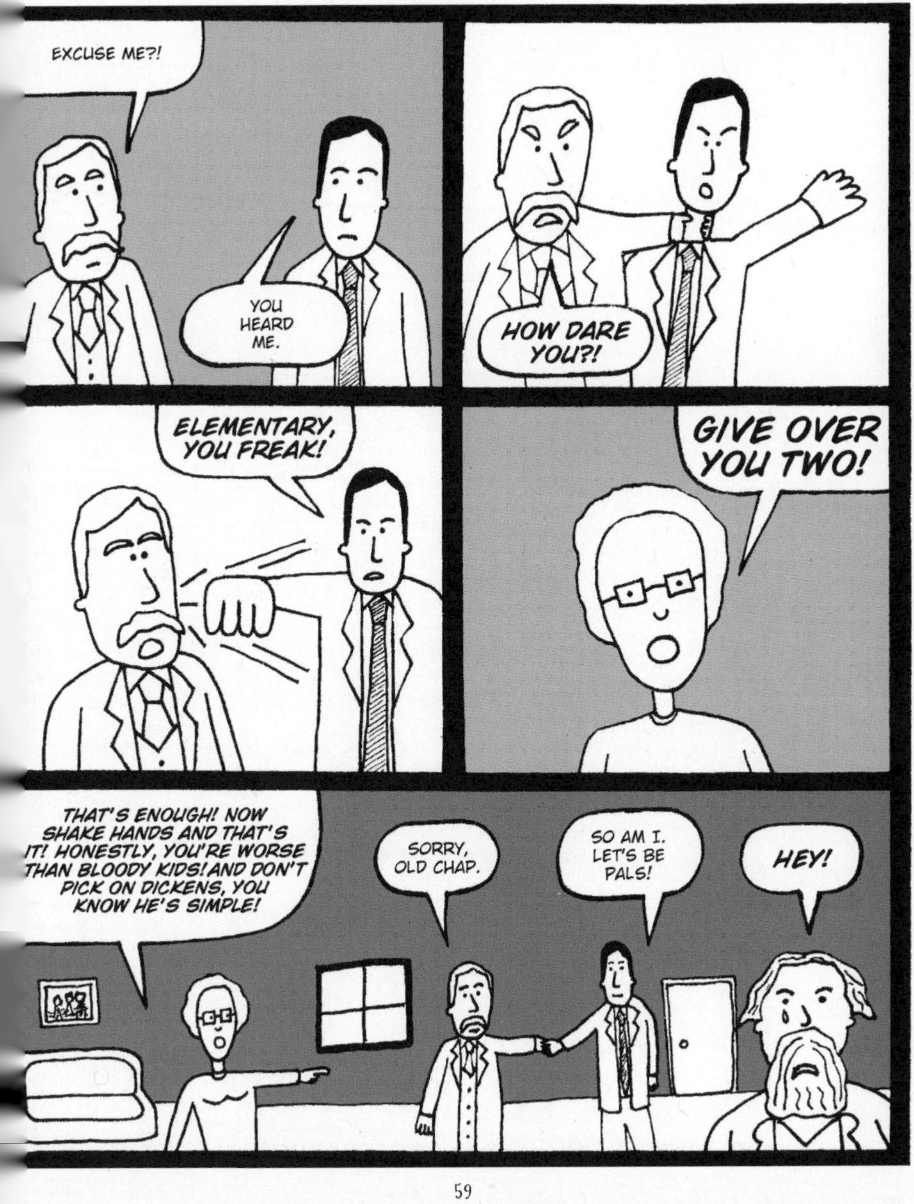
EXCUSE ME?!
YOU HEARD ME.
HOW DARE YOU?!
ELEMENTARY, YOU FREAK!
GIVE OVER YOU TWO!
THAT'S ENOUGH! NOW SHAKE HANDS AND THAT'S IT! HONESTLY, YOU'RE WORSE THAN BLOODY KIDS! AND DON'T PICK ON DICKENS, YOU KNOW HE'S SIMPLE!
SORRY, OLD CHAP.
SO AM I. LET'S BE PALS!
HEY!

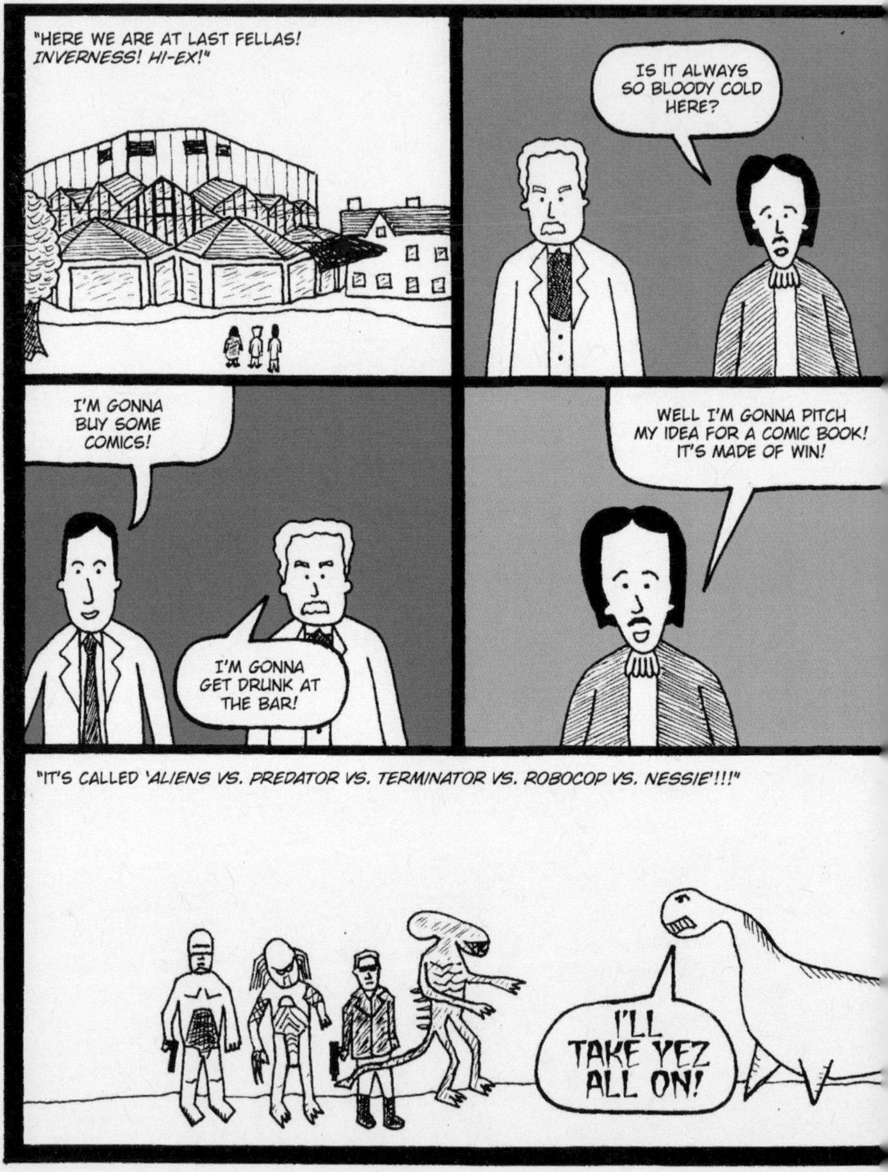
"HERE WE ARE AT LAST FELLAS! INVERNESS! HI-EX!"
IS IT ALWAYS SO BLOODY COLD HERE?
I'M GONNA BUY SOME COMICS!
I'M GONNA GET DRUNK AT THE BAR!
WELL I'M GONNA PITCH MY IDEA FOR A COMIC BOOK! IT'S MADE OF WIN!
"IT'S CALLED 'ALIENS VS. PREDATOR VS. TERMINATOR VS. ROBOCOP VS. NESSIE'!!!"
I'LL TAKE YEZ ALL ON!

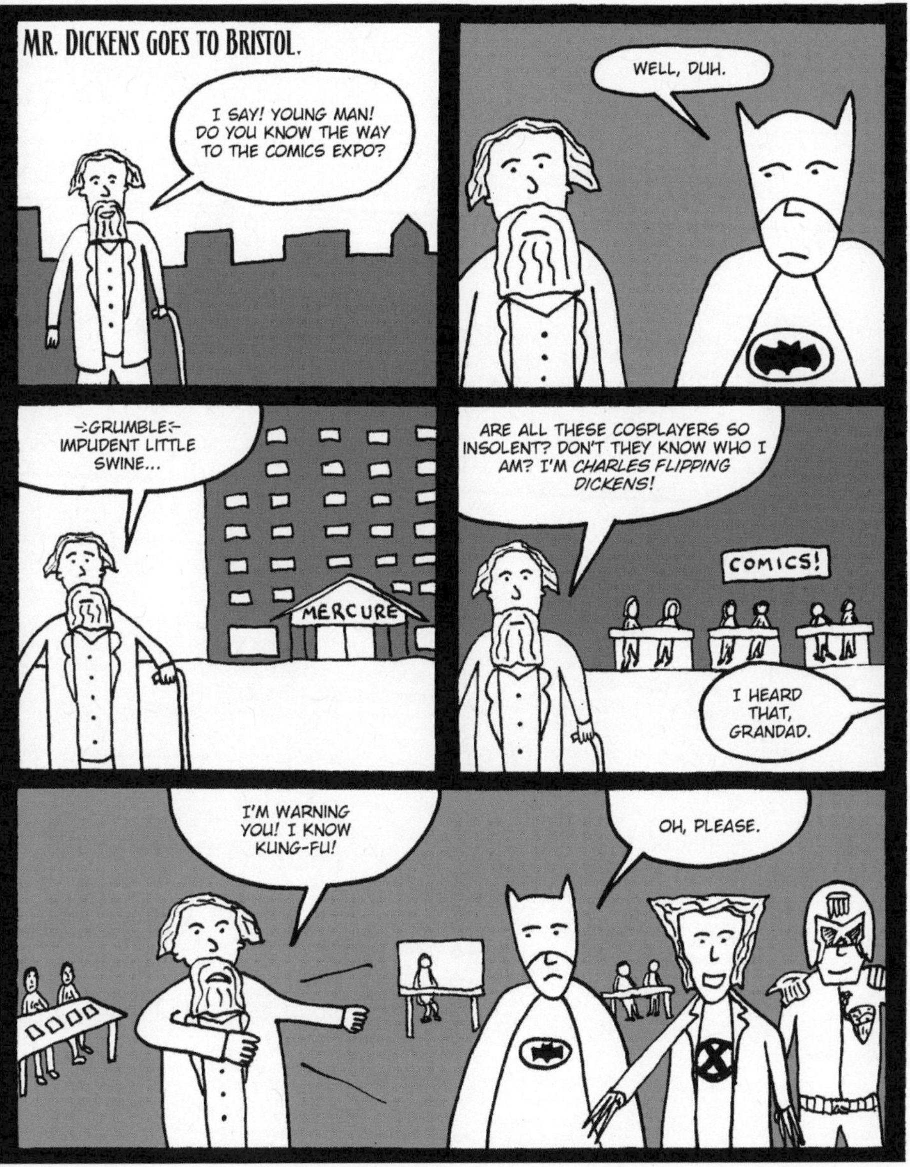
MR. DICKENS GOES TO BRISTOL.
I SAY! YOUNG MAN! DO YOU KNOW THE WAY TO THE COMICS EXPO?
WELL, DUH.
-GRUMBLE- IMPUDENT LITTLE SWINE...
MERCURE
ARE ALL THESE COSPLAYERS SO INSOLENT? DON'T THEY KNOW WHO I AM? I'M *CHARLES FLIPPING DICKENS!*
COMICS!
I HEARD THAT, GRANDAD.
I'M WARNING YOU! I KNOW KUNG-FU!
OH, PLEASE.

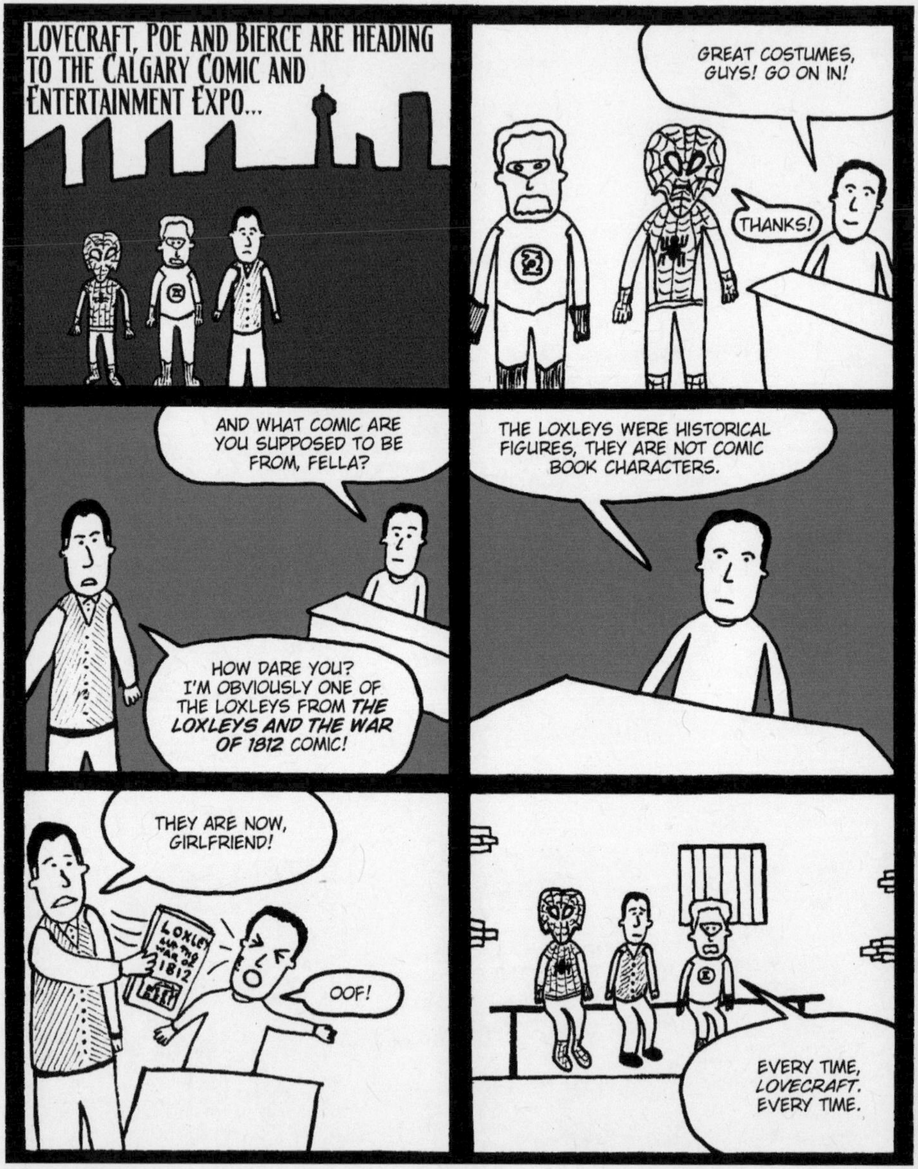
LOVECRAFT, POE AND BIERCE ARE HEADING TO THE CALGARY COMIC AND ENTERTAINMENT EXPO...
GREAT COSTUMES, GUYS! GO ON IN!
THANKS!
AND WHAT COMIC ARE YOU SUPPOSED TO BE FROM, FELLA?
HOW DARE YOU? I'M OBVIOUSLY ONE OF THE LOXLEYS FROM *THE LOXLEYS AND THE WAR OF 1812* COMIC!
THE LOXLEYS WERE HISTORICAL FIGURES, THEY ARE NOT COMIC BOOK CHARACTERS.
THEY ARE NOW, GIRLFRIEND!
OOF!
EVERY TIME, *LOVECRAFT*. EVERY TIME.

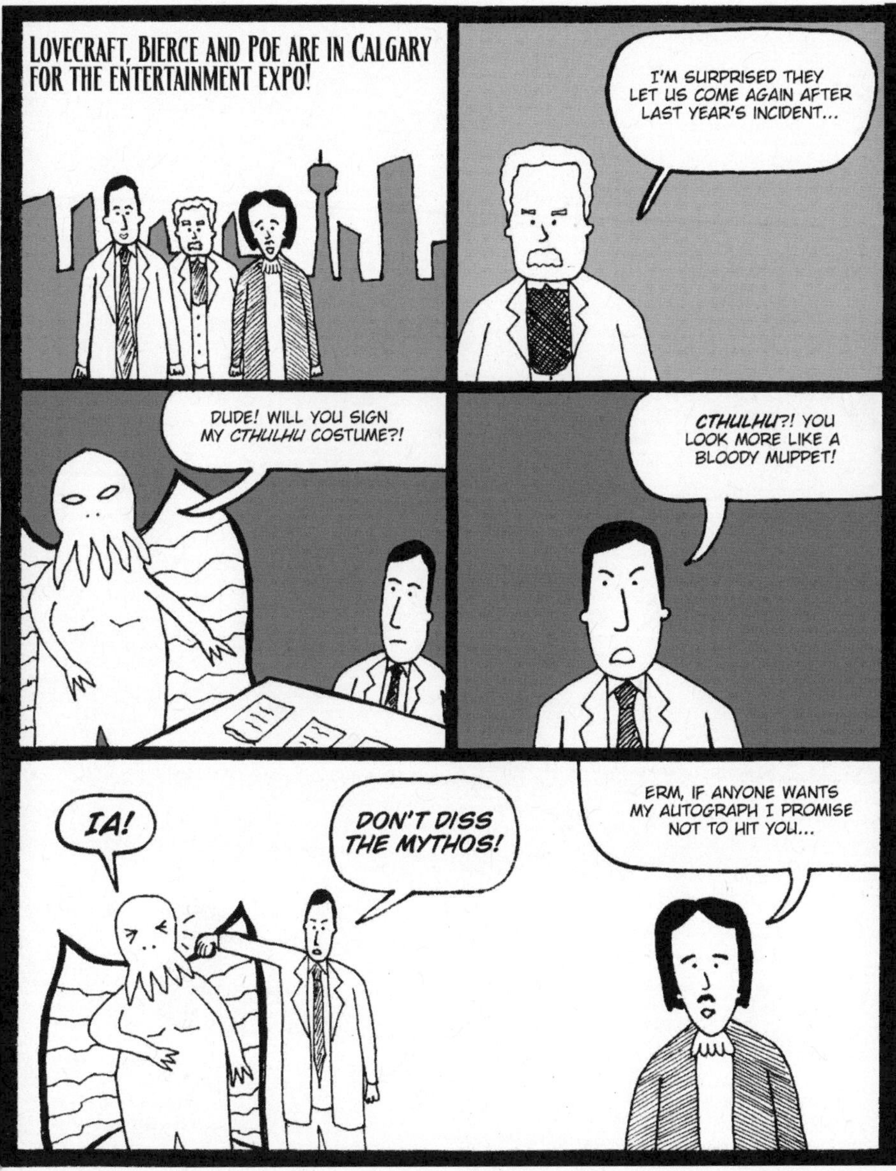
LOVECRAFT, BIERCE AND POE ARE IN CALGARY FOR THE ENTERTAINMENT EXPO!
I'M SURPRISED THEY LET US COME AGAIN AFTER LAST YEAR'S INCIDENT...
DUDE! WILL YOU SIGN MY CTHULHU COSTUME?!
CTHULHU?! YOU LOOK MORE LIKE A BLOODY MUPPET!
IA!
DON'T DISS THE MYTHOS!
ERM, IF ANYONE WANTS MY AUTOGRAPH I PROMISE NOT TO HIT YOU...

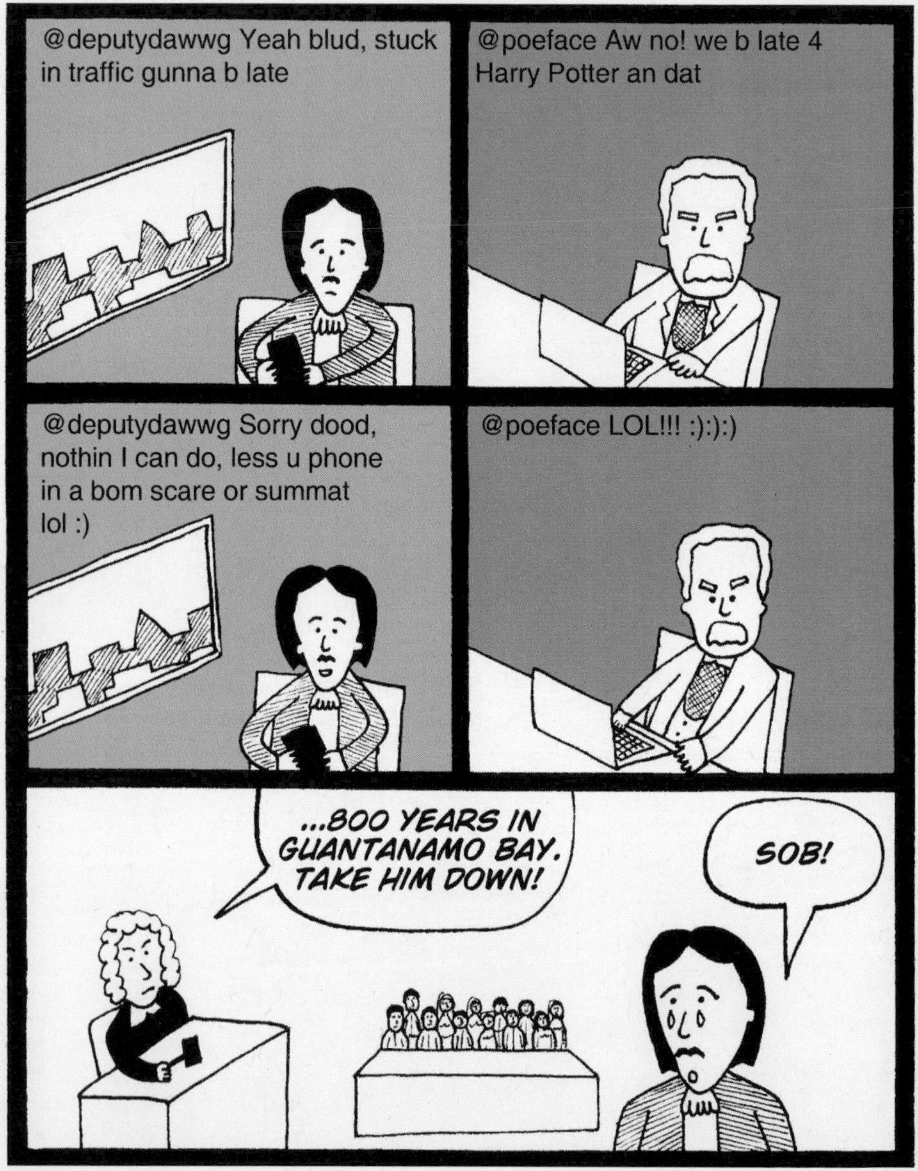
@deputydawwg Yeah blud, stuck in traffic gunna b late
@poeface Aw no! we b late 4 Harry Potter an dat
@deputydawwg Sorry dood, nothin I can do, less u phone in a bom scare or summat lol :)
@poeface LOL!!! :):):)
...800 YEARS IN GUANTANAMO BAY. TAKE HIM DOWN!
SOB!

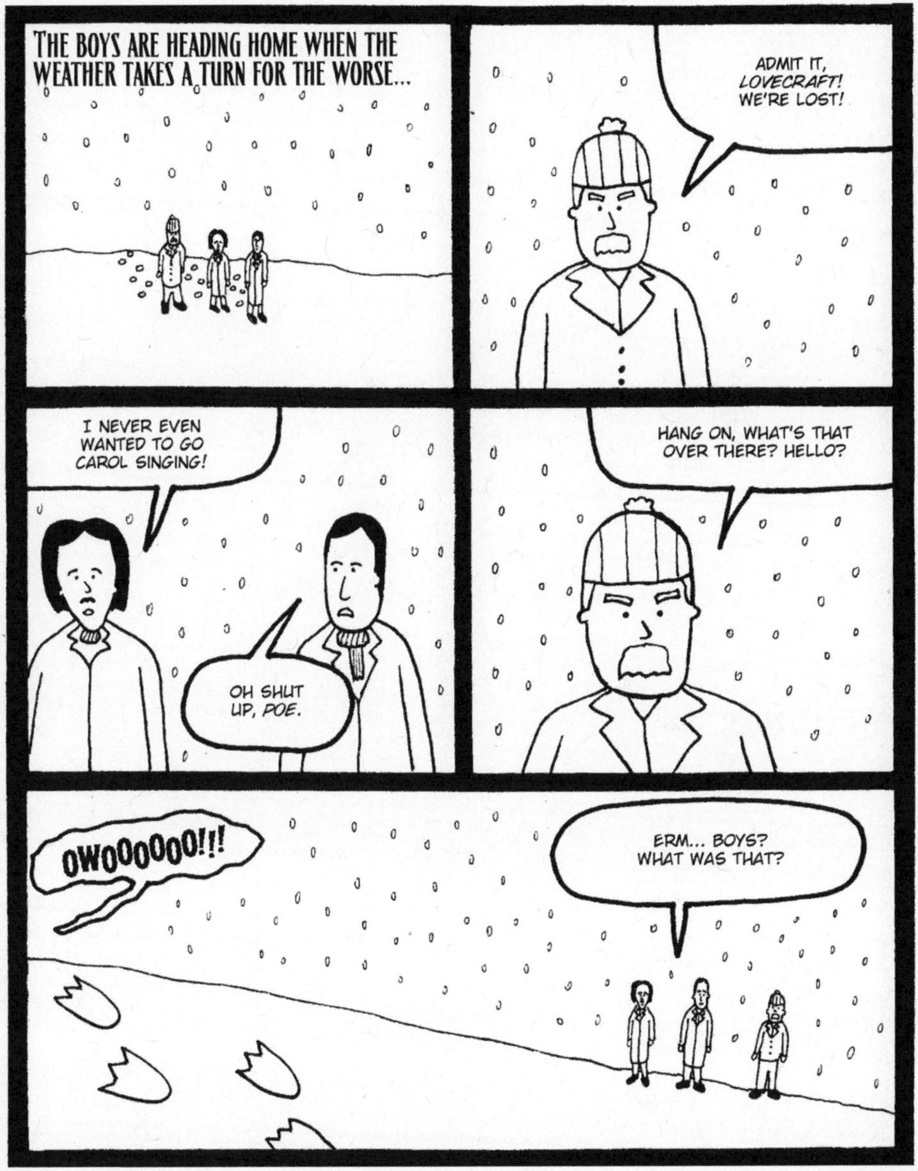
THE BOYS ARE HEADING HOME WHEN THE WEATHER TAKES A TURN FOR THE WORSE...
ADMIT IT, *LOVECRAFT!* WE'RE LOST!
I NEVER EVEN WANTED TO GO CAROL SINGING!
OH SHUT UP, *POE.*
HANG ON, WHAT'S THAT OVER THERE? HELLO?
OWOOOOOO!!!
ERM... BOYS? WHAT WAS THAT?

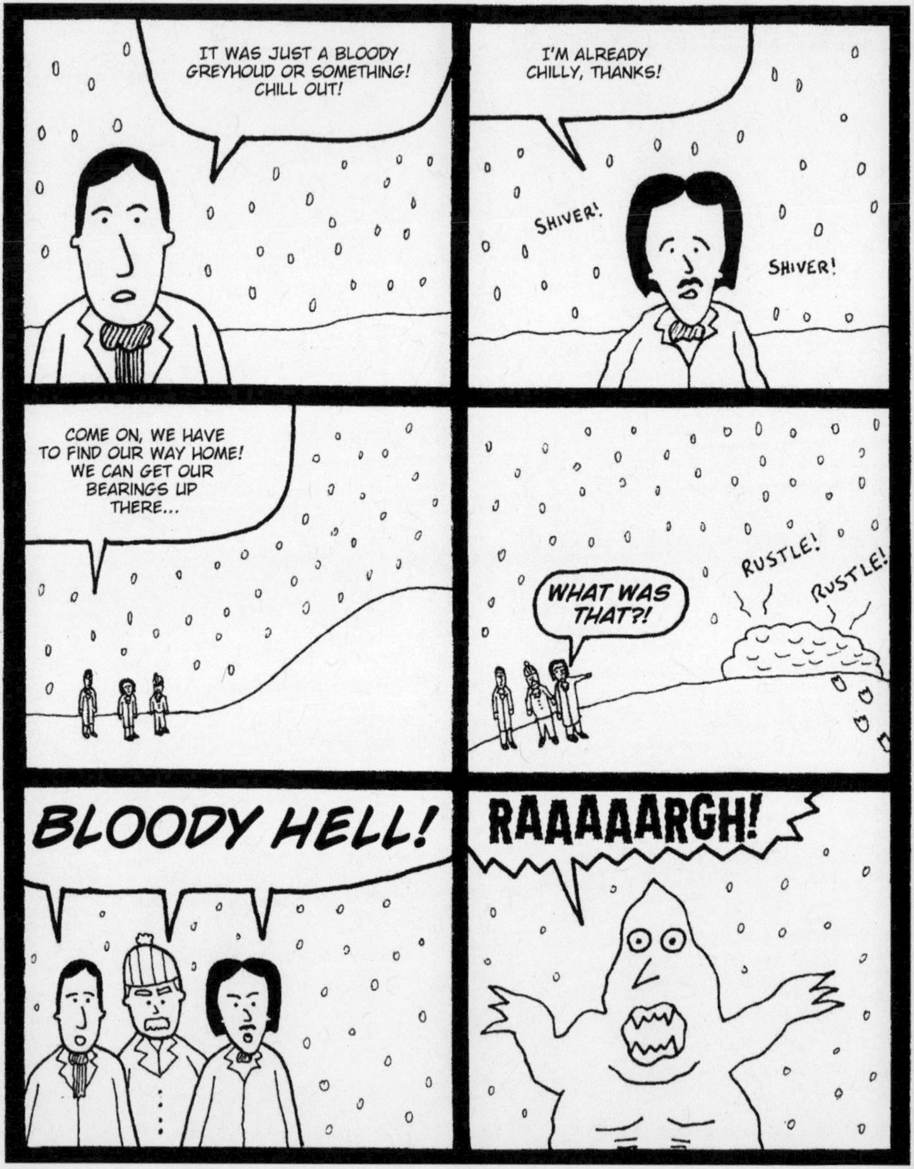
IT WAS JUST A BLOODY GREYHOUD OR SOMETHING! CHILL OUT!
I'M ALREADY CHILLY, THANKS!
SHIVER!
SHIVER!
COME ON, WE HAVE TO FIND OUR WAY HOME! WE CAN GET OUR BEARINGS UP THERE...
WHAT WAS THAT?!
RUSTLE!
RUSTLE!
BLOODY HELL!
RAAAAARGH!

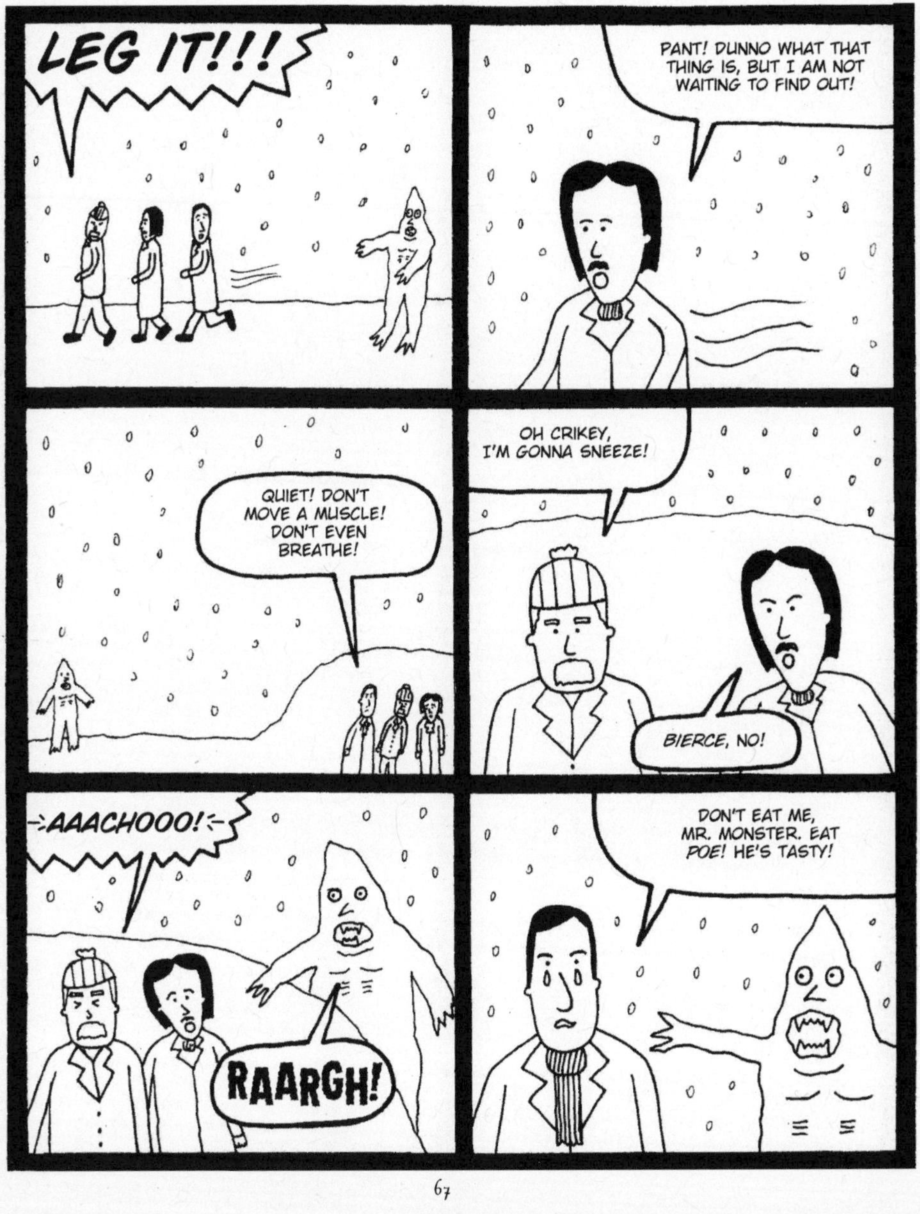
LEG IT!!!
PANT! DUNNO WHAT THAT THING IS, BUT I AM NOT WAITING TO FIND OUT!
QUIET! DON'T MOVE A MUSCLE! DON'T EVEN BREATHE!
OH CRIKEY, I'M GONNA SNEEZE!
BIERCE, NO!
AAACHOOO!
RAARGH!
DON'T EAT ME, MR. MONSTER. EAT POE! HE'S TASTY!

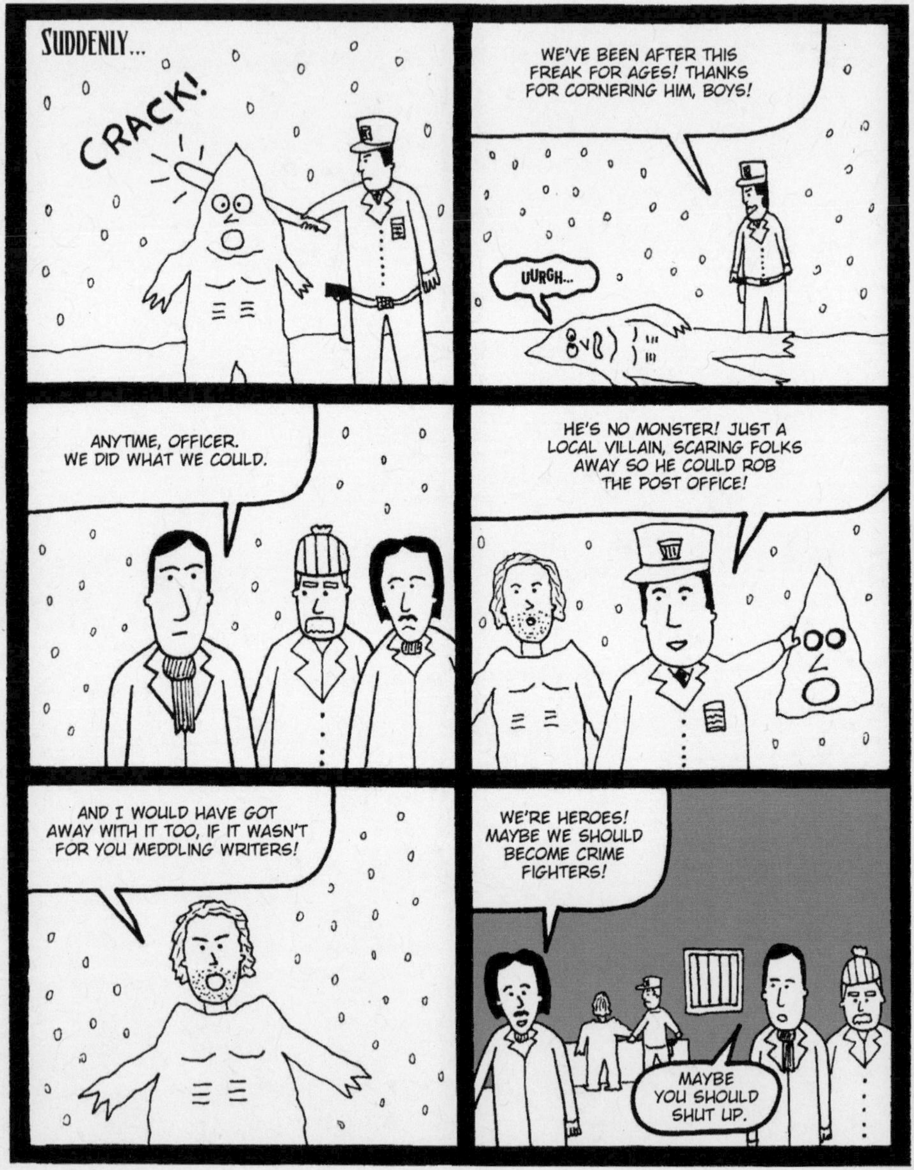
SUDDENLY...
CRACK!
WE'VE BEEN AFTER THIS FREAK FOR AGES! THANKS FOR CORNERING HIM, BOYS!
UURGH...
ANYTIME, OFFICER. WE DID WHAT WE COULD.
HE'S NO MONSTER! JUST A LOCAL VILLAIN, SCARING FOLKS AWAY SO HE COULD ROB THE POST OFFICE!
AND I WOULD HAVE GOT AWAY WITH IT TOO, IF IT WASN'T FOR YOU MEDDLING WRITERS!
WE'RE HEROES! MAYBE WE SHOULD BECOME CRIME FIGHTERS!
MAYBE YOU SHOULD SHUT UP.

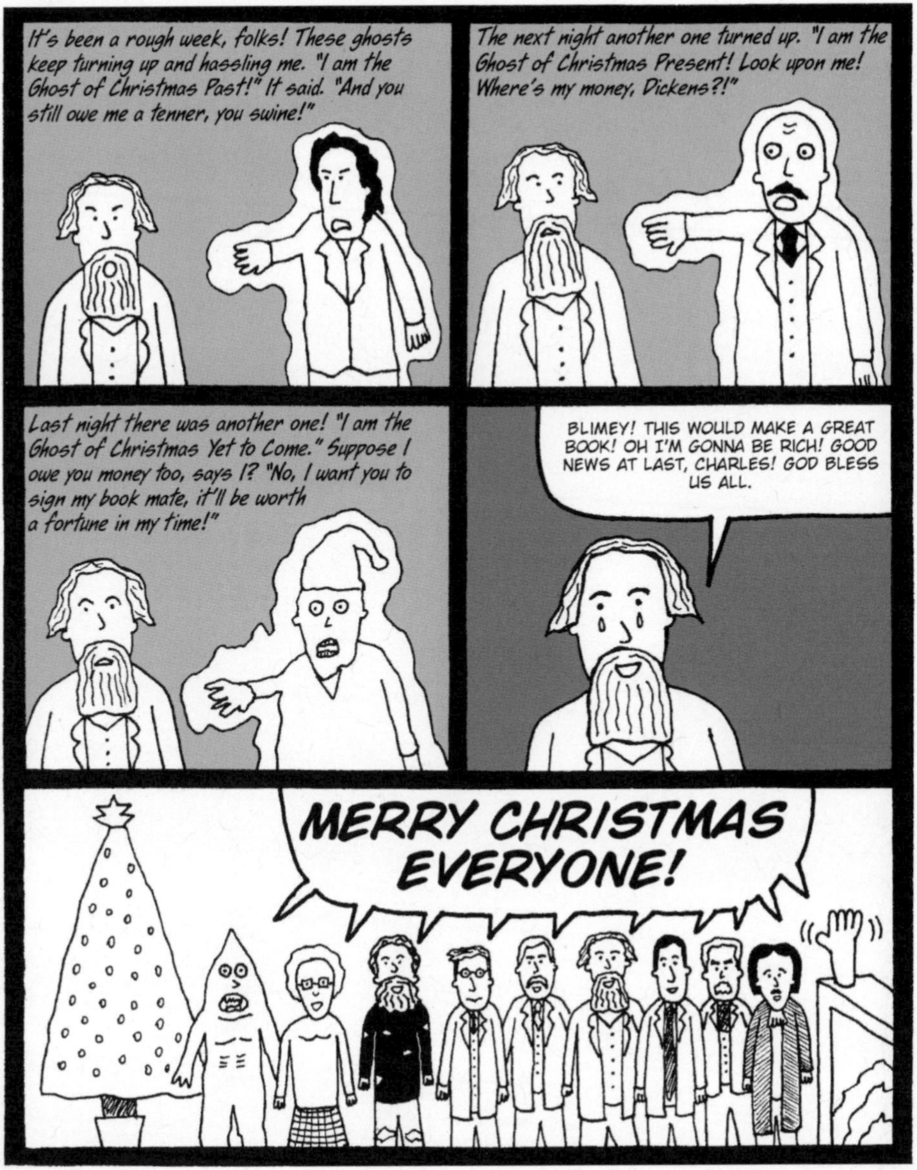

It's been a rough week, folks! These ghosts keep turning up and hassling me. "I am the Ghost of Christmas Past!" It said. "And you still owe me a tenner, you swine!"
The next night another one turned up. "I am the Ghost of Christmas Present! Look upon me! Where's my money, Dickens?!"
Last night there was another one! "I am the Ghost of Christmas Yet to Come." Suppose I owe you money too, says I? "No, I want you to sign my book mate, it'll be worth a fortune in my time!"
BLIMEY! THIS WOULD MAKE A GREAT BOOK! OH I'M GONNA BE RICH! GOOD NEWS AT LAST, CHARLES! GOD BLESS US ALL.
MERRY CHRISTMAS EVERYONE!

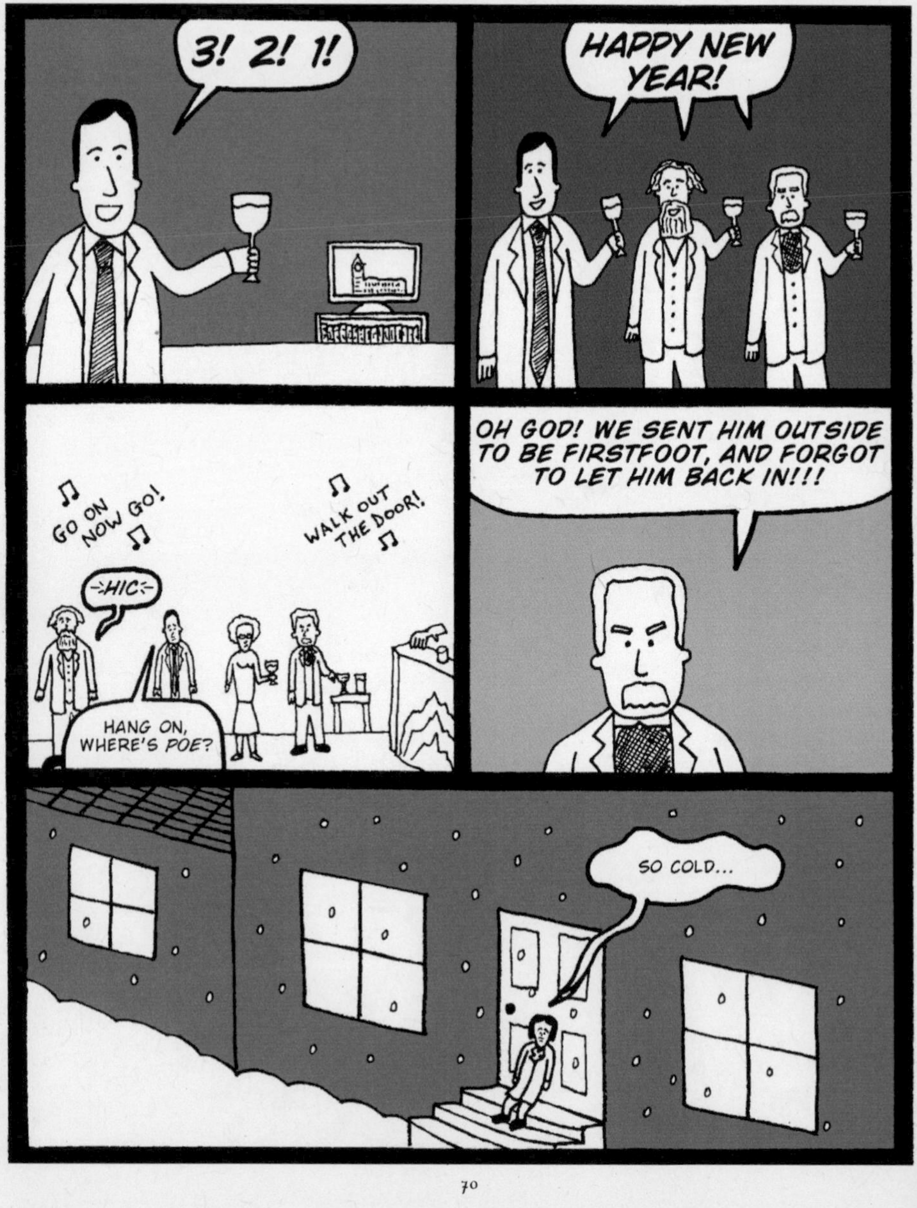
3! 2! 1!
HAPPY NEW YEAR!
♫ GO ON NOW GO! ♫
♫ WALK OUT THE DOOR! ♫
HIC
HANG ON, WHERE'S *POE*?
OH GOD! WE SENT HIM OUTSIDE TO BE FIRSTFOOT, AND FORGOT TO LET HIM BACK IN!!!
SO COLD...

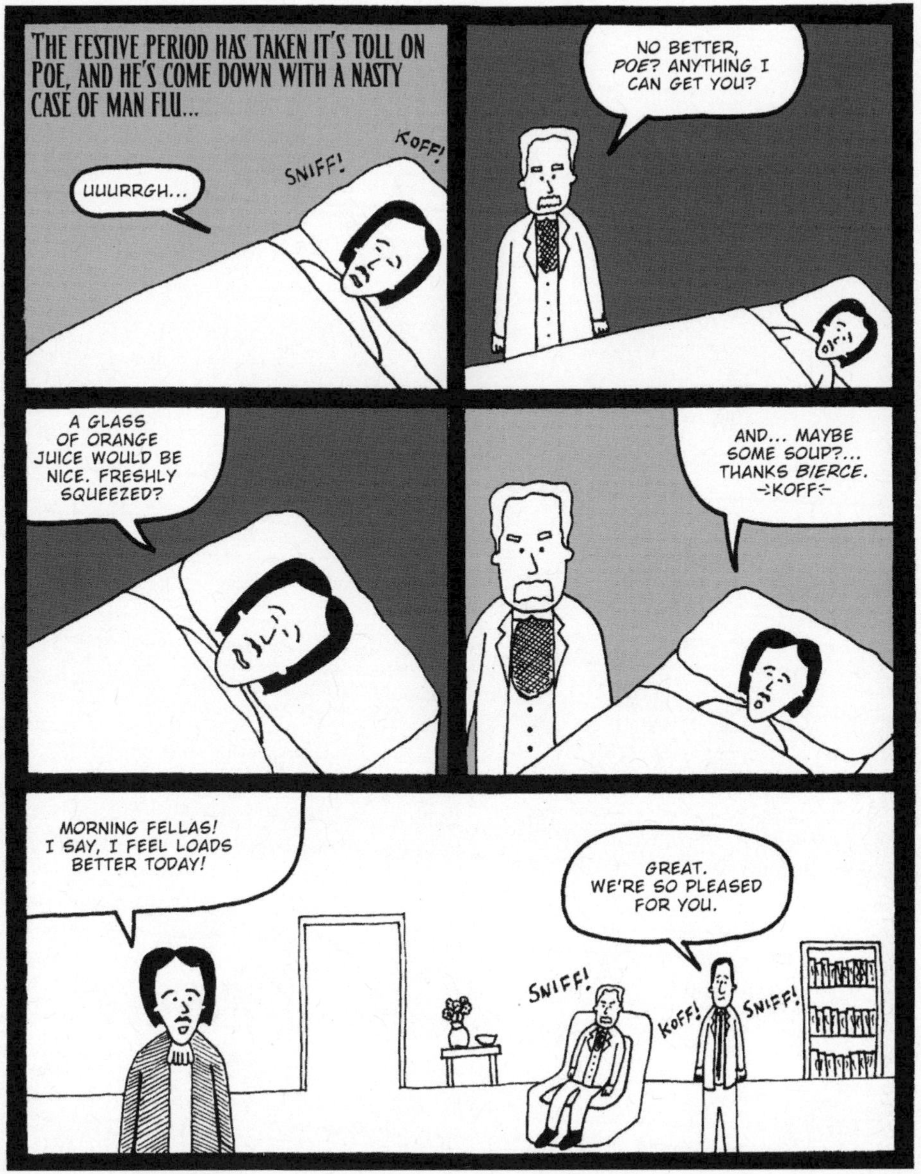

THE FESTIVE PERIOD HAS TAKEN IT'S TOLL ON POE, AND HE'S COME DOWN WITH A NASTY CASE OF MAN FLU...
UUURRGH...
SNIFF!
KOFF!
NO BETTER, *POE*? ANYTHING I CAN GET YOU?
A GLASS OF ORANGE JUICE WOULD BE NICE. FRESHLY SQUEEZED?
AND... MAYBE SOME SOUP?... THANKS *BIERCE*. KOFF
MORNING FELLAS! I SAY, I FEEL LOADS BETTER TODAY!
GREAT. WE'RE SO PLEASED FOR YOU.
SNIFF!
KOFF!
SNIFF!

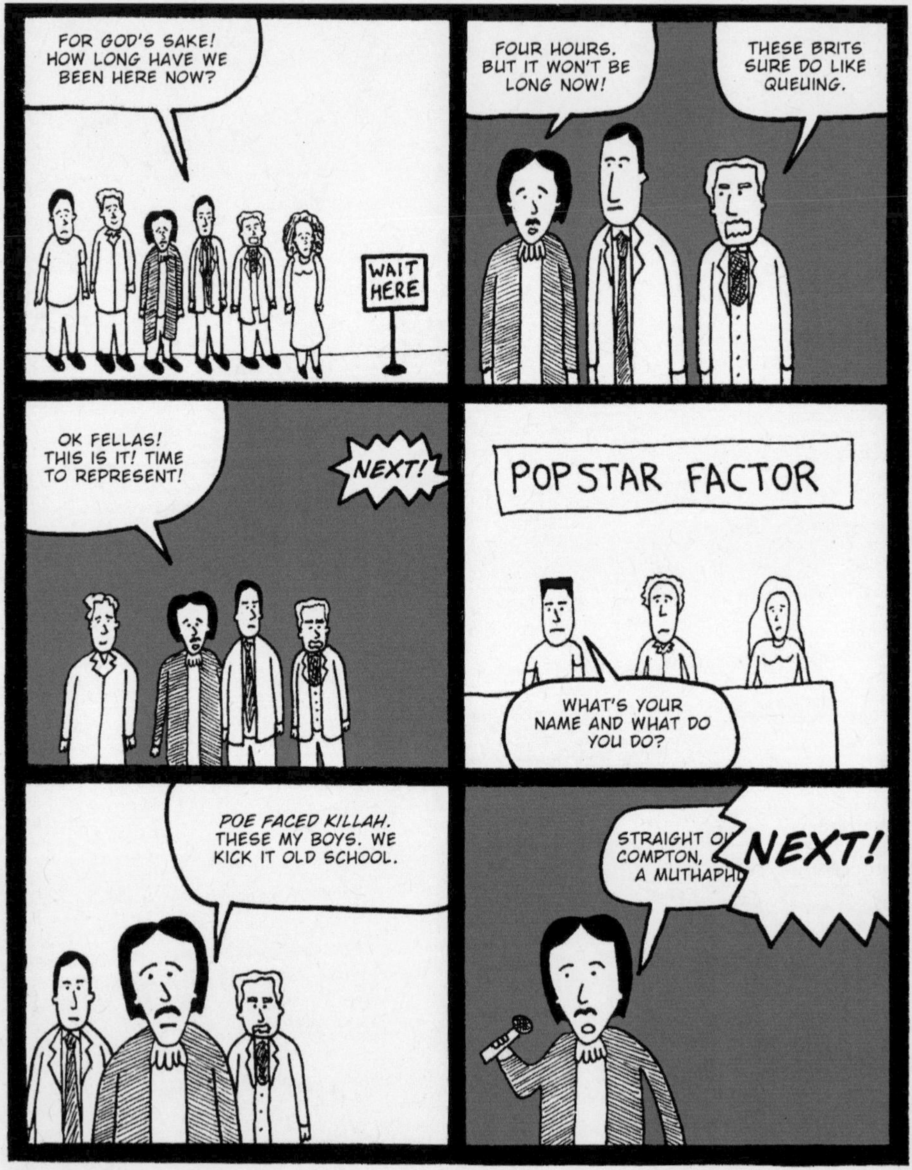
FOR GOD'S SAKE! HOW LONG HAVE WE BEEN HERE NOW?
WAIT HERE
FOUR HOURS. BUT IT WON'T BE LONG NOW!
THESE BRITS SURE DO LIKE QUEUING.
OK FELLAS! THIS IS IT! TIME TO REPRESENT!
NEXT!
POPSTAR FACTOR
WHAT'S YOUR NAME AND WHAT DO YOU DO?
POE FACED KILLAH. THESE MY BOYS. WE KICK IT OLD SCHOOL.
STRAIGHT O
COMPTON,
A MUTHAPH
NEXT!

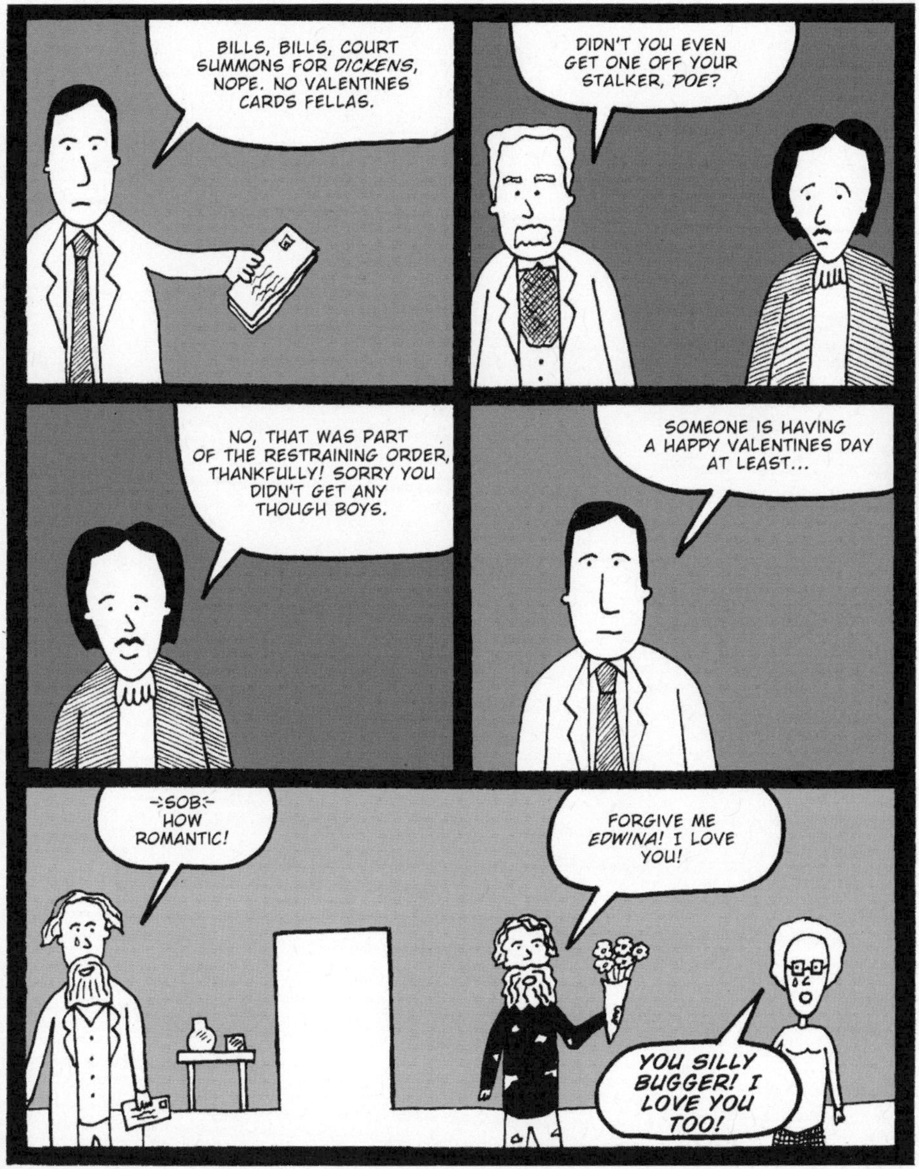
BILLS, BILLS, COURT SUMMONS FOR *DICKENS*, NOPE. NO VALENTINES CARDS FELLAS.
DIDN'T YOU EVEN GET ONE OFF YOUR STALKER, *POE*?
NO, THAT WAS PART OF THE RESTRAINING ORDER, THANKFULLY! SORRY YOU DIDN'T GET ANY THOUGH BOYS.
SOMEONE IS HAVING A HAPPY VALENTINES DAY AT LEAST...
-SOB- HOW ROMANTIC!
FORGIVE ME *EDWINA*! I LOVE YOU!
***YOU SILLY BUGGER! I LOVE YOU TOO!***

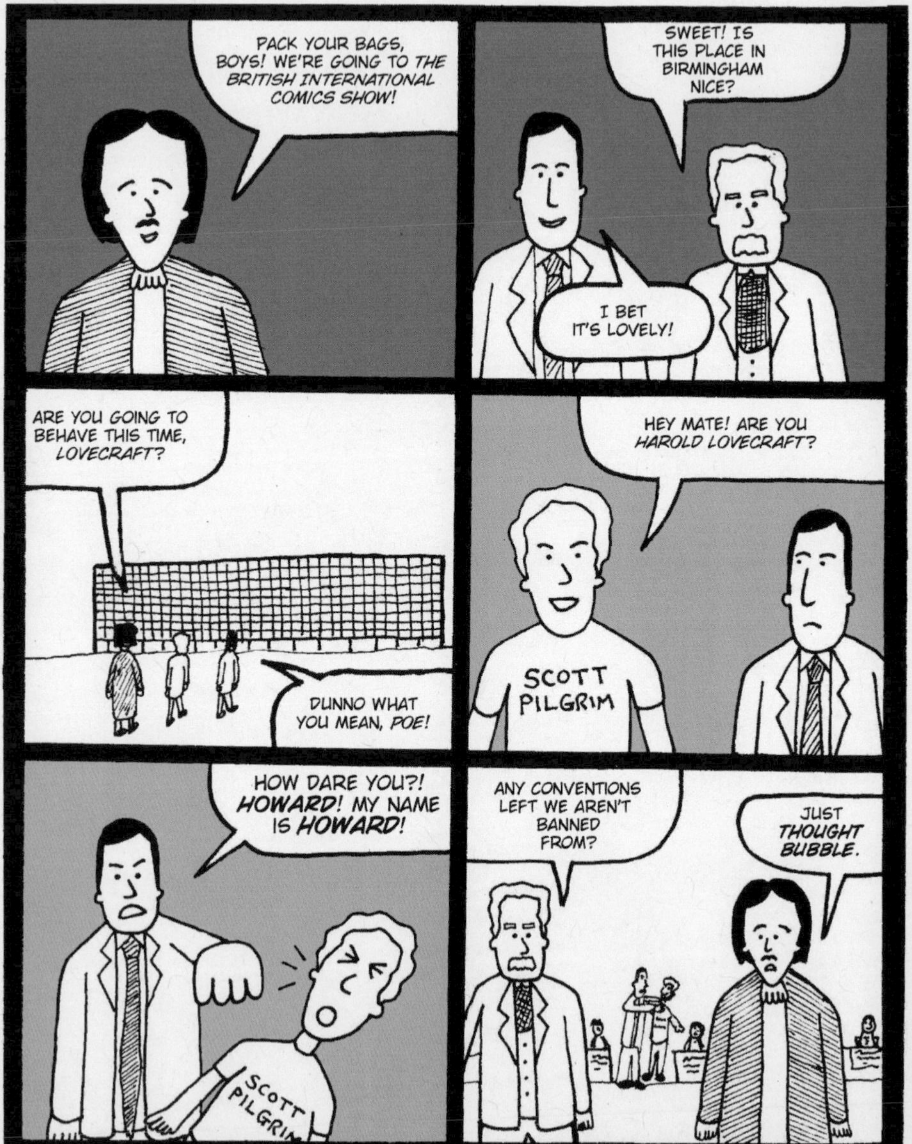
PACK YOUR BAGS, BOYS! WE'RE GOING TO THE BRITISH INTERNATIONAL COMICS SHOW!
SWEET! IS THIS PLACE IN BIRMINGHAM NICE?
I BET IT'S LOVELY!
ARE YOU GOING TO BEHAVE THIS TIME, LOVECRAFT?
DUNNO WHAT YOU MEAN, POE!
HEY MATE! ARE YOU HAROLD LOVECRAFT?
SCOTT PILGRIM
HOW DARE YOU?! HOWARD! MY NAME IS HOWARD!
SCOTT PILGRIM
ANY CONVENTIONS LEFT WE AREN'T BANNED FROM?
JUST THOUGHT BUBBLE.

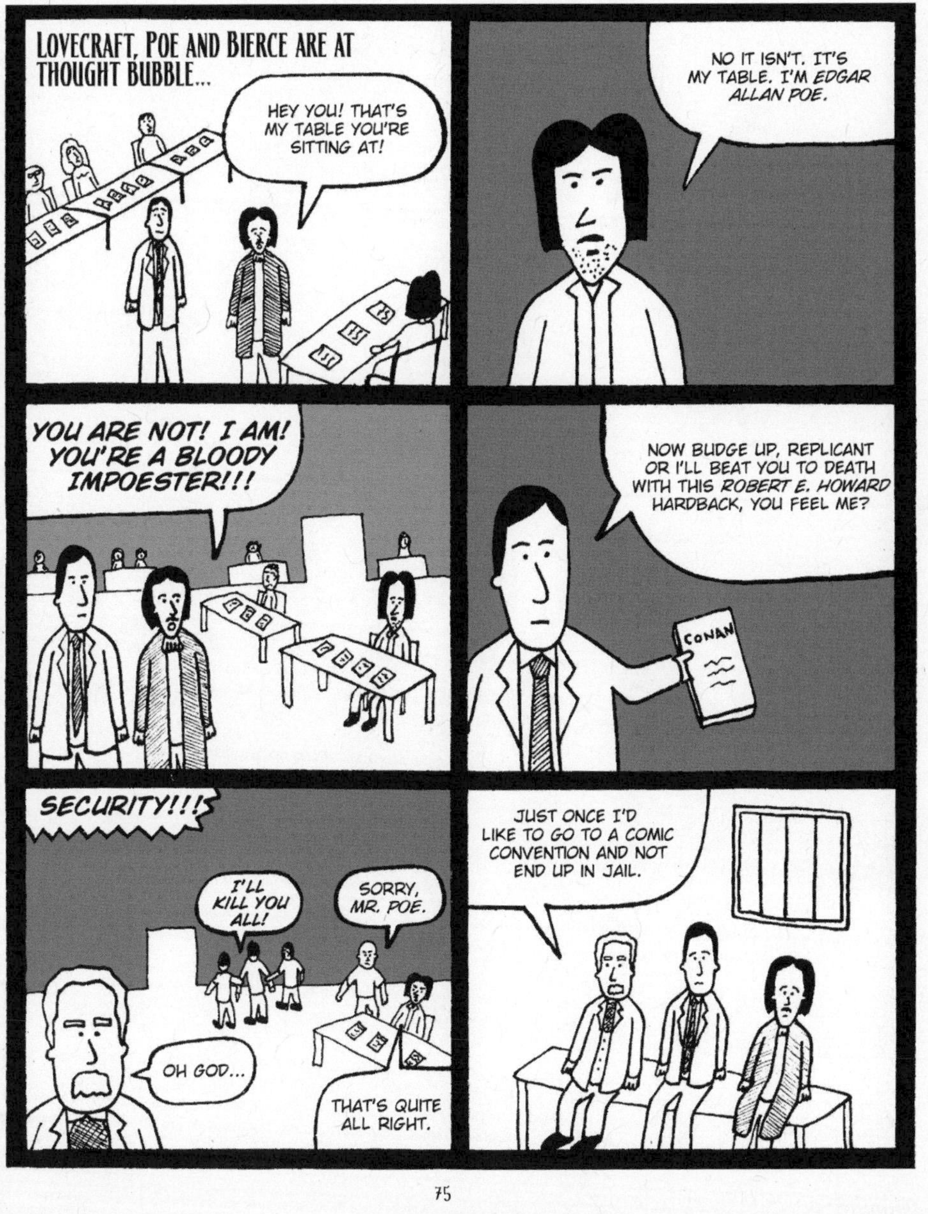
LOVECRAFT, POE AND BIERCE ARE AT THOUGHT BUBBLE...
HEY YOU! THAT'S MY TABLE YOU'RE SITTING AT!
NO IT ISN'T. IT'S MY TABLE. I'M *EDGAR ALLAN POE*.
YOU ARE NOT! I AM! YOU'RE A BLOODY IMPOESTER!!!
NOW BUDGE UP, REPLICANT OR I'LL BEAT YOU TO DEATH WITH THIS *ROBERT E. HOWARD* HARDBACK, YOU FEEL ME?
CONAN
SECURITY!!!
I'LL KILL YOU ALL!
SORRY, MR. POE.
OH GOD...
THAT'S QUITE ALL RIGHT.
JUST ONCE I'D LIKE TO GO TO A COMIC CONVENTION AND NOT END UP IN JAIL.

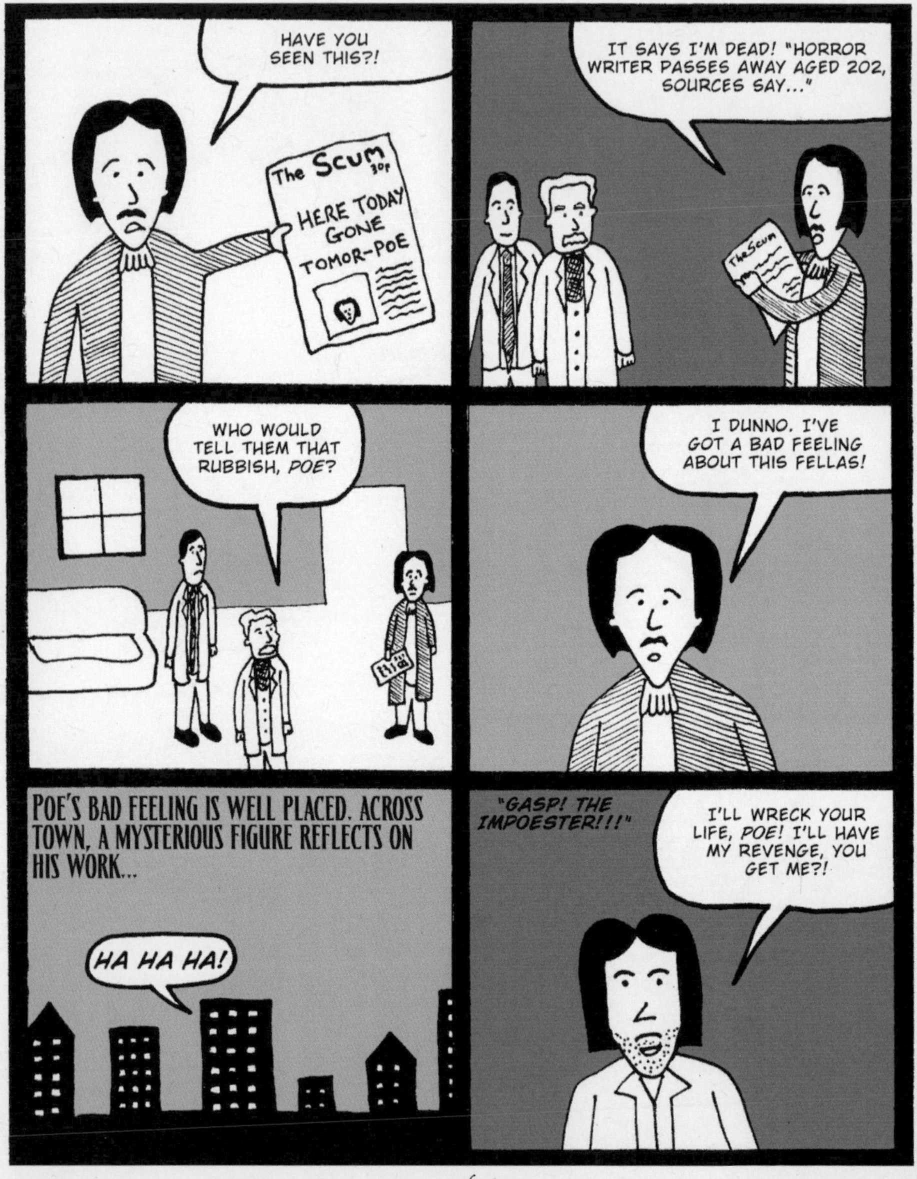
HAVE YOU SEEN THIS?!
The Scum 30p
HERE TODAY GONE TOMOR-POE
IT SAYS I'M DEAD! "HORROR WRITER PASSES AWAY AGED 202, SOURCES SAY..."
WHO WOULD TELL THEM THAT RUBBISH, *POE*?
I DUNNO. I'VE GOT A BAD FEELING ABOUT THIS FELLAS!
POE'S BAD FEELING IS WELL PLACED. ACROSS TOWN, A MYSTERIOUS FIGURE REFLECTS ON HIS WORK...
HA HA HA!
"GASP! THE IMPOESTER!!!"
I'LL WRECK YOUR LIFE, *POE*! I'LL HAVE MY REVENGE, YOU GET ME?!

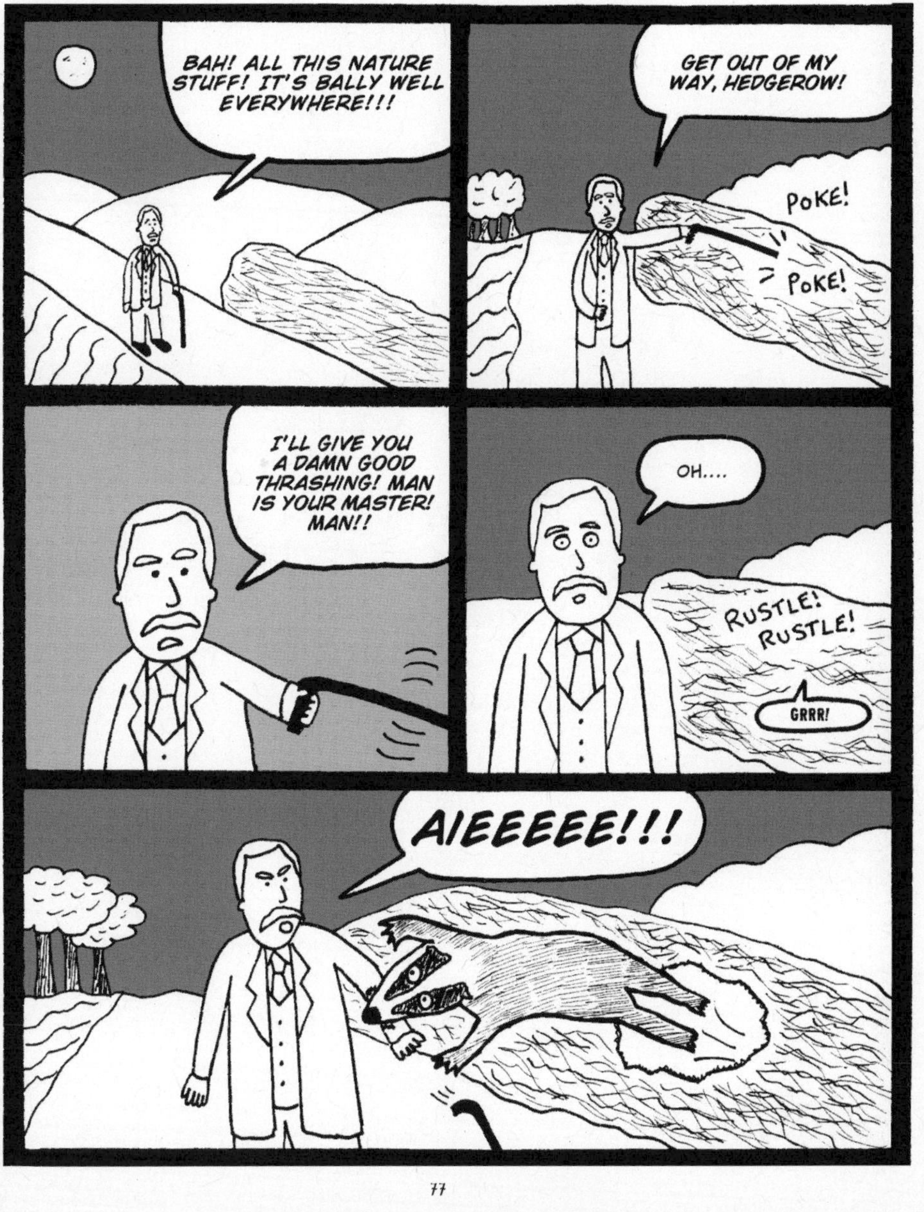
BAH! ALL THIS NATURE STUFF! IT'S BALLY WELL EVERYWHERE!!!
GET OUT OF MY WAY, HEDGEROW!
POKE!
POKE!
I'LL GIVE YOU A DAMN GOOD THRASHING! MAN IS YOUR MASTER! MAN!!
OH....
RUSTLE! RUSTLE!
GRRR!
AIEEEEEE!!!

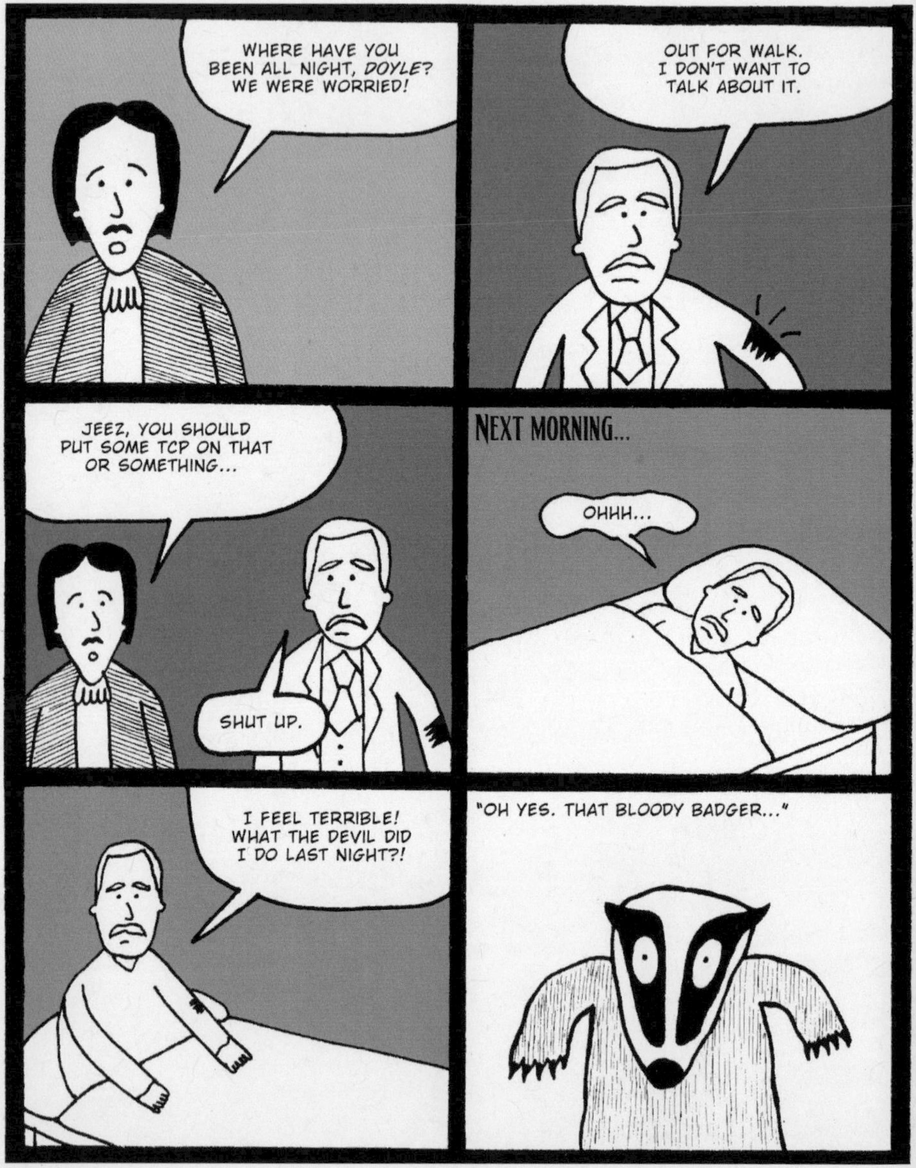
WHERE HAVE YOU BEEN ALL NIGHT, *DOYLE*? WE WERE WORRIED!
OUT FOR WALK. I DON'T WANT TO TALK ABOUT IT.
JEEZ, YOU SHOULD PUT SOME TCP ON THAT OR SOMETHING...
SHUT UP.
NEXT MORNING...
OHHH...
I FEEL TERRIBLE! WHAT THE DEVIL DID I DO LAST NIGHT?!
"OH YES. THAT BLOODY BADGER..."

THE FULL MOON LURKS ABOVE LIKE A LUMINOUS PIE...

WHILE INDOORS THE CHAPS ENJOY A THRILLING EPISODE OF THE FALL GUY.

I'M THE UNKNOWN STUNTMAN...

BUT ARTHUR CONAN DOYLE WAS MISSING THIS PARTICULAR EPISODE. HE WAS FEELING A BIT UNDER THE WEATHER...

GAH!

"SHOULDN'T... HAVE EATEN... THAT KEBAB GAAAAIIIEEEE!"

"WHAT'S HAPPENING TO ME?!"

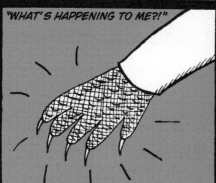

RAARGH!

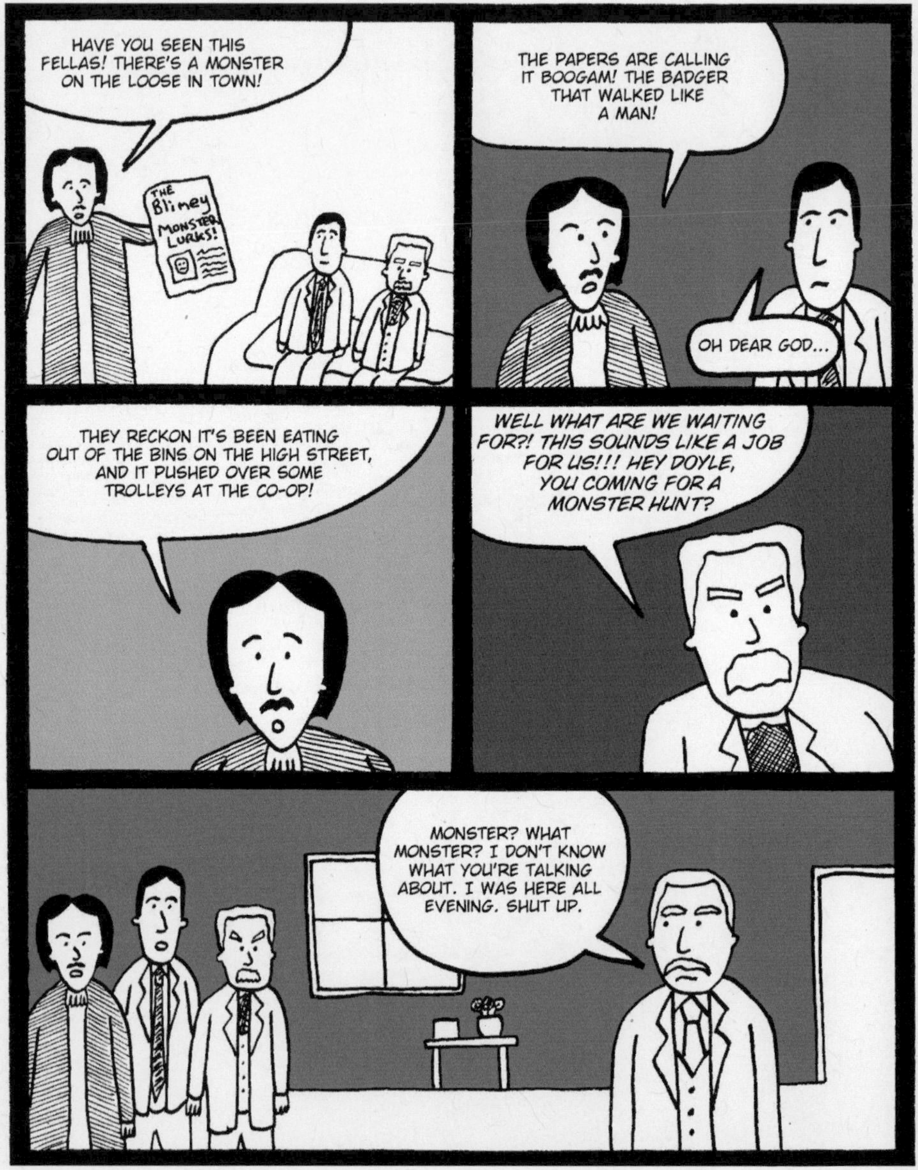
HAVE YOU SEEN THIS FELLAS! THERE'S A MONSTER ON THE LOOSE IN TOWN!
THE Blimey
MONSTER LURKS!
THE PAPERS ARE CALLING IT BOOGAM! THE BADGER THAT WALKED LIKE A MAN!
OH DEAR GOD...
THEY RECKON IT'S BEEN EATING OUT OF THE BINS ON THE HIGH STREET, AND IT PUSHED OVER SOME TROLLEYS AT THE CO-OP!
WELL WHAT ARE WE WAITING FOR?! THIS SOUNDS LIKE A JOB FOR US!!! HEY DOYLE, YOU COMING FOR A MONSTER HUNT?
MONSTER? WHAT MONSTER? I DON'T KNOW WHAT YOU'RE TALKING ABOUT. I WAS HERE ALL EVENING. SHUT UP.

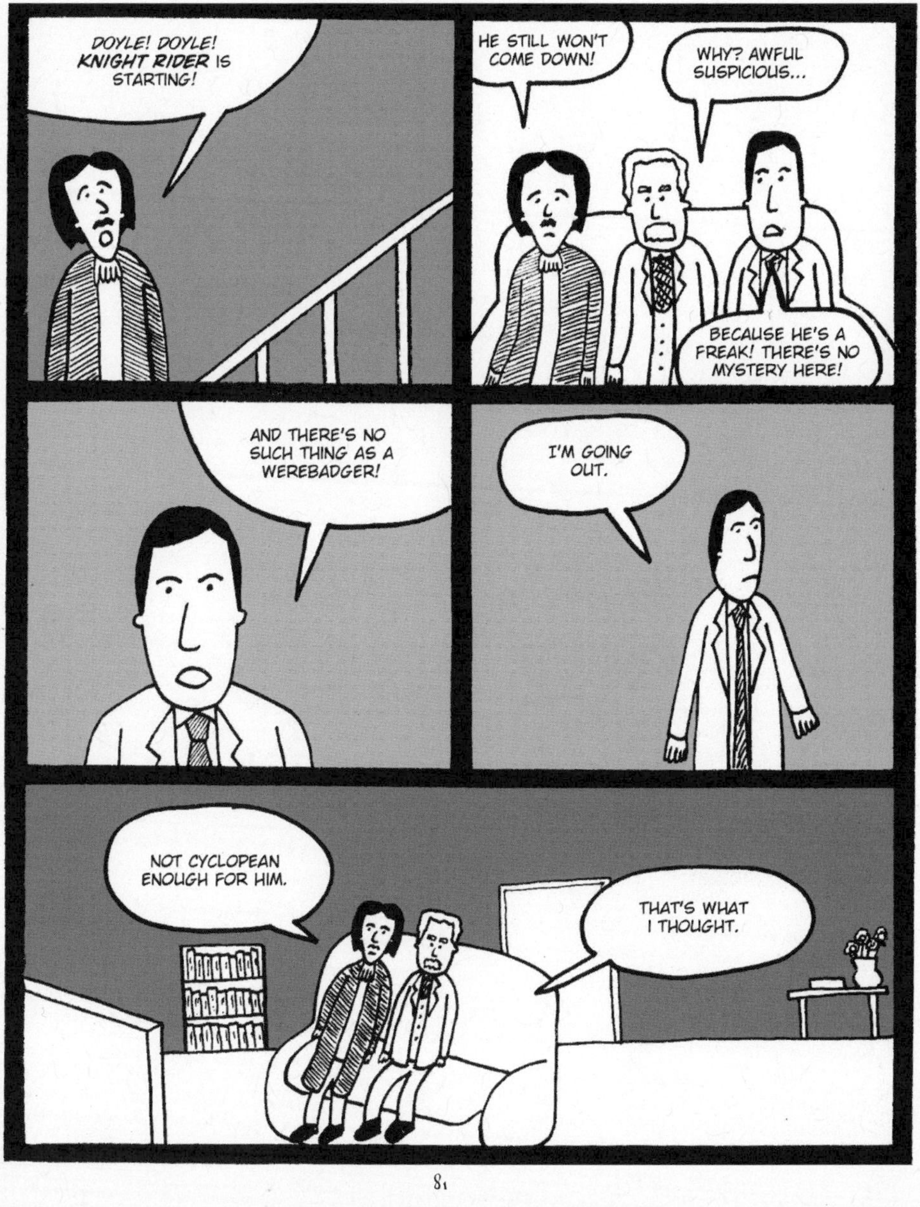
DOYLE! DOYLE! KNIGHT RIDER IS STARTING!
HE STILL WON'T COME DOWN!
WHY? AWFUL SUSPICIOUS...
BECAUSE HE'S A FREAK! THERE'S NO MYSTERY HERE!
AND THERE'S NO SUCH THING AS A WEREBADGER!
I'M GOING OUT.
NOT CYCLOPEAN ENOUGH FOR HIM.
THAT'S WHAT I THOUGHT.

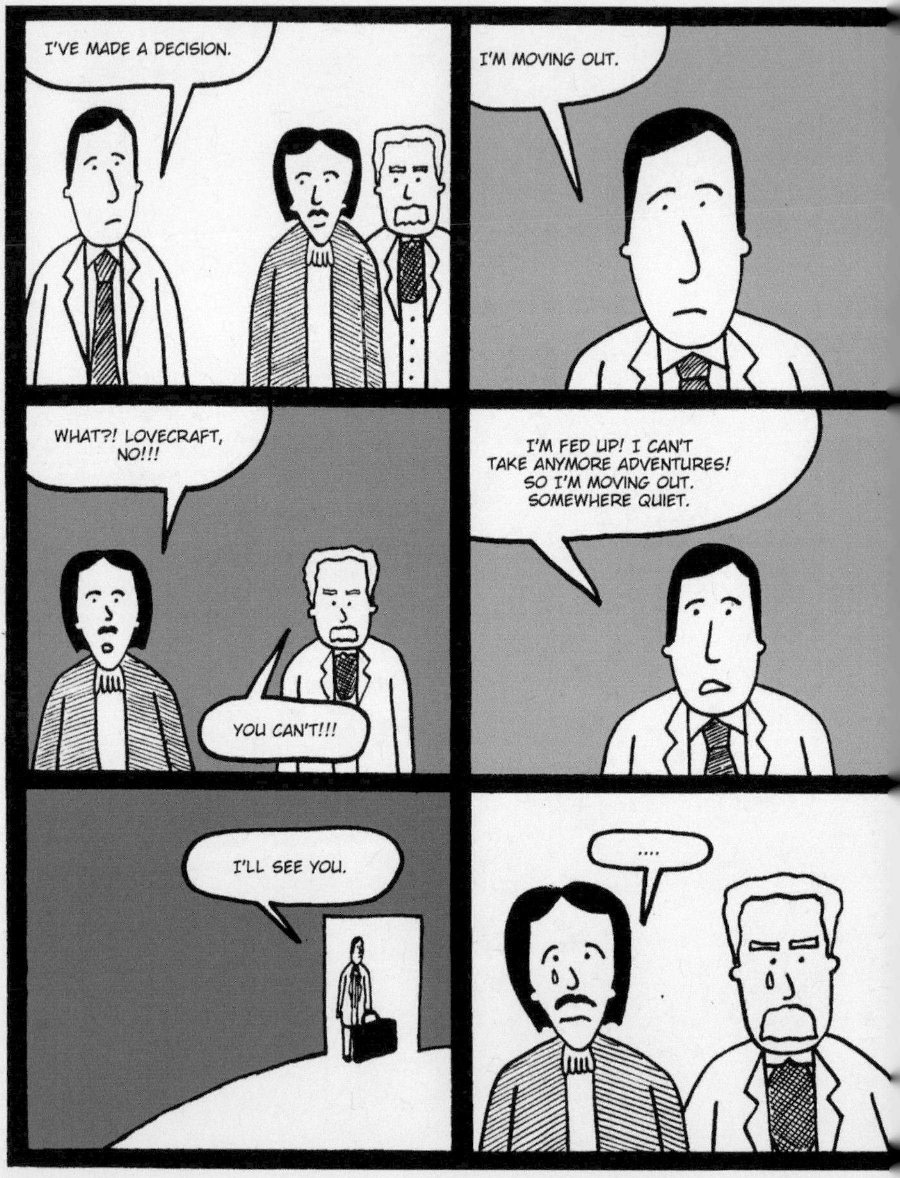
I'VE MADE A DECISION.
I'M MOVING OUT.
WHAT?! LOVECRAFT, NO!!!
YOU CAN'T!!!
I'M FED UP! I CAN'T TAKE ANYMORE ADVENTURES! SO I'M MOVING OUT. SOMEWHERE QUIET.
I'LL SEE YOU.
....

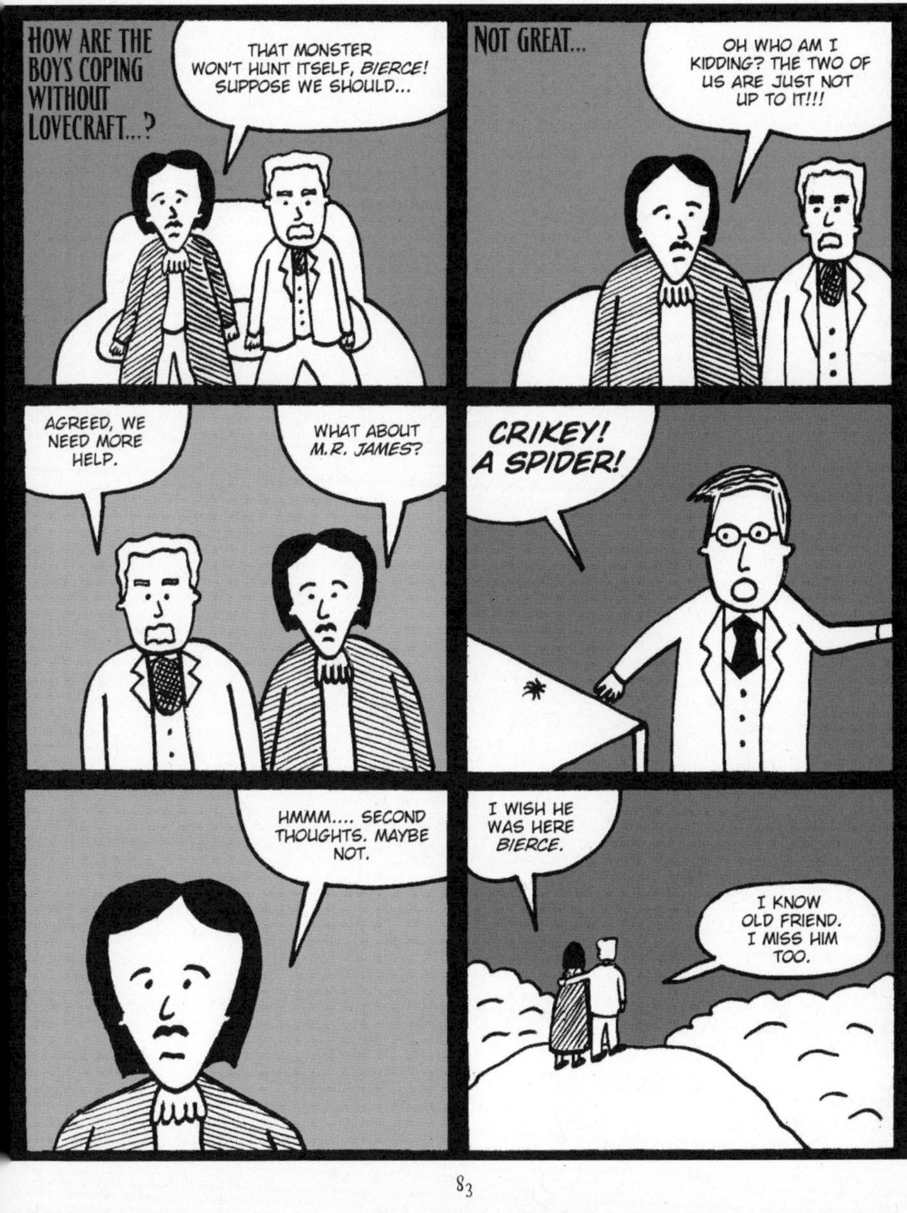
HOW ARE THE BOYS COPING WITHOUT LOVECRAFT...?
THAT MONSTER WON'T HUNT ITSELF, *BIERCE*! SUPPOSE WE SHOULD...
NOT GREAT...
OH WHO AM I KIDDING? THE TWO OF US ARE JUST NOT UP TO IT!!!
AGREED, WE NEED MORE HELP.
WHAT ABOUT *M.R. JAMES?*
*CRIKEY! A SPIDER!*
HMMM.... SECOND THOUGHTS. MAYBE NOT.
I WISH HE WAS HERE *BIERCE*.
I KNOW OLD FRIEND. I MISS HIM TOO.

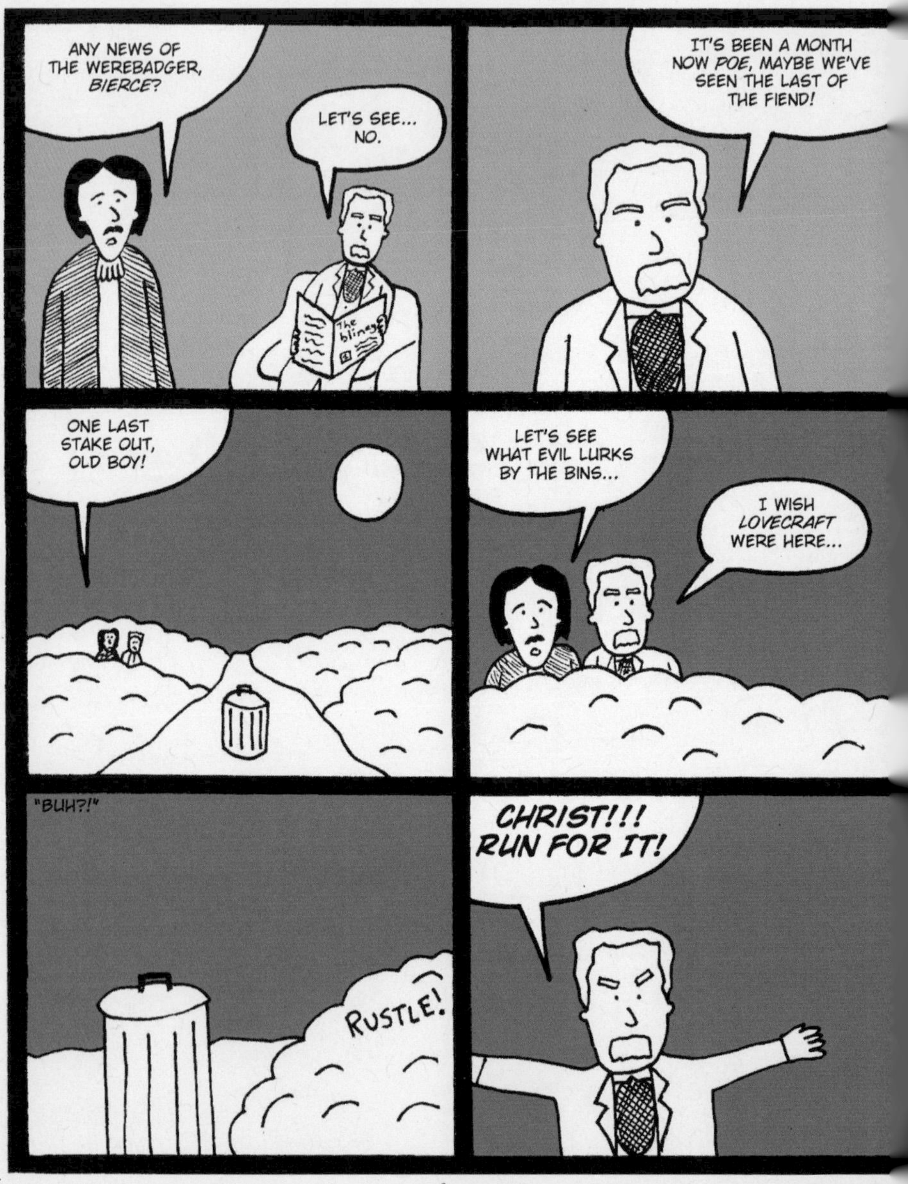

ANY NEWS OF THE WEREBADGER, *BIERCE*?
LET'S SEE... NO.
IT'S BEEN A MONTH NOW *POE*, MAYBE WE'VE SEEN THE LAST OF THE FIEND!
ONE LAST STAKE OUT, OLD BOY!
LET'S SEE WHAT EVIL LURKS BY THE BINS...
I WISH *LOVECRAFT* WERE HERE...
"BUH?!"
RUSTLE!
CHRIST!!! RUN FOR IT!

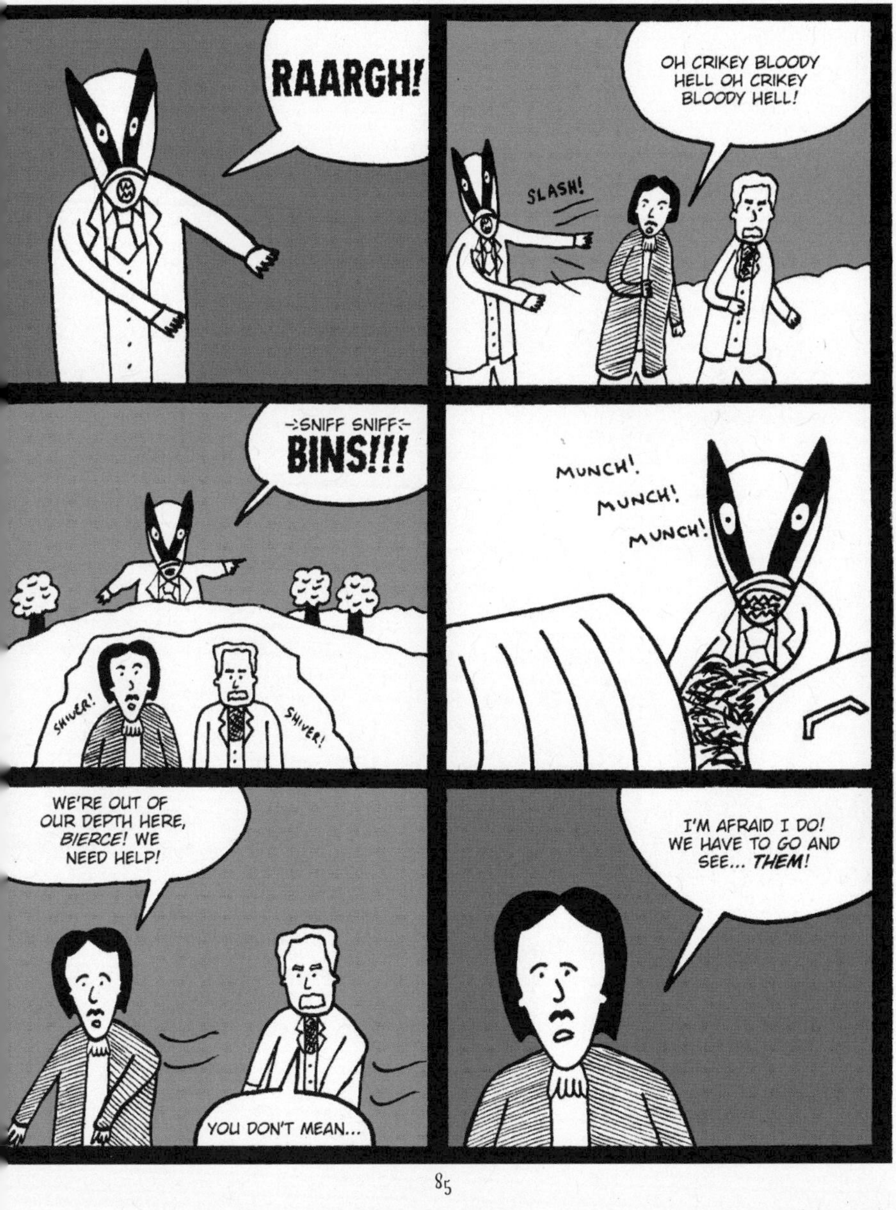
RAARGH!
OH CRIKEY BLOODY HELL OH CRIKEY BLOODY HELL!
SLASH!
SNIFF SNIFF
BINS!!!
SHIVER!
SHIVER!
MUNCH!
MUNCH!
MUNCH!
WE'RE OUT OF OUR DEPTH HERE, *BIERCE*! WE NEED HELP!
YOU DON'T MEAN...
I'M AFRAID I DO! WE HAVE TO GO AND SEE... *THEM*!

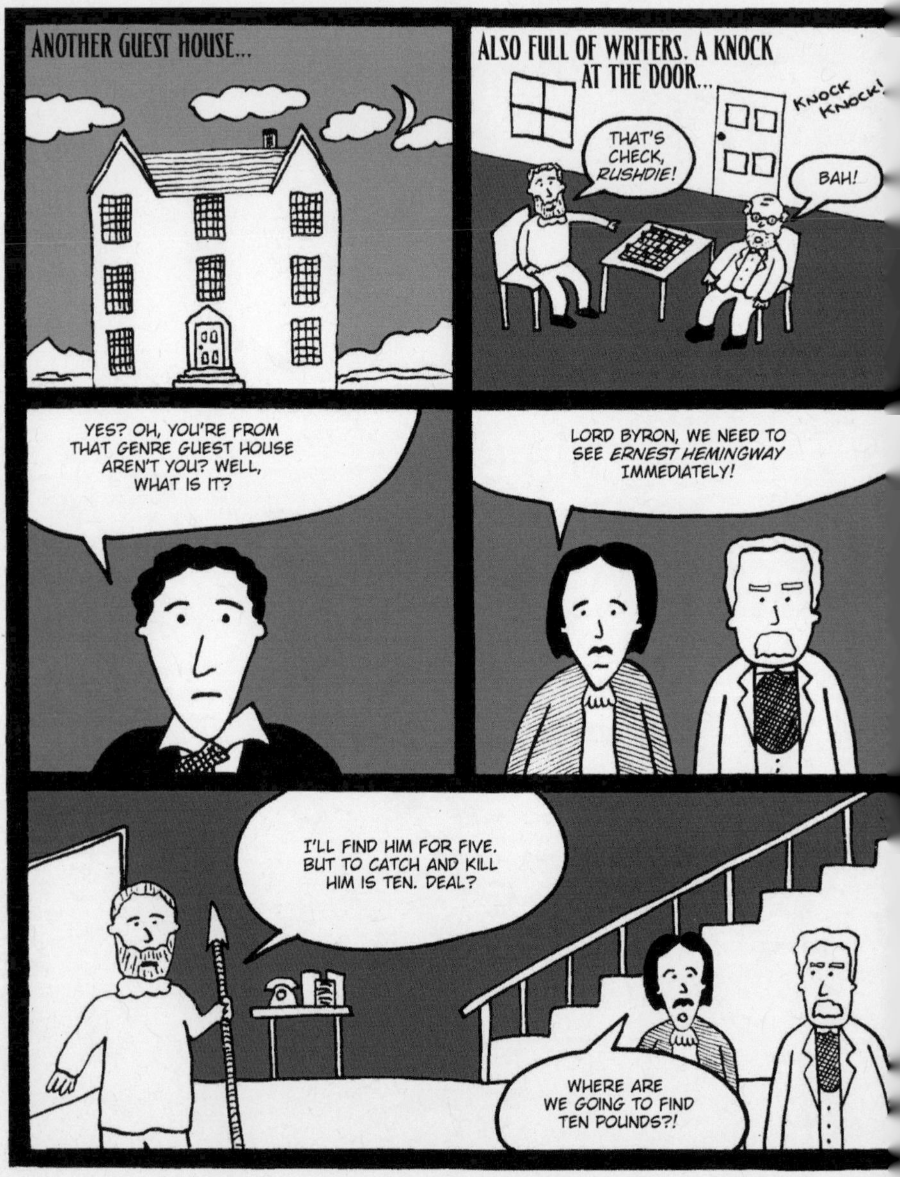
ANOTHER GUEST HOUSE...
ALSO FULL OF WRITERS. A KNOCK AT THE DOOR...
THAT'S CHECK, RUSHDIE!
KNOCK KNOCK!
BAH!
YES? OH, YOU'RE FROM THAT GENRE GUEST HOUSE AREN'T YOU? WELL, WHAT IS IT?
LORD BYRON, WE NEED TO SEE ERNEST HEMINGWAY IMMEDIATELY!
I'LL FIND HIM FOR FIVE. BUT TO CATCH AND KILL HIM IS TEN. DEAL?
WHERE ARE WE GOING TO FIND TEN POUNDS?!

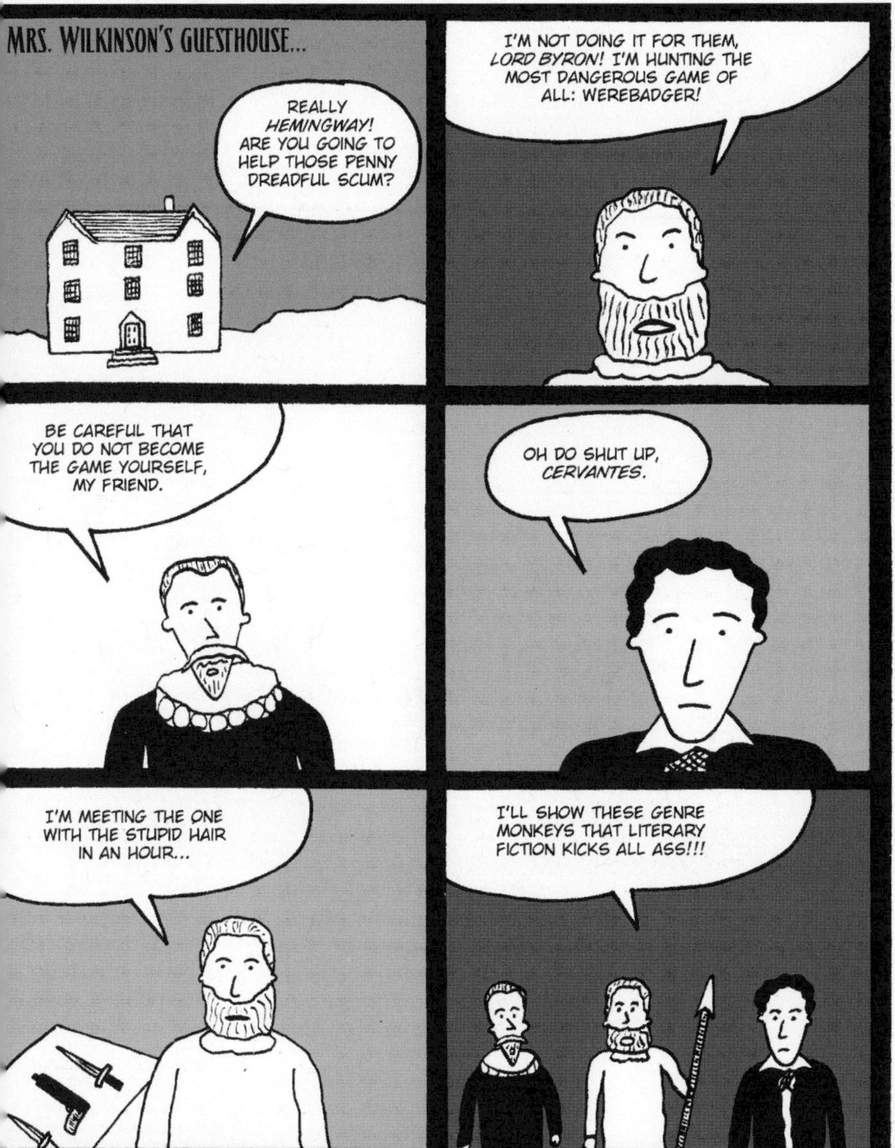
MRS. WILKINSON'S GUESTHOUSE...
REALLY HEMINGWAY! ARE YOU GOING TO HELP THOSE PENNY DREADFUL SCUM?
I'M NOT DOING IT FOR THEM, LORD BYRON! I'M HUNTING THE MOST DANGEROUS GAME OF ALL: WEREBADGER!
BE CAREFUL THAT YOU DO NOT BECOME THE GAME YOURSELF, MY FRIEND.
OH DO SHUT UP, CERVANTES.
I'M MEETING THE ONE WITH THE STUPID HAIR IN AN HOUR...
I'LL SHOW THESE GENRE MONKEYS THAT LITERARY FICTION KICKS ALL ASS!!!

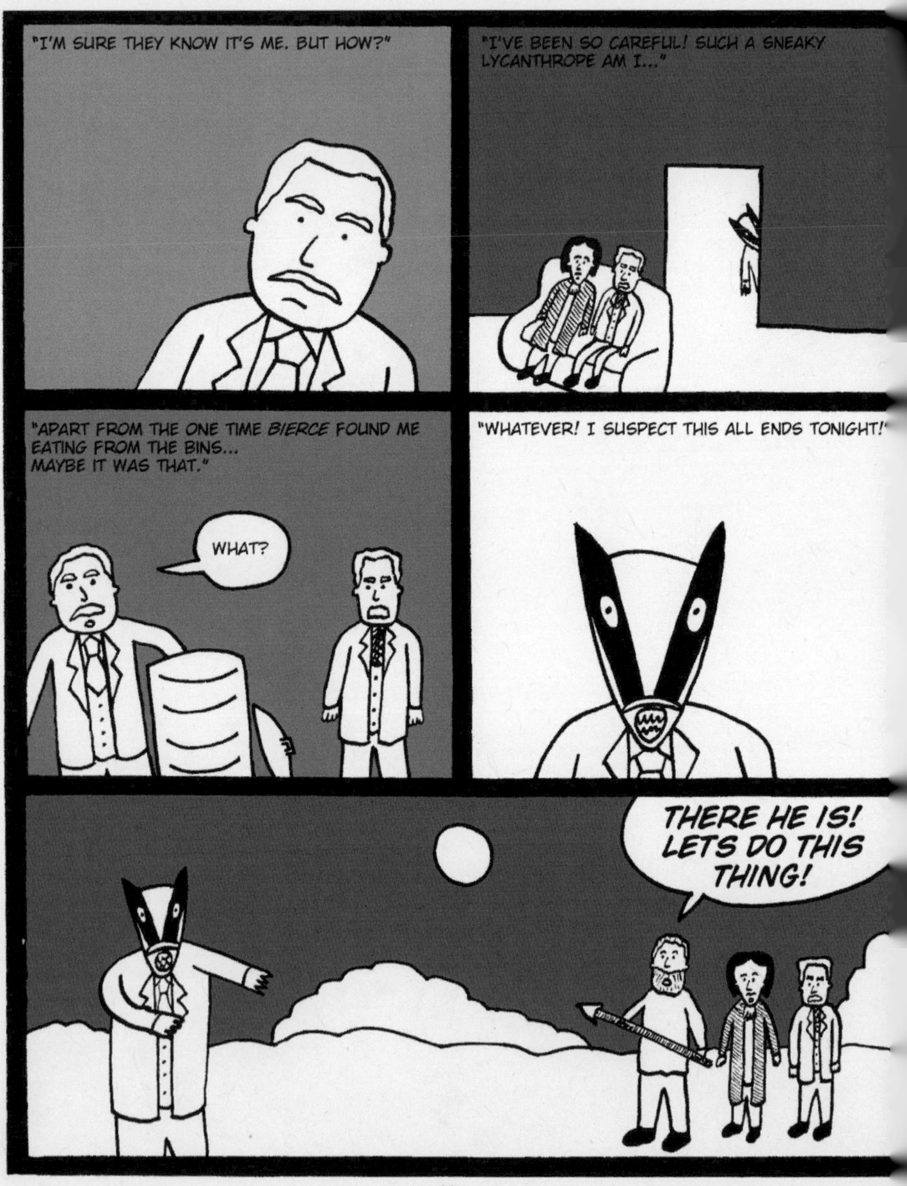
"I'M SURE THEY KNOW IT'S ME. BUT HOW?"
"I'VE BEEN SO CAREFUL! SUCH A SNEAKY LYCANTHROPE AM I..."
"APART FROM THE ONE TIME BIERCE FOUND ME EATING FROM THE BINS... MAYBE IT WAS THAT."
WHAT?
"WHATEVER! I SUSPECT THIS ALL ENDS TONIGHT!"
THERE HE IS! LETS DO THIS THING!

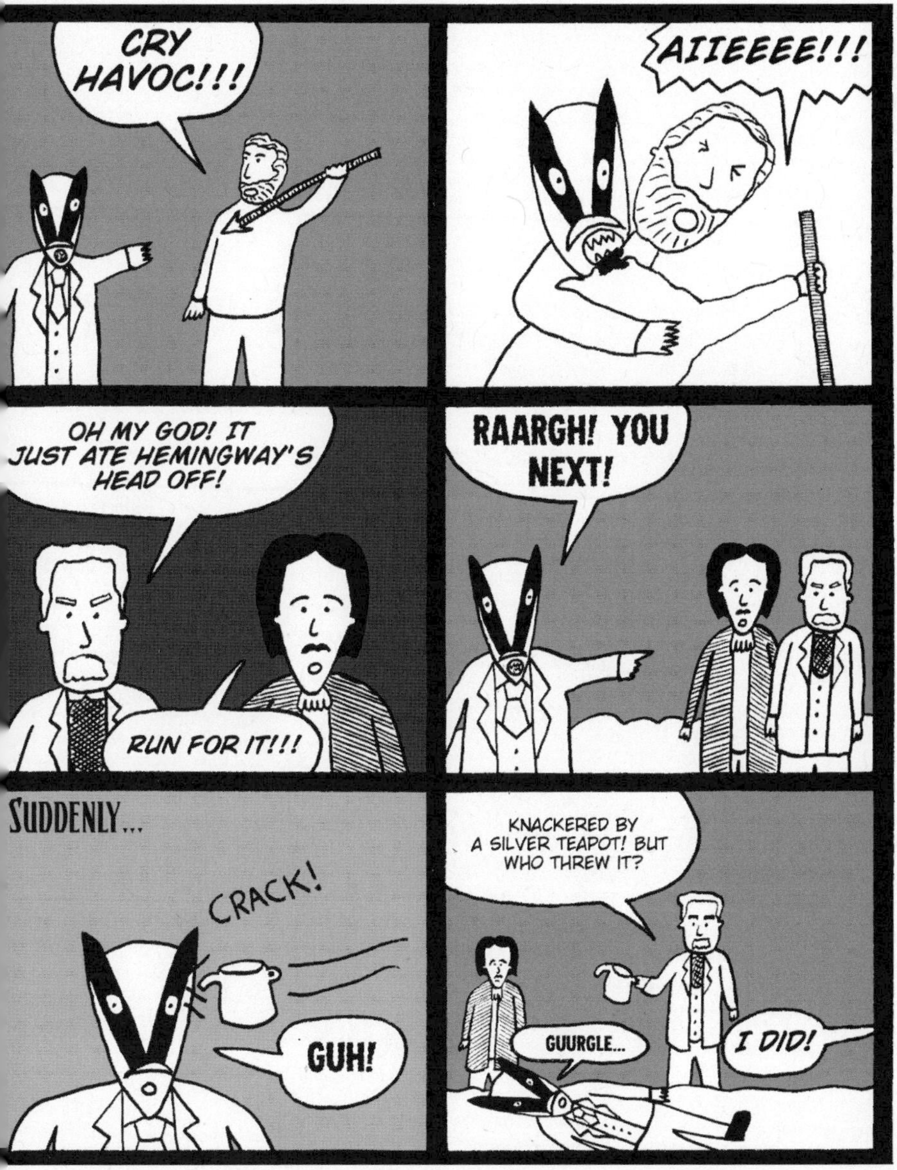
CRY HAVOC!!!
AIIEEEE!!!
OH MY GOD! IT JUST ATE HEMINGWAY'S HEAD OFF!
RUN FOR IT!!!
RAARGH! YOU NEXT!
SUDDENLY...
CRACK!
GUH!
KNACKERED BY A SILVER TEAPOT! BUT WHO THREW IT?
GUURGLE...
I DID!

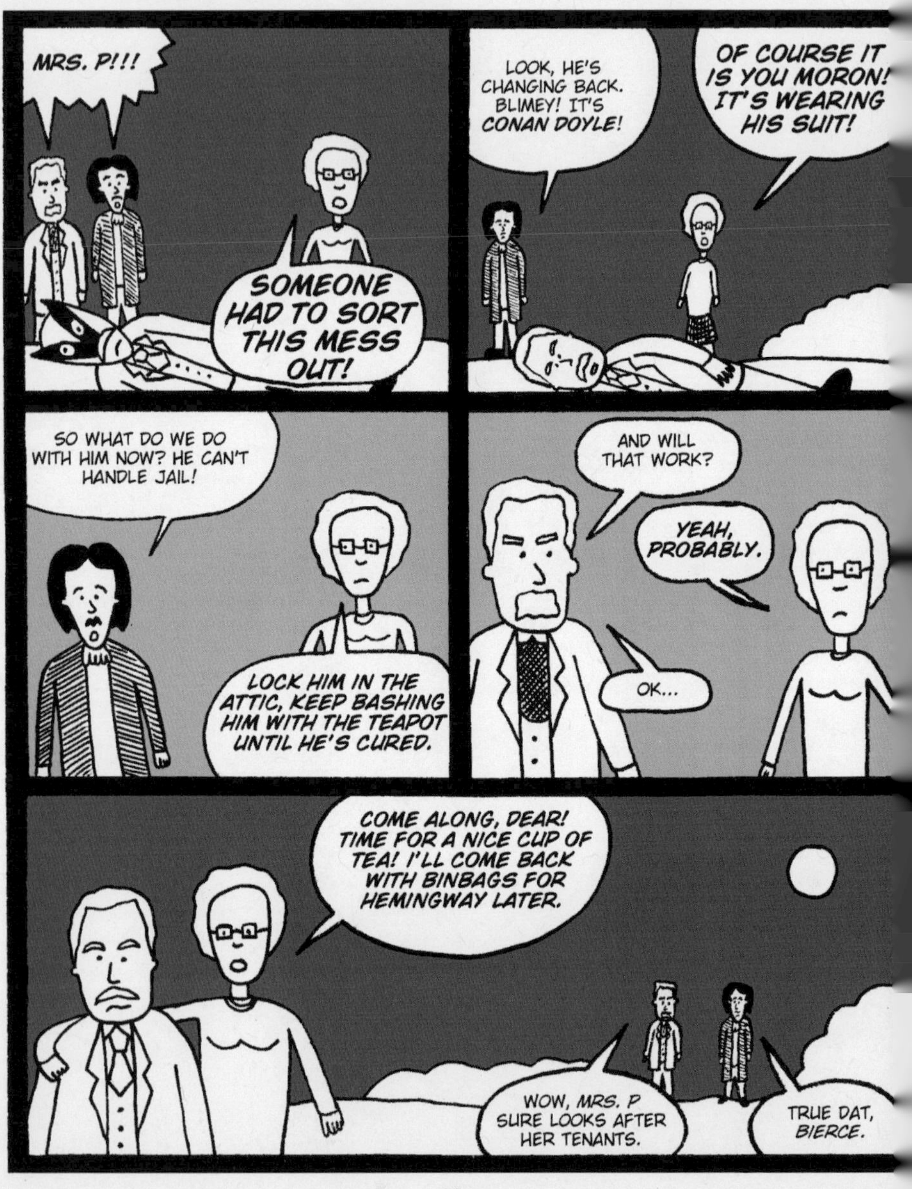
MRS. P!!!
SOMEONE HAD TO SORT THIS MESS OUT!
LOOK, HE'S CHANGING BACK. BLIMEY! IT'S CONAN DOYLE!
OF COURSE IT IS YOU MORON! IT'S WEARING HIS SUIT!
SO WHAT DO WE DO WITH HIM NOW? HE CAN'T HANDLE JAIL!
LOCK HIM IN THE ATTIC, KEEP BASHING HIM WITH THE TEAPOT UNTIL HE'S CURED.
AND WILL THAT WORK?
YEAH, PROBABLY.
OK...
COME ALONG, DEAR! TIME FOR A NICE CUP OF TEA! I'LL COME BACK WITH BINBAGS FOR HEMINGWAY LATER.
WOW, MRS. P SURE LOOKS AFTER HER TENANTS.
TRUE DAT, BIERCE.

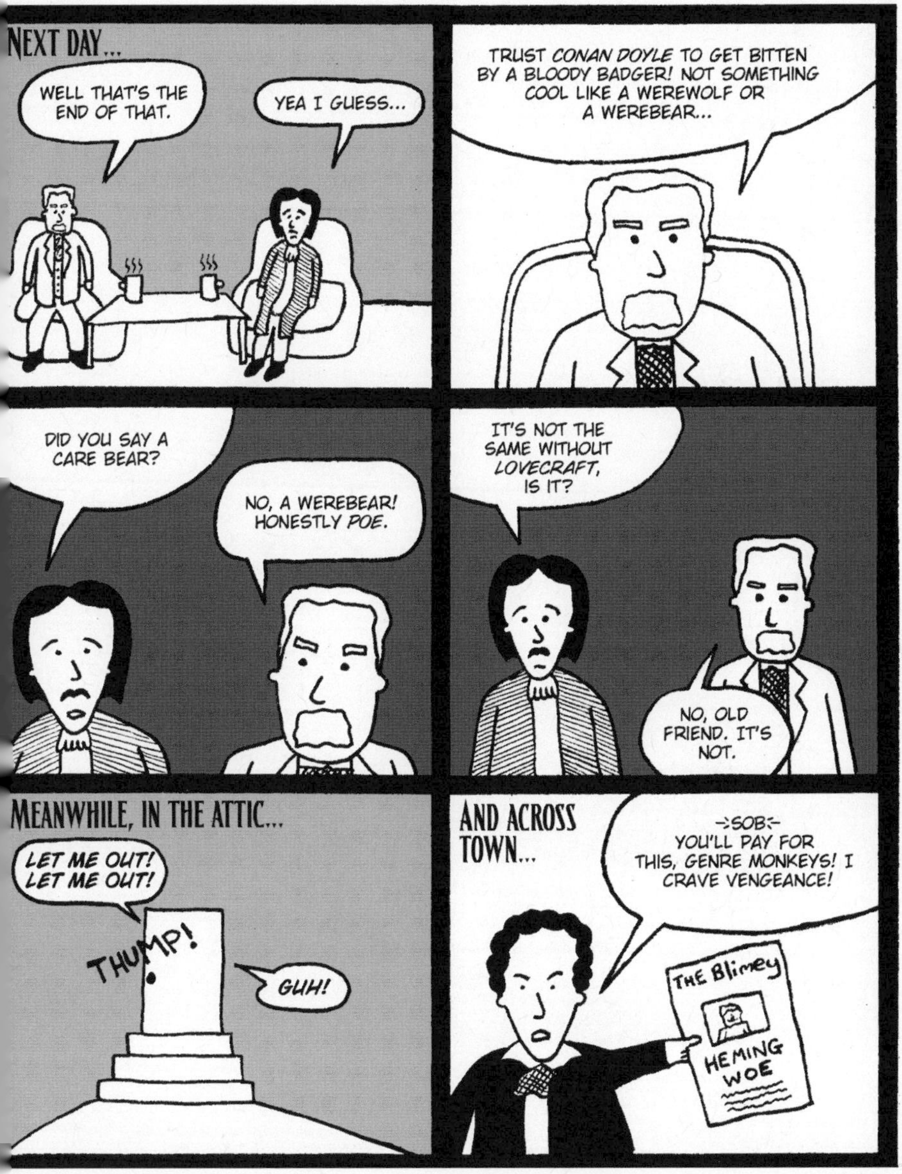
NEXT DAY...
WELL THAT'S THE END OF THAT.
YEA I GUESS...
TRUST *CONAN DOYLE* TO GET BITTEN BY A BLOODY BADGER! NOT SOMETHING COOL LIKE A WEREWOLF OR A WEREBEAR...
DID YOU SAY A CARE BEAR?
NO, A WEREBEAR! HONESTLY *POE*.
IT'S NOT THE SAME WITHOUT *LOVECRAFT*, IS IT?
NO, OLD FRIEND. IT'S NOT.
MEANWHILE, IN THE ATTIC...
*LET ME OUT! LET ME OUT!*
THUMP!
*GUH!*
AND ACROSS TOWN...
SOB
YOU'LL PAY FOR THIS, GENRE MONKEYS! I CRAVE VENGEANCE!
THE Blimey
HEMING WOE

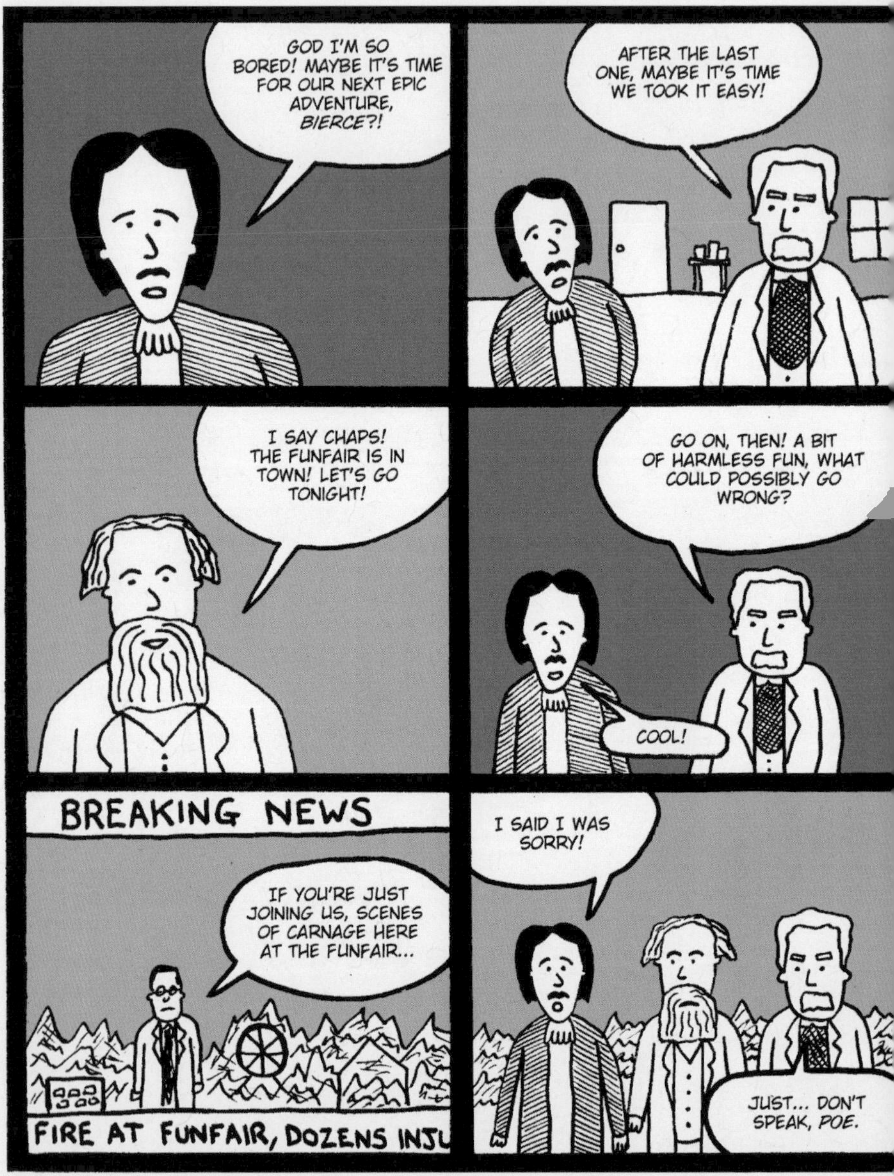
GOD I'M SO BORED! MAYBE IT'S TIME FOR OUR NEXT EPIC ADVENTURE, *BIERCE*?!
AFTER THE LAST ONE, MAYBE IT'S TIME WE TOOK IT EASY!
I SAY CHAPS! THE FUNFAIR IS IN TOWN! LET'S GO TONIGHT!
GO ON, THEN! A BIT OF HARMLESS FUN, WHAT COULD POSSIBLY GO WRONG?
COOL!
BREAKING NEWS
IF YOU'RE JUST JOINING US, SCENES OF CARNAGE HERE AT THE FUNFAIR...
FIRE AT FUNFAIR, DOZENS INJU
I SAID I WAS SORRY!
JUST... DON'T SPEAK, *POE*.

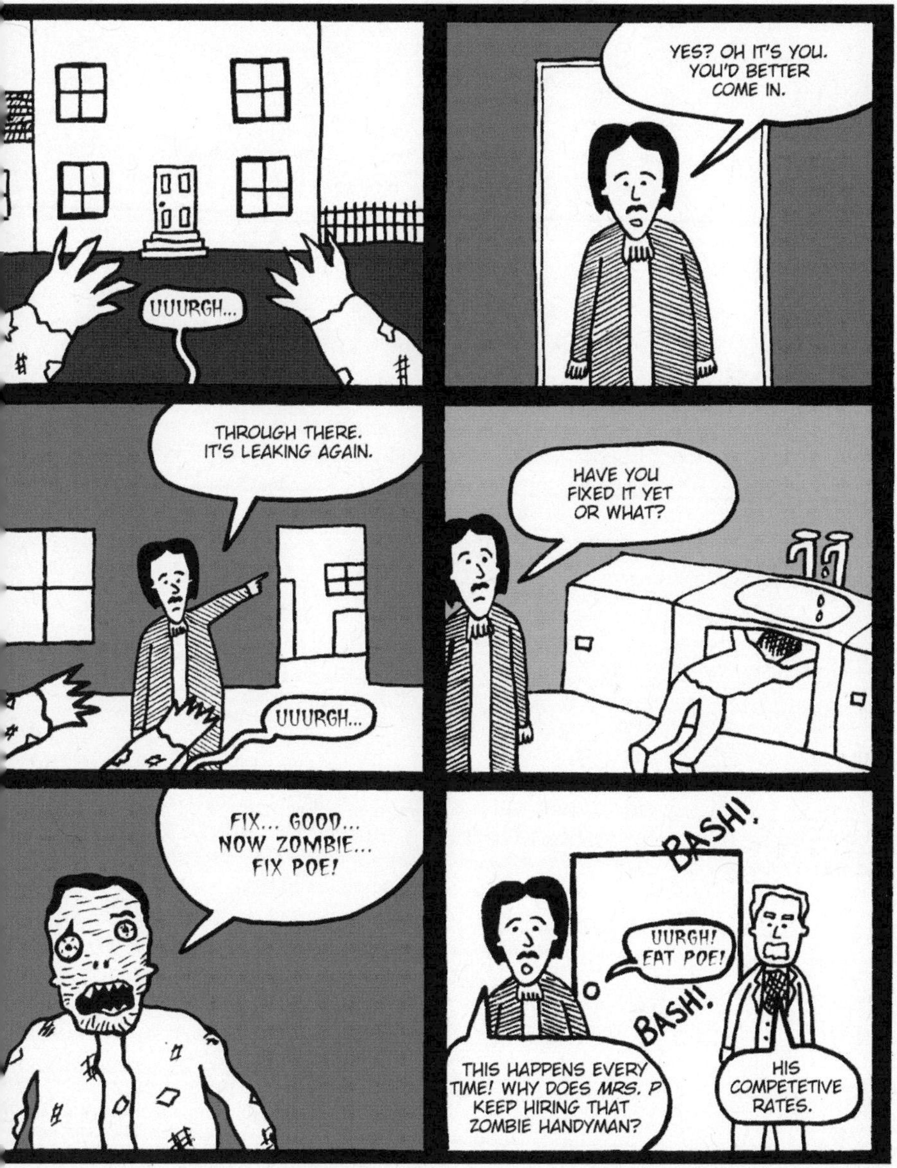
UUURGH...
YES? OH IT'S YOU. YOU'D BETTER COME IN.
THROUGH THERE. IT'S LEAKING AGAIN.
UUURGH...
HAVE YOU FIXED IT YET OR WHAT?
FIX... GOOD... NOW ZOMBIE... FIX POE!
BASH!
UURGH! EAT POE!
BASH!
THIS HAPPENS EVERY TIME! WHY DOES MRS. P KEEP HIRING THAT ZOMBIE HANDYMAN?
HIS COMPETETIVE RATES.

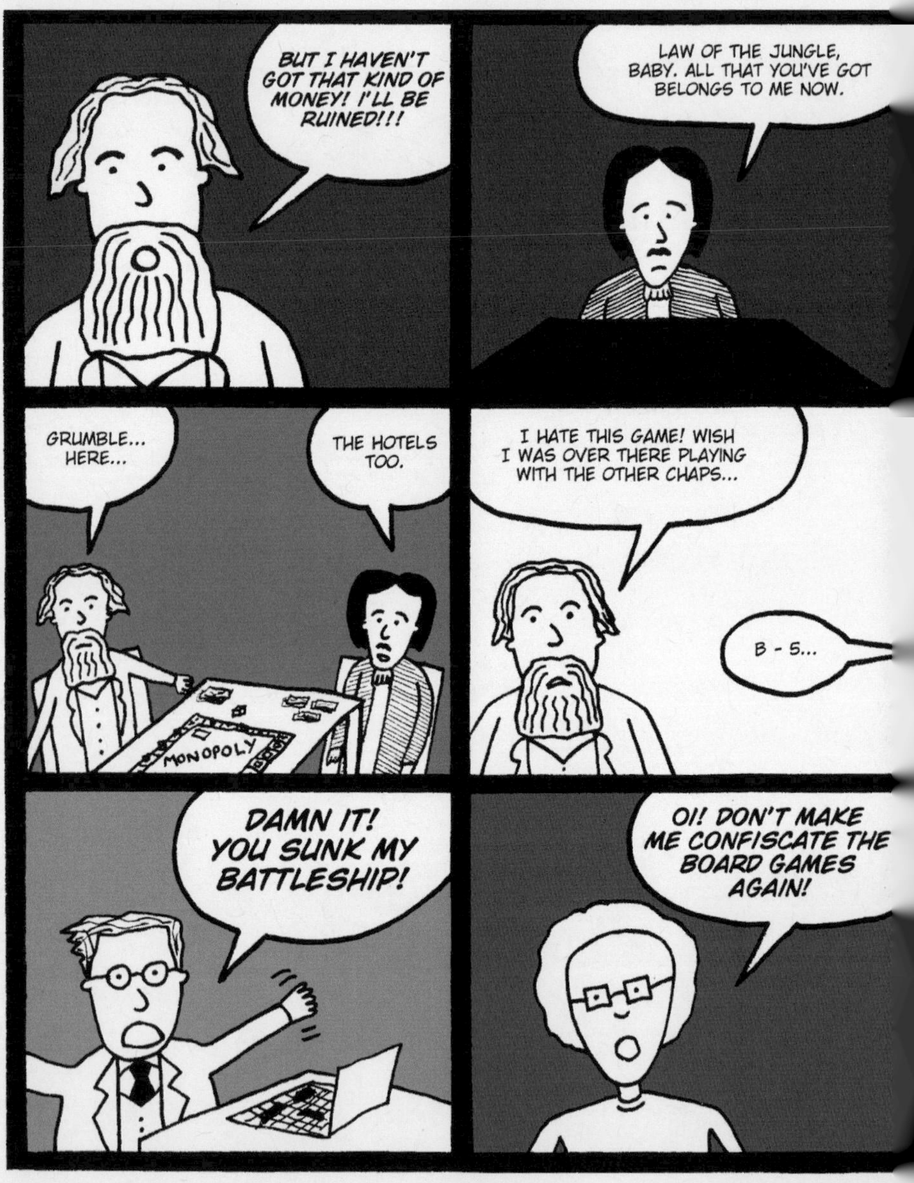
BUT I HAVEN'T GOT THAT KIND OF MONEY! I'LL BE RUINED!!!
LAW OF THE JUNGLE, BABY. ALL THAT YOU'VE GOT BELONGS TO ME NOW.
GRUMBLE... HERE...
THE HOTELS TOO.
MONOPOLY
I HATE THIS GAME! WISH I WAS OVER THERE PLAYING WITH THE OTHER CHAPS...
B - 5...
DAMN IT! YOU SUNK MY BATTLESHIP!
OI! DON'T MAKE ME CONFISCATE THE BOARD GAMES AGAIN!

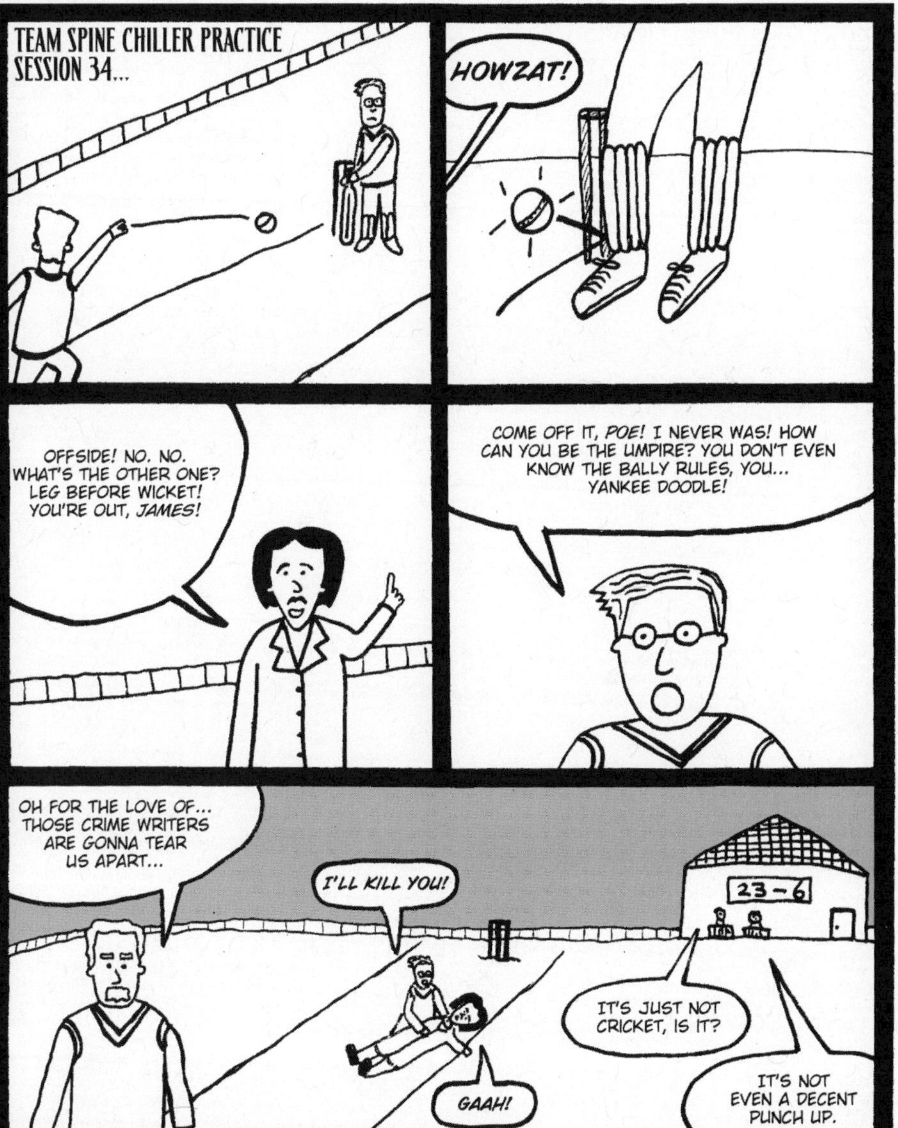

TEAM SPINE CHILLER PRACTICE SESSION 34...
HOWZAT!
OFFSIDE! NO. NO. WHAT'S THE OTHER ONE? LEG BEFORE WICKET! YOU'RE OUT, *JAMES!*
COME OFF IT, *POE!* I NEVER WAS! HOW CAN YOU BE THE UMPIRE? YOU DON'T EVEN KNOW THE BALLY RULES, YOU... YANKEE DOODLE!
OH FOR THE LOVE OF... THOSE CRIME WRITERS ARE GONNA TEAR US APART...
I'LL KILL YOU!
23 – 6
GAAH!
IT'S JUST NOT CRICKET, IS IT?
IT'S NOT EVEN A DECENT PUNCH UP.

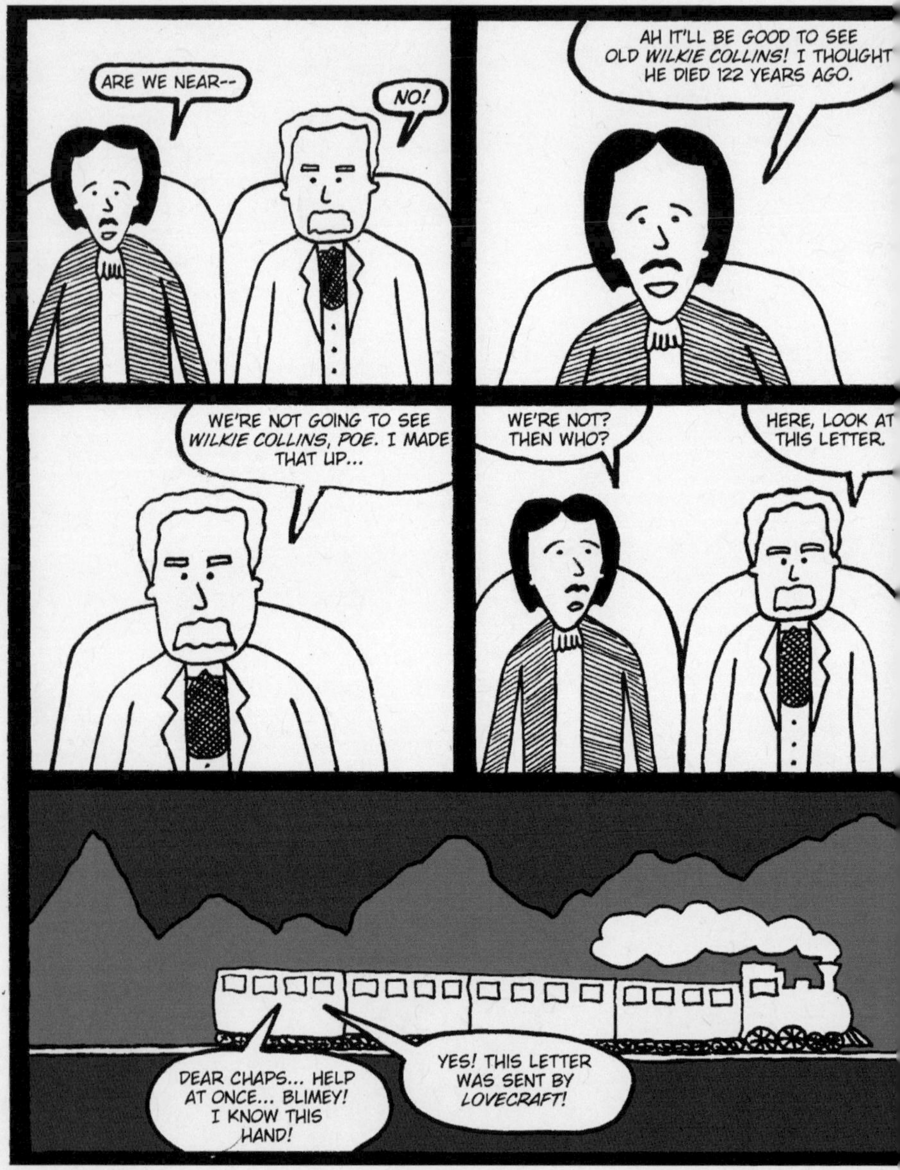
ARE WE NEAR--
NO!
AH IT'LL BE GOOD TO SEE OLD *WILKIE COLLINS*! I THOUGHT HE DIED 122 YEARS AGO.
WE'RE NOT GOING TO SEE *WILKIE COLLINS, POE*. I MADE THAT UP...
WE'RE NOT? THEN WHO?
HERE, LOOK AT THIS LETTER.
DEAR CHAPS... HELP AT ONCE... BLIMEY! I KNOW THIS HAND!
YES! THIS LETTER WAS SENT BY *LOVECRAFT*!

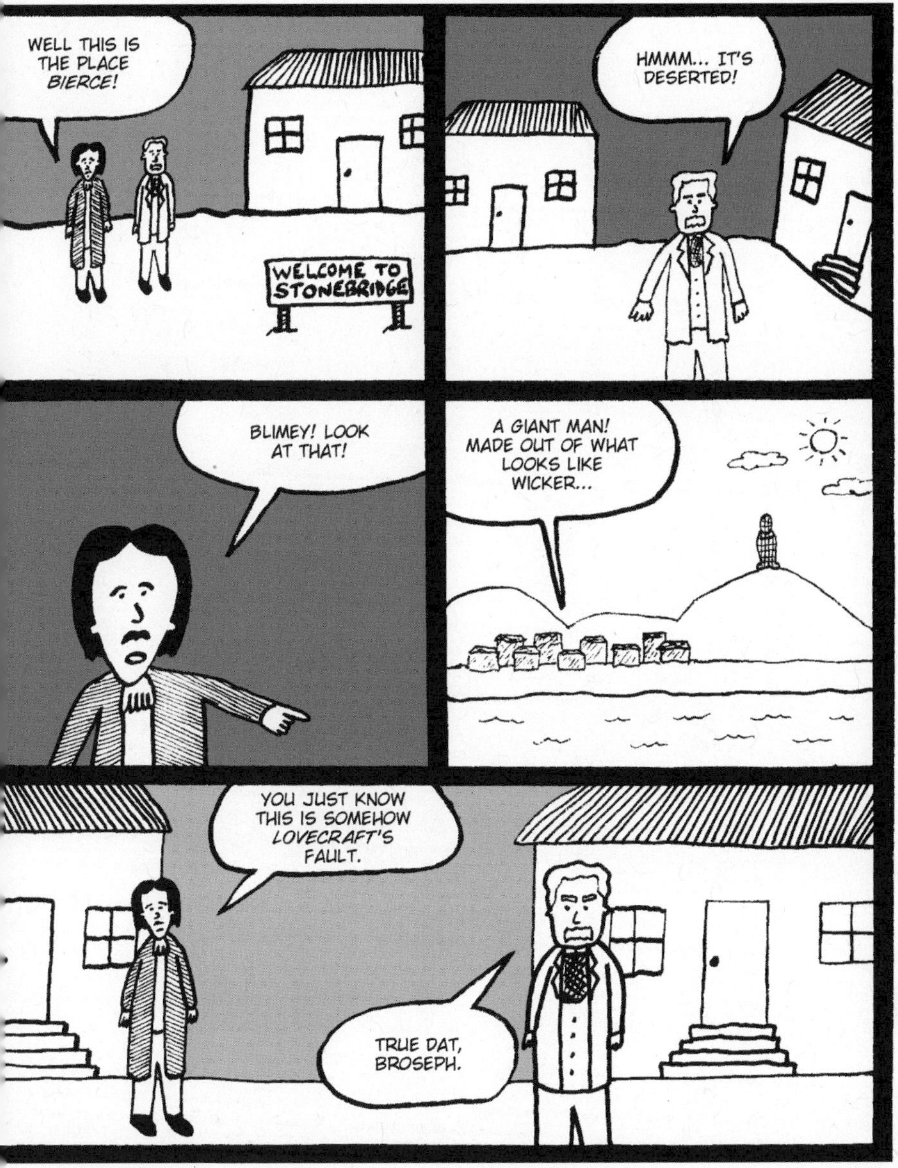
WELL THIS IS THE PLACE *BIERCE!*
WELCOME TO STONEBRIDGE
HMMM... IT'S DESERTED!
BLIMEY! LOOK AT THAT!
A GIANT MAN! MADE OUT OF WHAT LOOKS LIKE WICKER...
YOU JUST KNOW THIS IS SOMEHOW *LOVECRAFT'S* FAULT.
TRUE DAT, BROSEPH.

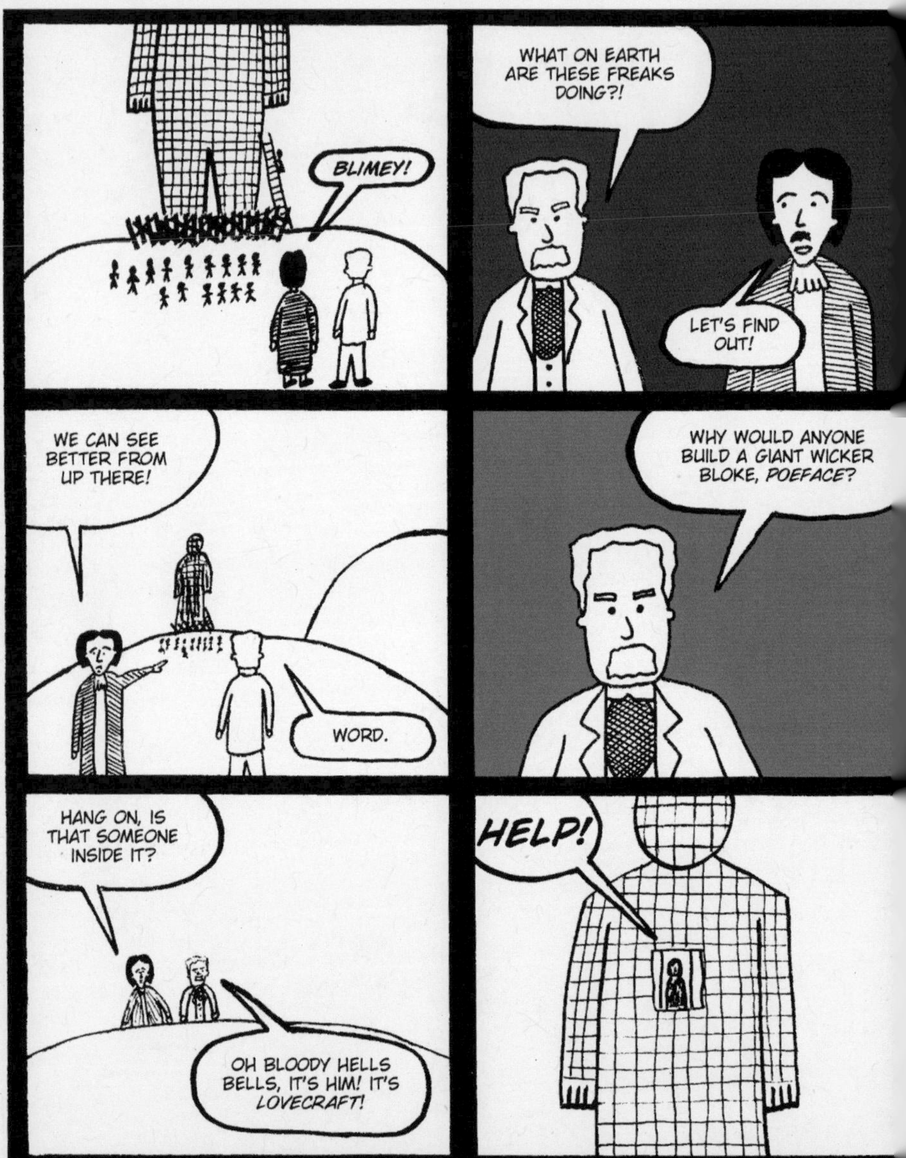
BLIMEY!
WHAT ON EARTH ARE THESE FREAKS DOING?!
LET'S FIND OUT!
WE CAN SEE BETTER FROM UP THERE!
WORD.
WHY WOULD ANYONE BUILD A GIANT WICKER BLOKE, *POEFACE*?
HANG ON, IS THAT SOMEONE INSIDE IT?
OH BLOODY HELLS BELLS, IT'S HIM! IT'S *LOVECRAFT*!
HELP!

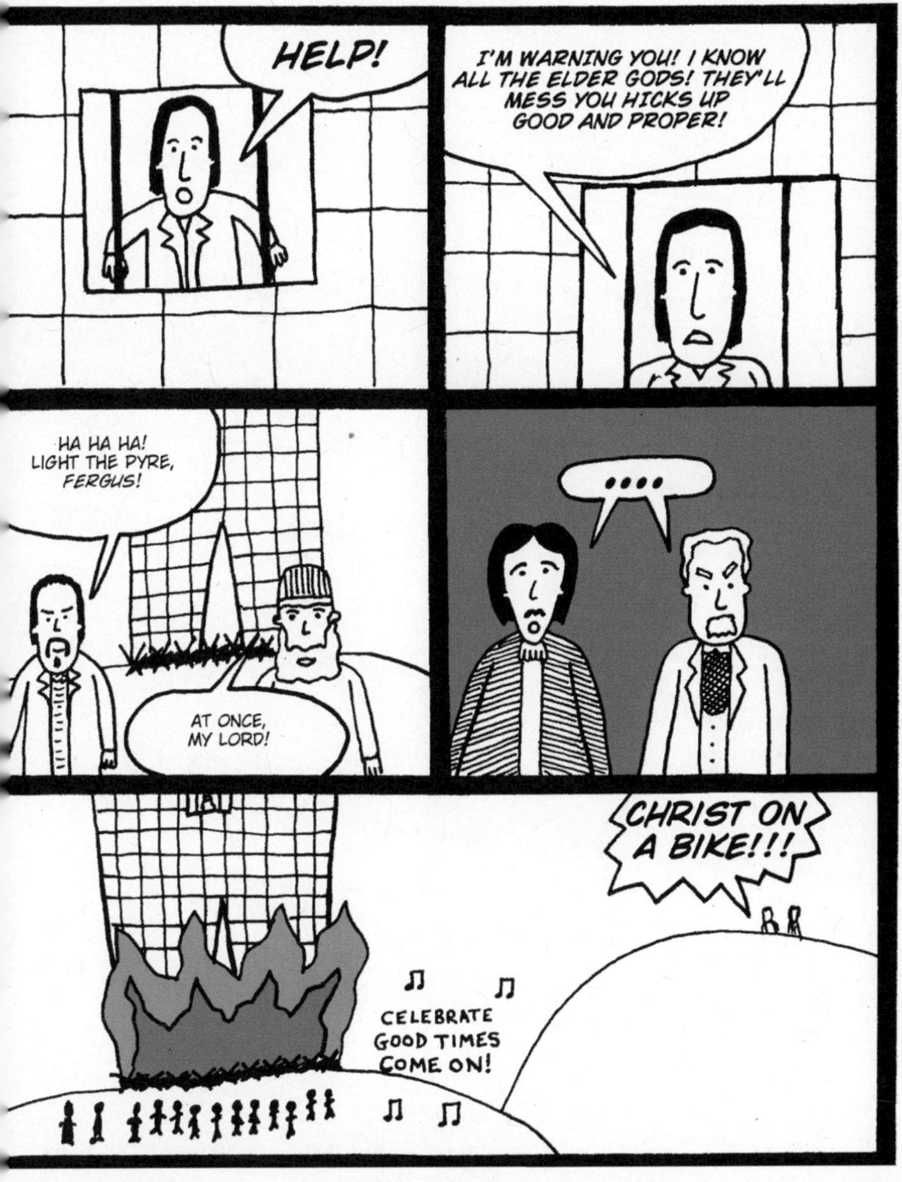
HELP!
I'M WARNING YOU! I KNOW ALL THE ELDER GODS! THEY'LL MESS YOU HICKS UP GOOD AND PROPER!
HA HA HA! LIGHT THE PYRE, FERGUS!
AT ONCE, MY LORD!
....
CHRIST ON A BIKE!!!
CELEBRATE GOOD TIMES COME ON!

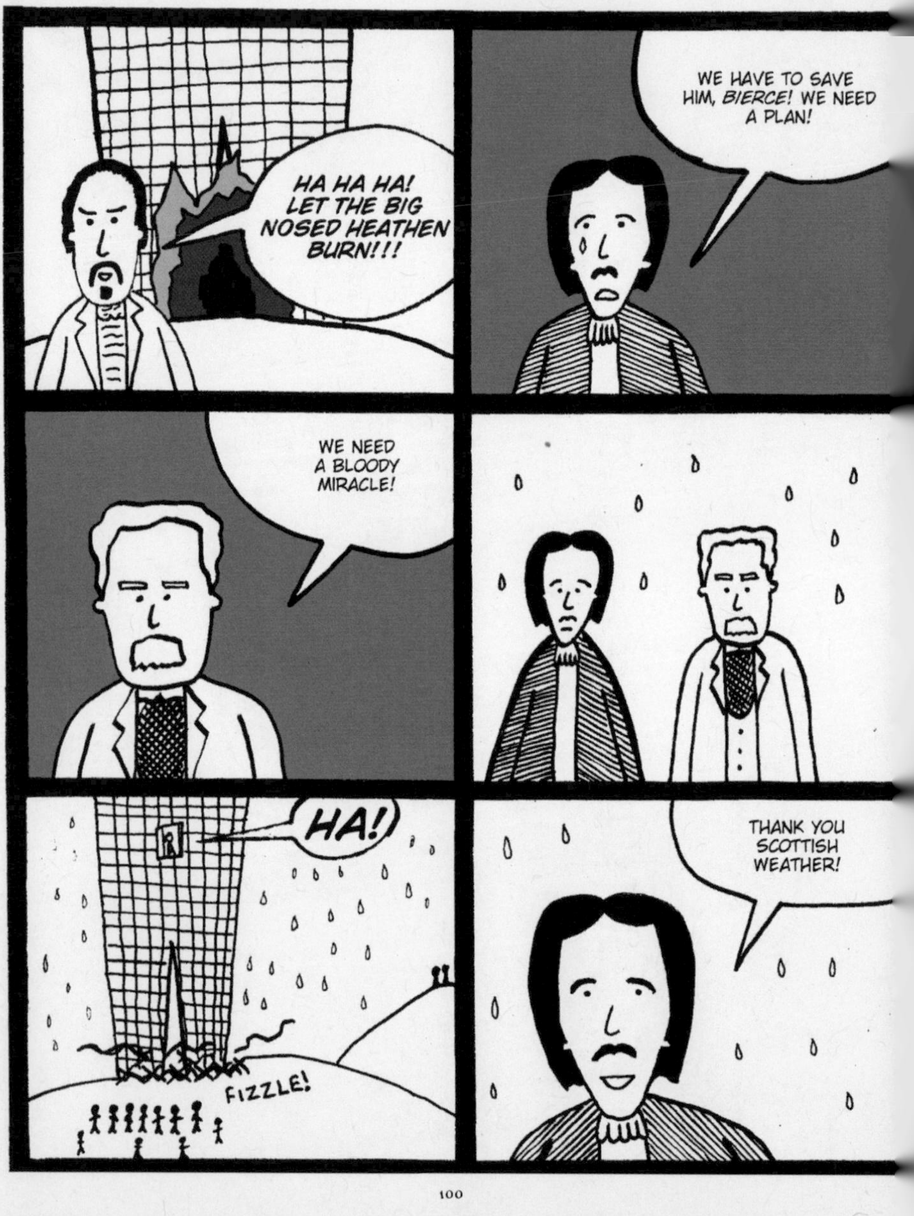
HA HA HA! LET THE BIG NOSED HEATHEN BURN!!!
WE HAVE TO SAVE HIM, *BIERCE!* WE NEED A PLAN!
WE NEED A BLOODY MIRACLE!
HA!
FIZZLE!
THANK YOU SCOTTISH WEATHER!

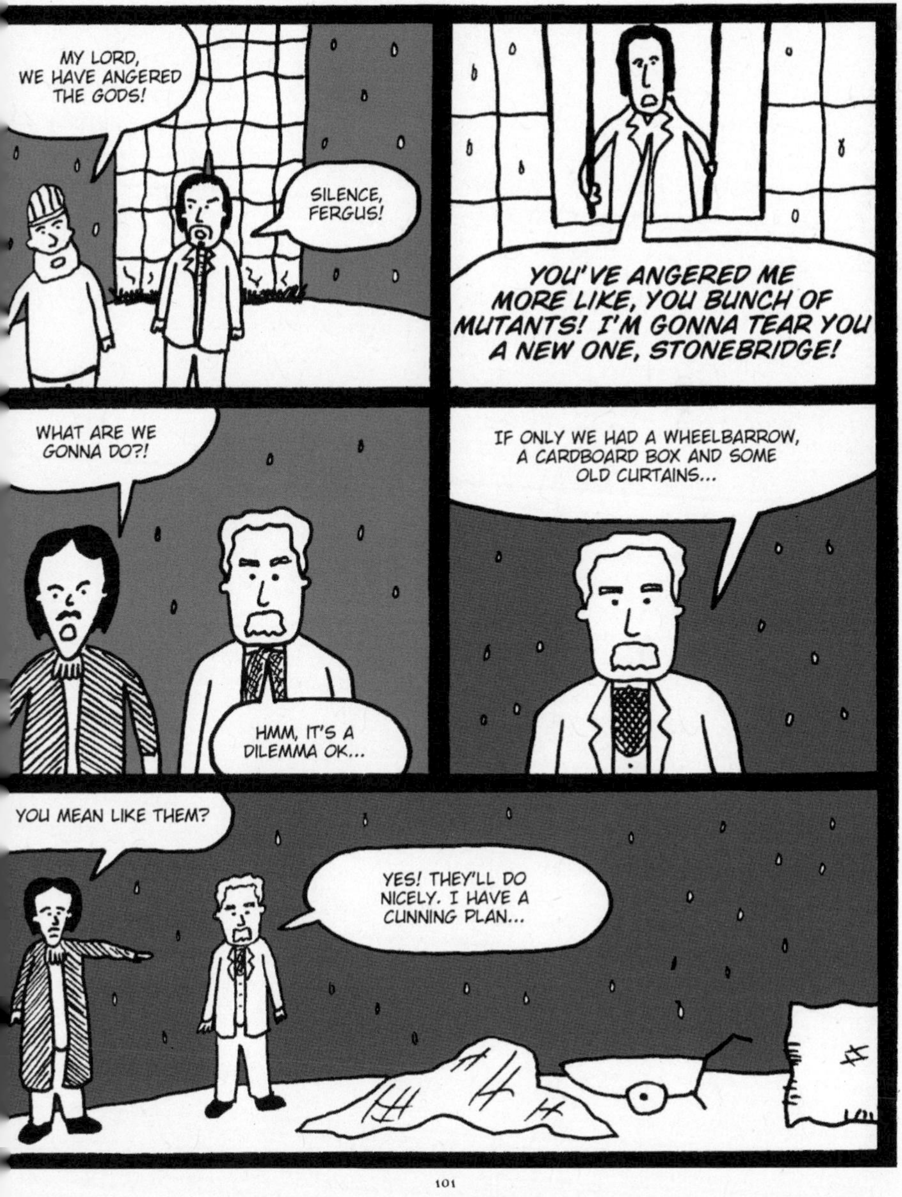
MY LORD, WE HAVE ANGERED THE GODS!
SILENCE, FERGUS!
YOU'VE ANGERED ME MORE LIKE, YOU BUNCH OF MUTANTS! I'M GONNA TEAR YOU A NEW ONE, STONEBRIDGE!
WHAT ARE WE GONNA DO?!
HMM, IT'S A DILEMMA OK...
IF ONLY WE HAD A WHEELBARROW, A CARDBOARD BOX AND SOME OLD CURTAINS...
YOU MEAN LIKE THEM?
YES! THEY'LL DO NICELY. I HAVE A CUNNING PLAN...

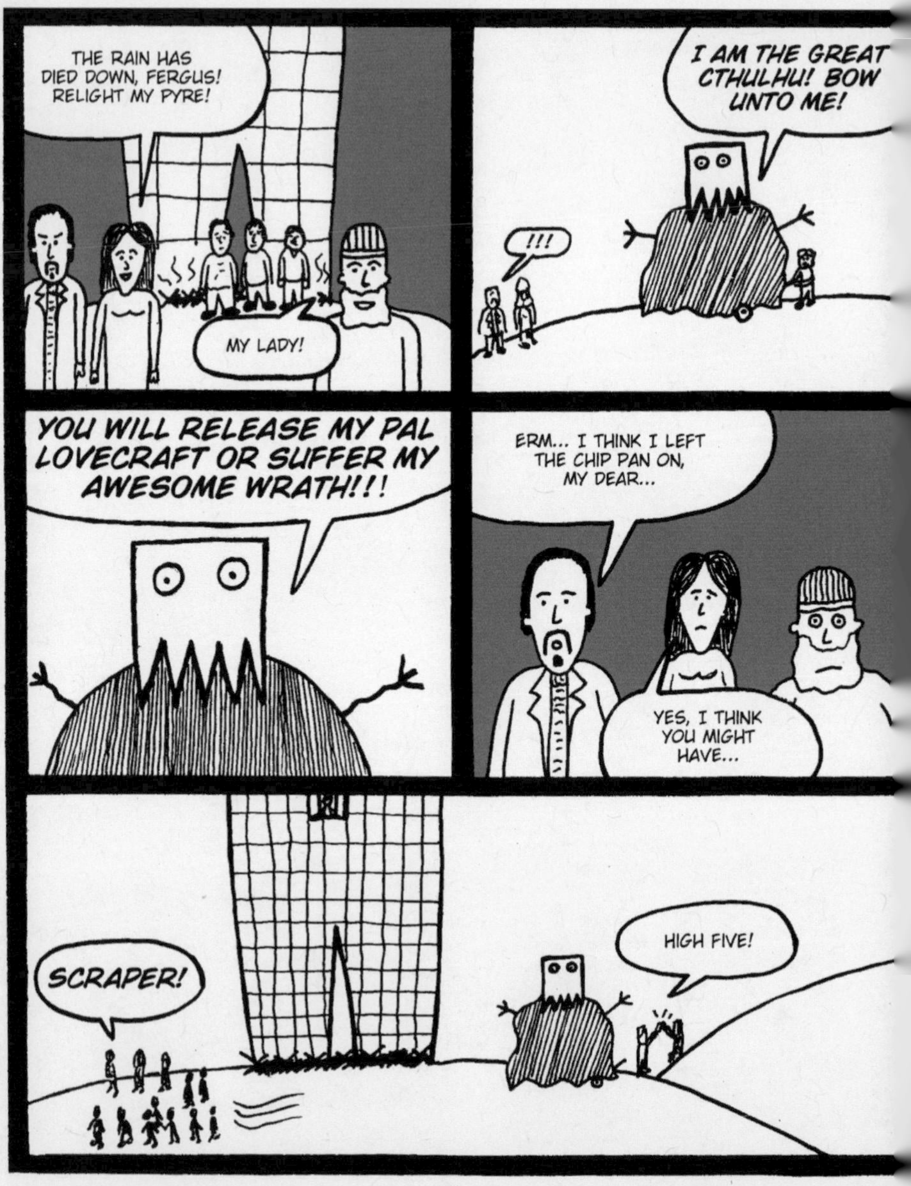
THE RAIN HAS DIED DOWN, FERGUS! RELIGHT MY PYRE!
MY LADY!
I AM THE GREAT CTHULHU! BOW UNTO ME!
!!!
YOU WILL RELEASE MY PAL LOVECRAFT OR SUFFER MY AWESOME WRATH!!!
ERM... I THINK I LEFT THE CHIP PAN ON, MY DEAR...
YES, I THINK YOU MIGHT HAVE...
SCRAPER!
HIGH FIVE!

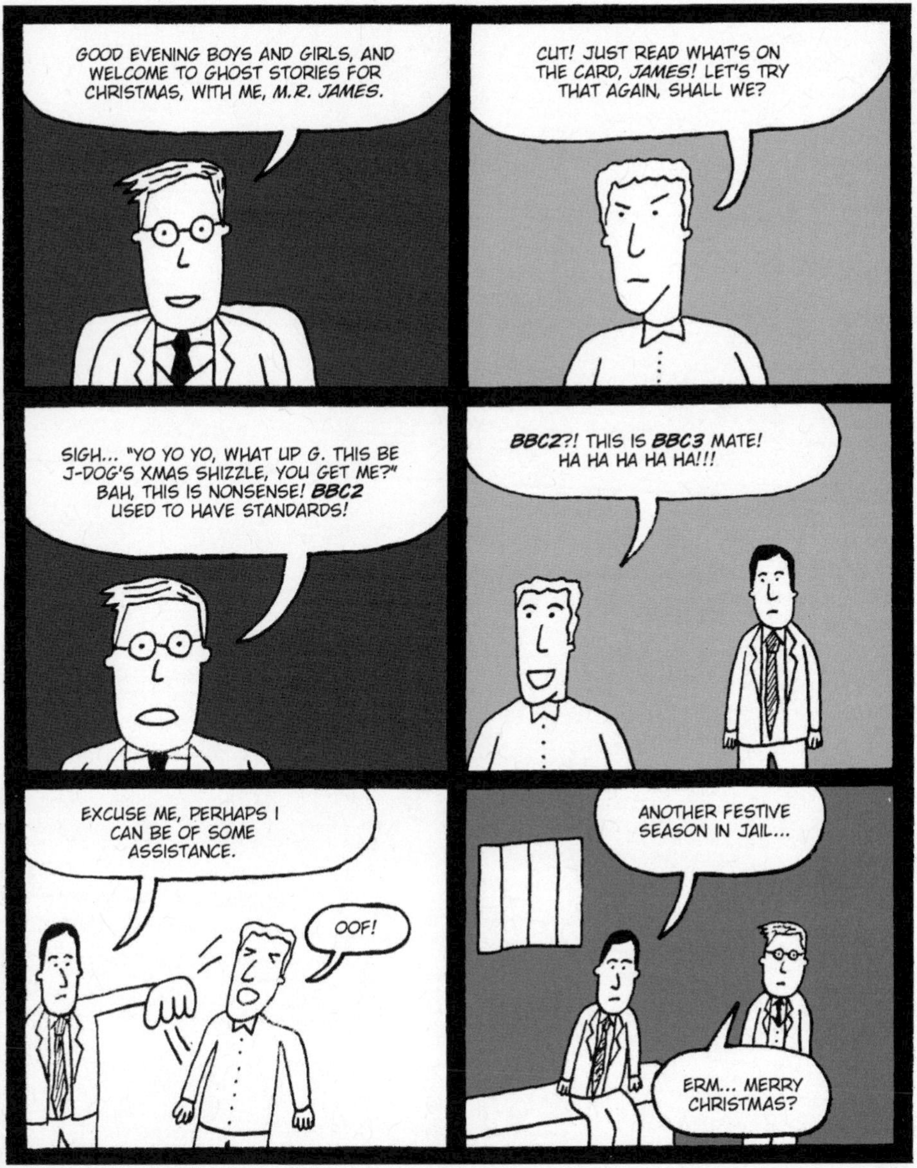
GOOD EVENING BOYS AND GIRLS, AND WELCOME TO GHOST STORIES FOR CHRISTMAS, WITH ME, *M.R. JAMES*.
CUT! JUST READ WHAT'S ON THE CARD, *JAMES!* LET'S TRY THAT AGAIN, SHALL WE?
SIGH... "YO YO YO, WHAT UP G. THIS BE J-DOG'S XMAS SHIZZLE, YOU GET ME?" BAH, THIS IS NONSENSE! ***BBC2*** USED TO HAVE STANDARDS!
***BBC2****?!* THIS IS ***BBC3*** MATE! HA HA HA HA HA!!!
EXCUSE ME, PERHAPS I CAN BE OF SOME ASSISTANCE.
*OOF!*
ANOTHER FESTIVE SEASON IN JAIL...
ERM... MERRY CHRISTMAS?

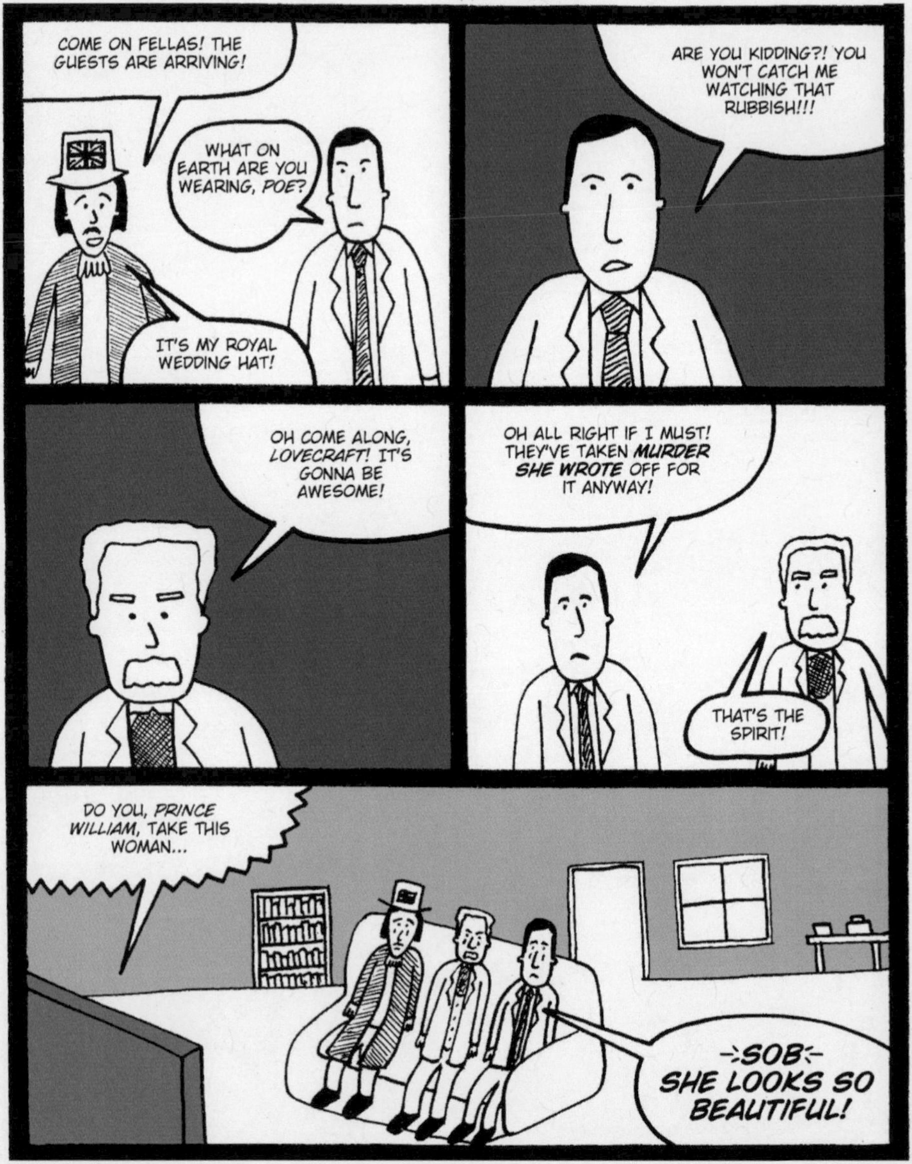
COME ON FELLAS! THE GUESTS ARE ARRIVING!
WHAT ON EARTH ARE YOU WEARING, POE?
IT'S MY ROYAL WEDDING HAT!
ARE YOU KIDDING?! YOU WON'T CATCH ME WATCHING THAT RUBBISH!!!
OH COME ALONG, LOVECRAFT! IT'S GONNA BE AWESOME!
OH ALL RIGHT IF I MUST! THEY'VE TAKEN MURDER SHE WROTE OFF FOR IT ANYWAY!
THAT'S THE SPIRIT!
DO YOU, PRINCE WILLIAM, TAKE THIS WOMAN...
SOB
SHE LOOKS SO BEAUTIFUL!

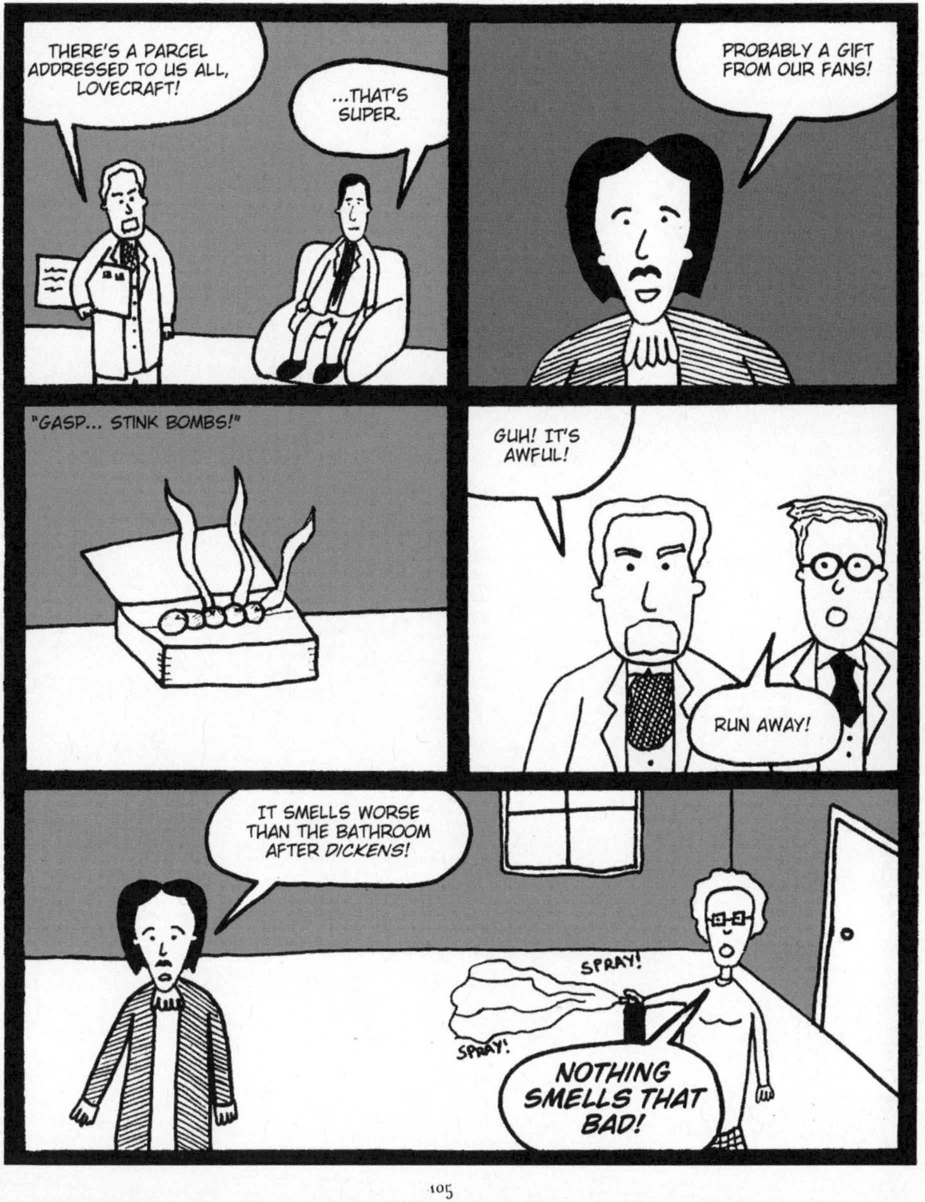
THERE'S A PARCEL ADDRESSED TO US ALL, LOVECRAFT!
...THAT'S SUPER.
PROBABLY A GIFT FROM OUR FANS!
"GASP... STINK BOMBS!"
GUH! IT'S AWFUL!
RUN AWAY!
IT SMELLS WORSE THAN THE BATHROOM AFTER DICKENS!
SPRAY!
SPRAY!
NOTHING SMELLS THAT BAD!

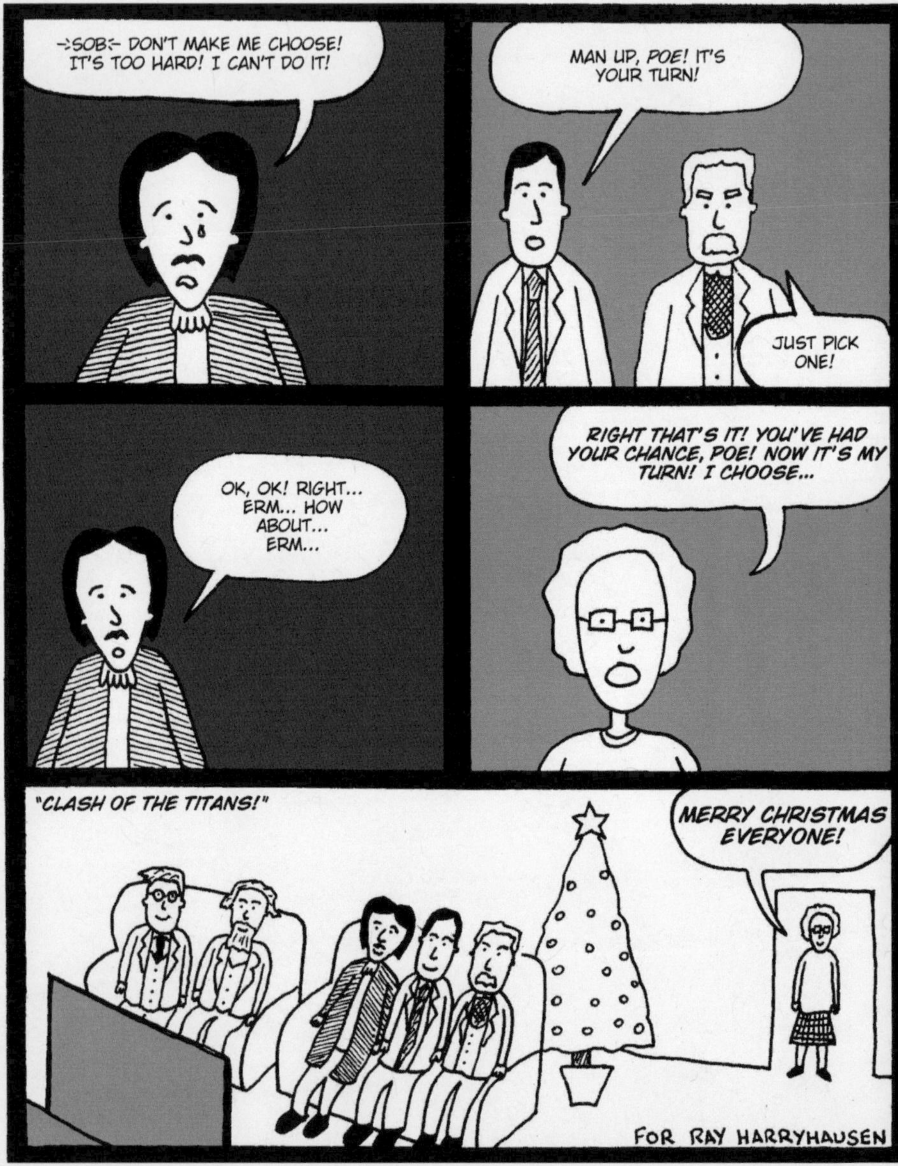
-:SOB:- DON'T MAKE ME CHOOSE! IT'S TOO HARD! I CAN'T DO IT!
MAN UP, POE! IT'S YOUR TURN!
JUST PICK ONE!
OK, OK! RIGHT... ERM... HOW ABOUT... ERM...
RIGHT THAT'S IT! YOU'VE HAD YOUR CHANCE, POE! NOW IT'S MY TURN! I CHOOSE...
"CLASH OF THE TITANS!"
MERRY CHRISTMAS EVERYONE!
FOR RAY HARRYHAUSEN

GENTLEMEN, I COULDN'T HELP MYSELF...

I HAVE ENTERED MRS P'S ATTIC.

THE MYSTERY FINALLY SOLVED? DO TELL POE!

WHAT IS MRS P'S GREAT SECRET? I BET IT'S CYCLOPEAN, BIERCE.

EVEN WORSE! THE ACTOR DOUG BRADLEY IS HER PRISONER.

CHAINED TO A DESK.

"SHE'S FORCING THE POOR LAD TO RECORD OUR EPIC STORIES. ALL FOR HER OWN PROFIT!"

NO, THE REAL HORROR IS ME. I USED THE POOR MAN TO CREATE MY MOST ORIGINAL AND FEARED MONSTER OF ALL TIME.

TRUE HELL PERSONIFIED IN MAN. MEET **STAPLEHEAD!**

dum dumm
dumm DUMMM
WHA--?
DUMMM DUM DUM
GAAGGH! HELP!
WHAT IS IT, POE?
WAS IT THE NIGHTMARE ABOUT THE MONKEY AGAIN?
NO! LISTEN! CAN YOU HEAR IT?
DUM DUMMM
AH, THAT'S WHERE IT IS...
WHERE WHAT IS?
I KNEW I'D LEFT IT SOMEWHERE! CAN'T BE DOING WITHOUT MY DAILY DOSE OF TUPAC, DOG.
DUMM DUMMM... DUMM... thug for life... DUMMM DUMM

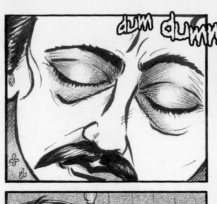

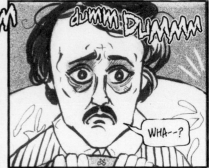

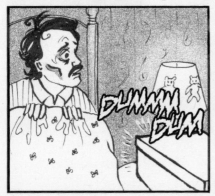

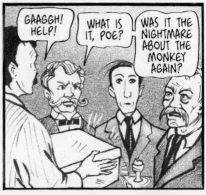

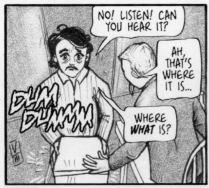

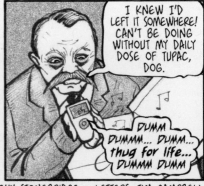

WORDS: RICHMOND CLEMENTS • PICTURES: VICKY STONEBRIDGE • LETTERS: JIM CAMPBELL

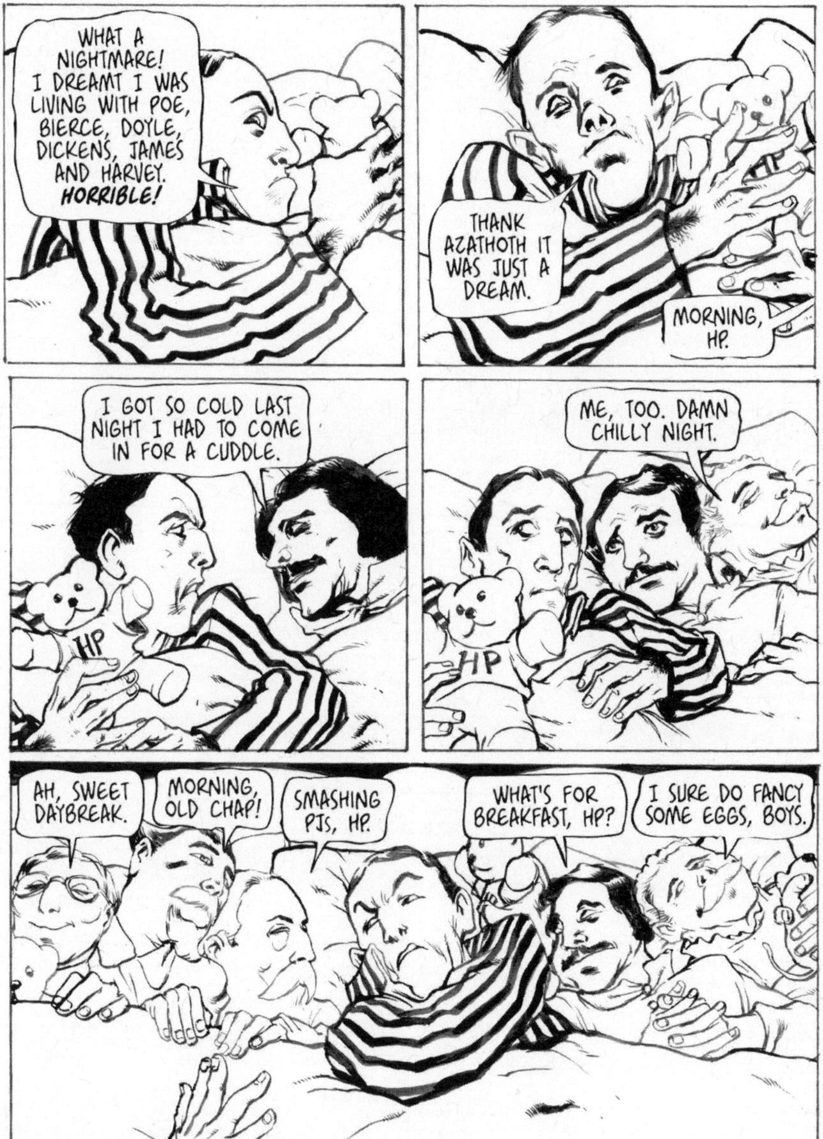
WHAT A NIGHTMARE! I DREAMT I WAS LIVING WITH POE, BIERCE, DOYLE, DICKENS, JAMES AND HARVEY. **HORRIBLE!**
THANK AZATHOTH IT WAS JUST A DREAM.
MORNING, HP.
I GOT SO COLD LAST NIGHT I HAD TO COME IN FOR A CUDDLE.
HP
ME, TOO. DAMN CHILLY NIGHT.
HP
AH, SWEET DAYBREAK.
MORNING, OLD CHAP!
SMASHING PJs, HP.
WHAT'S FOR BREAKFAST, HP?
I SURE DO FANCY SOME EGGS, BOYS.

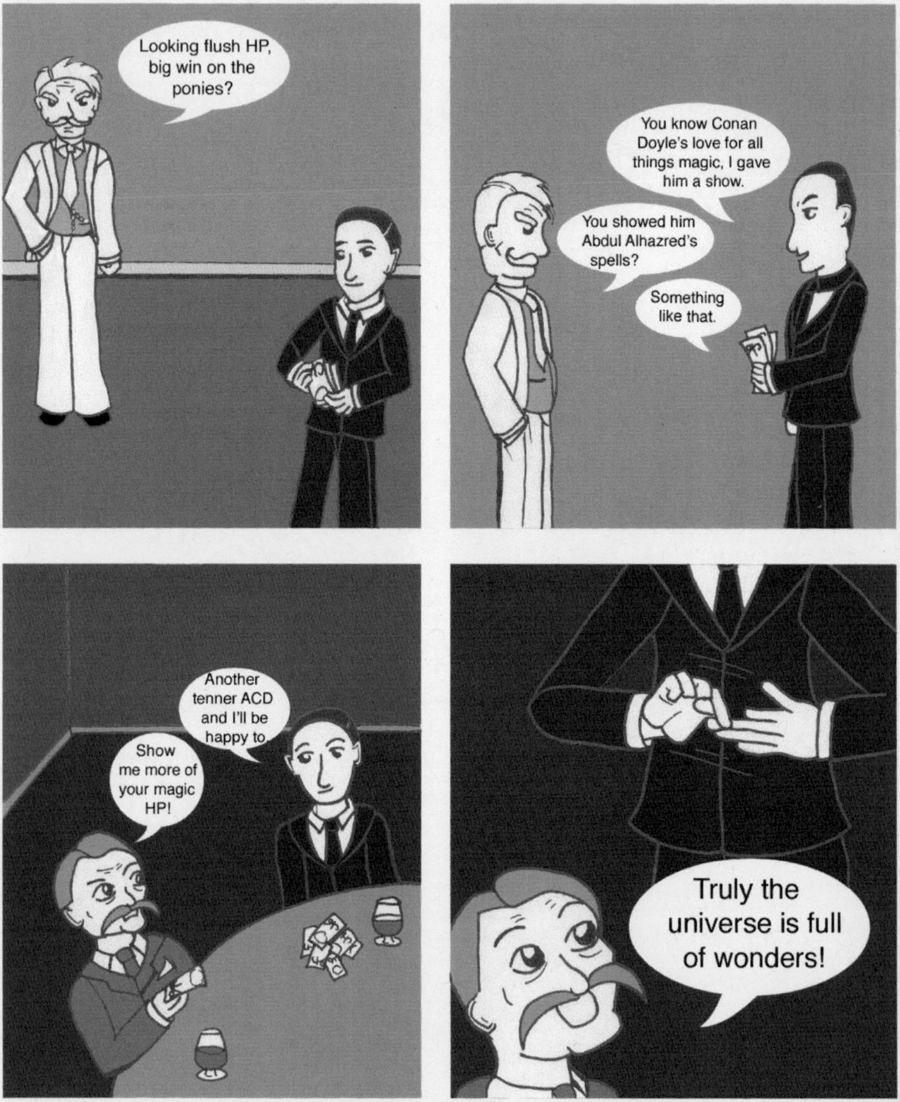
Looking flush HP, big win on the ponies?
You know Conan Doyle's love for all things magic, I gave him a show.
You showed him Abdul Alhazred's spells?
Something like that.
Show me more of your magic HP!
Another tenner ACD and I'll be happy to.
Truly the universe is full of wonders!

# The Bio of Ben Clark

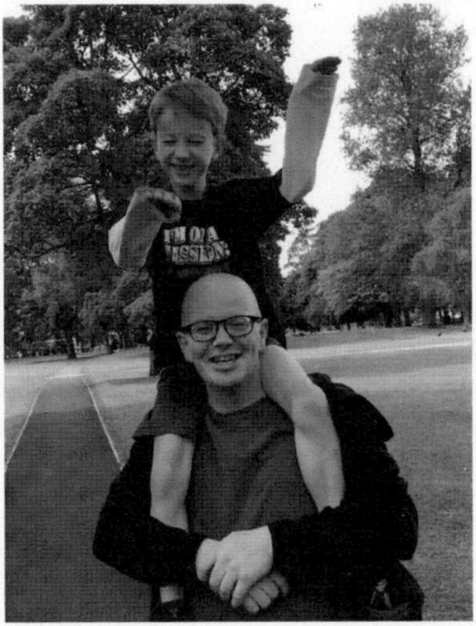

I'M ON A
MISSION


Early exposure to 2000AD left Ben Clark unfit for anything but a life in comics. One of the mainstays of the award winning anthology Solar Wind, his work has also appeared in Zarjaz, Omnivistascope, and his own line of Magic Beans Comics like Mothman About The House, Lenny Biscuits, I Cashed A Dead Man's Pension, Nessie Vs Dracula and Mike Neville Adventures. He is currently working on his first children's book, about a Vampire that owns a submarine. He lives in the North East of England and eats a lot of crisps.

Read more of Ben's comic strips at magicbeanscomics.blogspot.com

Many thanks to the wonderful writers and artists who created the guest comic strips. whilst I was busy helping to welcome my son Dylan to the world. You are truly appreciated!

Ben Clark

The Spine Chillers will return